THANKSGIVING ANGELS

A MERCY ALLCUTT MYSTERY

THANKSGIVING ANGELS

ALICE DUNCAN

FIVE STAR
A part of Gale, Cengage Learning

GALE
CENGAGE Learning·

Farmington Hills, Mich • San Francisco • New York • Waterville, Maine
Meriden, Conn • Mason, Ohio • Chicago

LIBRARY OF CONGRESS CATALOGING-IN-PUBLICATION DATA

Duncan, Alice, 1945–
    Thanksgiving angels : a Mercy Allcutt mystery / Alice Duncan.
    — First edition.
        pages ; cm
    ISBN 978-1-4328-3056-4 (hardcover) — ISBN 1-4328-3056-2 (hardcover) — ISBN 978-1-4328-3053-3 (ebook) — ISBN 1-4328-3053-8 (ebook)
        I. Title.
    PS3554.U463394T48 2015
    813'.54—dc23   2014041556

First Edition. First Printing: April 2015
Find us on Facebook– https://www.facebook.com/FiveStarCengage
Visit our website– http://www.gale.cengage.com/fivestar/
Contact Five Star™ Publishing at FiveStar@cengage.com

Printed in the United States of America
1 2 3 4 5 6 7 19 18 17 16 15

CHAPTER ONE

I stood before my boss's desk, my hands folded in front of me, my head bowed, my eyes closed, praying like mad that he'd deny my request.

I should have known better.

"Sure," said Ernie Templeton, P.I., with his usual air of insouciance. Naturally, he was sitting back in his swivel chair with his hands cupping his head. His feet were crossed at the ankles and residing on his desktop. The flask he generally carried in his hip pocket lay on his desk. I'd been shocked when I first saw that flask, until I learned it carried nothing more illegal than apple cider. "Why not? It's never busy around here, and this time of year it's dead."

My eyes opened like a shot, and I glared at him. "You're consigning me to my mother's care at *Thanksgiving*? How can you be so cruel?"

With a chuckle, Ernie said, "Not my fault, Mercy. She's your mother. If you don't want to spend Thanksgiving with her, don't."

"She'd kill me." I sounded sulky. I felt sulky. "Besides, Chloe begged me to come with her and Harvey to Pasadena so she wouldn't be Mother's only target during the season of thanksgiving—which ought to change its name when Mother's around."

"Well, then," said Ernie with a shrug. "There you go. You're saving your sister's life."

"Bother."

I slumped into one of the chairs in front of Ernie's desk and frowned at my irritating employer. "The least you could do is let me take only a couple of days off—Thursday and Friday maybe. What am I going to do during a whole week at my parents' house?"

Another shrug. "Beats me. Glad it's you and not me, actually. Your mother gives me the shivers."

I glared some more. "Nothing gives you the shivers, Ernie Templeton, my mother least of all."

"Hey, I've met the woman. If she were my mother, I wouldn't go anywhere near her. You don't have to either, although that would be a mean trick to play on your nice sister."

He was right, of course. My mother, known to her friends, my father and her associates back East as Honoria and to her children as the Wrath of God, was a formidable female. I'd escaped the confines of my ivory tower in Boston in June of this same year in order to move to Los Angeles and get a—gasp!—*job.* This was something unheard of for the women in my family, and every single one of them except Chloe had told me how rebellious and undutiful I was being.

Nuts to them. I wanted to see how *real* people lived. I wanted to see the mean streets, although I must admit I didn't want to live on them. I wanted to *learn,* darn it, because my ambition was to write novels about the world as most people lived in it, not as how the people in my social set on Beacon Hill lived in it. The Beacon Hill folks could be nice, but they had no idea how the majority of people had to scramble for a living.

Truth to tell, I didn't *have* to scramble for a living, either. I'd inherited a nice chunk of money from my late great-aunt, Agatha. But I didn't use her money. Since I'd come West and been hired as Ernie's secretary, I'd been living on my earnings. For the most part.

Very well, so I'd dipped into Great-Aunt Agatha's legacy in order to purchase my lovely home on Bunker Hill from Chloe and Harvey, her movie-mogul husband. But I'd since then rented out rooms—at an extremely fair rate—to other working women, to whom I wanted to give the chance to have a safe and reliable place to live. After all, *some* women really did have to earn their own livings. It was also true that I'd rented an apartment to one bad apple, but she was gone. And I'd also given employment to Mrs. Emerald Buck, wife of the custodian at the Figueroa Building, in which Ernie had his office.

Lulu LaBelle, the receptionist at the Figueroa Building, rented rooms from me, too, as did Miss Caroline Terry, who worked the hosiery counter at the Broadway Department Store; and Miss Susan Krekeler, receptionist at a dentist's office near our building. I was proud of myself for achieving my goal of helping three worthy working women find a safe place to live. Besides which, Mrs. Buck cooked for us, and her cooking was simply scrumptious.

Mr. Buck did maintenance on my home, too, which was lucky for me. In exchange, they lived in a suite of rooms off the breakfast room and I paid both of them a decent wage. I tell you, I was succeeding, if in a minor way, in achieving the goals in my life. I was even writing a book! Mind you, I hadn't written much of it, but I worked on it every chance I got.

And did I mention my adorable apricot toy poodle, Buttercup? Well, she was an achievement, too, and I loved her dearly.

"Take heart, Mercy. Maybe something exciting will happen at your parents' place while you're there."

"Mother would never stand for that. She despises excitement."

Ernie chuckled.

"This isn't funny, Ernest Templeton! I have to spend an entire *week* with my parents. I can't think of anything worse than that."

"You might've been born poor," Ernie suggested.

He always ragged me about being a "rich girl." I frowned at him some more. "It's not my fault I was born into a wealthy family and you weren't."

"I s'pose not. But it'll be all right, Mercy. It's only a week."

"Only a week," I grumbled. "That one week will seem like a lifetime."

Ernie only chuckled some more, so I got up from the chair and walked stiffly to my own room, which was outside Ernie's office. Technically, I suppose I occupied the "front" office. People coming in to see Ernie saw me first, and I'd decide whether or not to allow them in to see my boss. Well . . . we had so little business that I'd never yet turned anyone away. Sobering thought. We made so little money, I was surprised Ernie hadn't let me go before that day.

Egad. That would be terrible. I loved this job. I was quite fond of my annoying employer. And I had other friends in the Figueroa Building, the primary ones being Lulu LaBelle and Mr. Emerald Buck.

Bother. I still had to take Thanksgiving week off and spend it in Pasadena with my mother, the mere thought of whom made me quail in terror.

I checked the time on the little Chinese clock on my desk. Our offices weren't far from Chinatown, and I'd decorated them with lots of items I'd purchased there. Using my own money.

Oh, dear. I did wish business would pick up.

Anyhow, the clock told me it was lunchtime, so I took my hat and handbag from my desk drawer—God knows there weren't enough file folders to fill the thing—got up and again went to Ernie's office.

"Heading out for lunch?" he said, turning from the window out of which he'd been staring. "Hang on. I'll go with you."

"Lulu's going too," I told him.

"Excellent. How about Chinatown?"

Ernie loved a little hole-in-the-wall diner in Chinatown called Charlie's, on the east side of Hill Street.

"Sounds good to me."

So we headed out the door and to the stairs at the end of the corridor. The building had a self-operating elevator, but I'd had a bad experience there shortly after Ernie'd hired me, and I didn't like to use the thing. The stairs were noisy and cramped, but climbing them several times a day kept me in shape—and away from that creepy elevator.

That day I was clad in a dark blue suit, infinitely suited to my job as a P.I.'s secretary. P.I. stands for Private Investigator, by the way, in case you didn't know. I didn't until Ernie told me. Anyhow, with my dark blue suit, I also wore a pair of sensible black shoes and carried a black handbag. My hat was also black. I looked every inch the professional secretary.

When Ernie got to the bottom of the stairs, he held the door open for me, and I stepped into the lobby of our building. Sure enough, there was Lulu, filing her nails, an open bottle of vivid red nail varnish before her on her desk.

Lulu, as usual, did not look at all the professional working woman. A bottle blonde, today she wore a red-and-green polka-dotted dress that tied around her hips with a bright red ribbon. Along with the dress, she'd chosen to wear bright red shoes, hat and handbag. All of this red went well with her flame-colored fingernails, which she filed pretty much all day long as she handled the receptionist's job at the Figueroa Building. Lulu was the first person in Los Angeles I'd met, on the first day I'd set out to seek honest employment. She was generally quite . . . flamboyant, I guess is the right word for it, and today she'd surpassed all of her prior efforts in that regard.

Lulu, you see, didn't aim to keep her receptionist's job

forever. She intended to be "discovered" by a moving-picture producer or director any day now. If such had been my own ambition, I don't think I'd have sat at the Figueroa Building's reception desk filing my nails all day every day, but would do something more . . . well, active, to achieve my goal. But I wasn't Lulu, and I didn't want her to leave her job, so her plans were all right by me.

"Hey, Lulu, want to get Chinese?" I called across the lobby.

She looked up and smiled. "Sure. Hey, Ern. You going with us?"

"Sure am," said Ernie, shrugging into the overcoat he'd snagged just before leaving the office.

"He gave me the time off at Thanksgiving," I told Lulu, a hint of tragedy in my voice.

"I'm sorry, Mercy." She turned her big blue eyes on my boss. "That wasn't very nice of you, Ernie."

He chuckled again, the beast. "Hell, Lulu, we don't have enough work to justify me even having a secretary. I sure can't keep her from her family on Thanksgiving, now can I?"

Lulu swished to the coat rack beside the front door and lifted down her own coat, a green number she'd found somewhere, undoubtedly on sale. She looked like one of Santa Claus's gaudier Christmas elves in all her red and green. Wrong season, I told myself.

Ernie walked over and held Lulu's coat for her. I looked on a little jealously. He never did that for *me*. Then his words struck me, and I turned abruptly, horrified. "Ernie! You're not thinking of firing me, are you? I love this job!"

"Don't worry, kiddo. What would I do for entertainment if you left my employ?"

Frowning, I said, "What do you mean by that? Entertainment?"

"You do keep me amused. Both of you. Remember when you

12

were picked up for streetwalking?"

How could we ever forget? Lulu and I exchanged a glance of embarrassment. "That wasn't our fault." My voice didn't carry conviction, even though I'd only spoken the truth.

"Right. And it wasn't your fault you tackled that insane lady at the Angelica Gospel Hall, either."

"Well, it wasn't." I sounded downright whiny, and I told myself to knock it off. Still and all, those things *weren't* my fault. "I only went to the hall trying to gather information so that *you,* Ernest Templeton, wouldn't be arrested and hanged for murder."

"Yeah, Ern. You're not being fair."

"We use the electric chair in these parts, kiddo."

I shuddered.

"All right, all right." Ernie opened the front door of the Figueroa Building, and we saw Mr. Buck standing beside Ernie's dilapidated Studebaker, holding the rear passenger-side door open for either Lulu or me.

We exchanged another couple of glances, and Lulu slipped into the backseat. Mr. Buck then opened the front passenger door, and I sat next to Ernie.

"Thanks, Buck," Ernie said, flipping a coin to the building's maintenance manager.

"You're more than welcome, Mr. Ernie."

Mr. Buck's black face beamed. He adored Ernie, who had managed to get his son cleared of a charge of murder a few weeks earlier. Well . . . truth to tell, I'd played a big part in that investigation, too, but I wasn't going to remind Ernie of the fact. If I did, he'd then point out that it was my fault I'd rented rooms to a murderer, the mere thought of whom made me shudder. And she was only eighteen years old! It boggled my mind then, and it boggles my mind now.

A brilliant idea struck me. I swiveled in the seat so I could look at Lulu. The sight of her in all her red and green made me blink a little, but I didn't turn around again. "Lulu! I have a wonderful idea! Why don't you come to Pasadena with me at Thanksgiving?"

"Not on your life, Mercy. I love you dearly, but I've met your mother."

Ernie laughed out loud. I turned in my seat, defeated. "Bother."

"It's only for a week, kiddo," Ernie said.

As if that would soothe me. And I hated when he called me *kiddo,* which made me feel like his little sister or something like that.

But we'd made it to Chinatown by then, so Ernie slid into a parking space on Hill, and we all scrambled out and headed for Charlie's. There we ate Chinese pork and noodles. By that point in time, I was quite adept with the old chopsticks. I'd even overcome my Boston upbringing enough so that I was able to pick up my bowl of broth and vegetables and slurp it down just like the rest of the folks in the restaurant did. Except for us, they were all Chinese.

Even though I had to spend an entire week with my mother and father, I felt a surge of triumph at the knowledge that I'd at least conquered chopsticks.

CHAPTER TWO

On Saturday morning, November 20, 1926, and with an ache in my heart, I dutifully packed my bags and headed downstairs. A sense of doom settled over me.

Lulu, who'd been lounging in the living room reading *Motion Picture Story Magazine,* glanced over to the staircase as I descended it. She knew how glum I felt. "It's all right, Mercy. You'll survive, although I sure don't envy you."

I heaved one of my bigger sighs. "I suppose so, Lulu." I cast her a pleading glance. "Are you *sure* you won't come with me?"

She shuddered. I saw her. "I'm sorry, Mercy, but I don't ever want to meet your mother again. She made me feel like a worm."

"She makes everyone feel like that, Lulu. It's not just you."

"Oh, Mercy," said Caroline Terry, walking into the room from the kitchen with Buttercup prancing behind her. "I'm sure it won't be *that* bad."

Lulu and I just stared at her for a moment. Then Lulu said, "You haven't met Mercy's mother, have you, Caroline?"

"Well, no. But I visit my parents in Alhambra every Sunday. They're lovely people."

"Trust me, Caroline, your parents aren't anything like Mercy's. Mercy's folks are real stuffy. Especially her mother. She's kind of a dragon, actually."

"But your sister's very nice. I've met her when she's visited you here."

"Chloe's a peach," I said. "God alone knows how she man-

15

aged to escape the family curse and turn into a pleasant human being. I guess Harvey has helped her."

"Hey, Mercy, *you're* a peach, too," said the loyal Lulu. Well, she was loyal to a point. Clearly her faithfulness didn't extend to visiting my parents in Pasadena to aid and support me.

Buttercup trotted over to me, and I set my suitcases down and picked her up. "At least I'm taking Buttercup along with me. I don't care what Mother says about not liking dogs. Nobody can not like Buttercup."

I nuzzled my dog's soft fur. I'd bathed her the night before, and she smelled heavenly. At least Mother wouldn't be able to complain about dog hair all over the place, because poodles didn't shed. Much. My shoulders slumped as I put my darling doggie down. She danced around my feet for a second or two, then dashed over to Lulu and leapt up on her lap.

"Ah, Buttercup, we'll miss you."

"Oh, are you ready to go?" Susan Krekeler walked into the room in what looked like a nurse's uniform. She wore it for her job at the dentist's office.

"Yes. Unfortunately," I said.

"I know you don't want to go," said Susan. "I'm sorry your parents aren't nicer. But I hope you'll have a good time anyway. I have to go to work, so I'll be off now." She waved as she headed for the front door.

" 'Bye," I said, thinking sadly that I'd rather be going to work than to Pasadena. Not that Pasadena isn't a charming city, but its beauties had been sullied for me ever since my parents bought a winter home there.

Oh, Lord. Did that mean I'd have to spend *Christmas* there, too? The thought was too ghastly to think about, so I didn't.

"You take this basket along with you, Miss Mercy," said Lottie Buck, carrying a picnic basket from the kitchen. "You'll want to stop and have lunch somewhere along the way."

"I'm only going to Pasadena," I reminded her. "Pasadena's only twenty-two miles away from here. But thank you. This way I can stop at that park Ernie and I saw when we went to Pasadena in June. That'll delay my arrival at the mansion of misfortune a little bit."

Mrs. Buck shook her head. "And don't you be carrying them heavy suitcases to your car, either, young lady. Mr. Buck will take those things out for you."

"Thank you. I appreciate everything you do for us, Mrs. Buck. Wish I could partake of your delicious Thanksgiving dinner this coming Thursday." I actually wept a tear or two and felt silly.

"Oh, you poor thing. Everything will be all right. You'll see. I'm sorry you have a family that burdens you," said the nice Mrs. Buck. "We can't all have kindhearted relations."

"I'm glad I have you," I said, and I gave her a huge hug.

She patted me on the back. "You'll be back here as soon as can be, child, and you'll see. Everything will be better for you having gone through a trial this week."

"Do you really think so?"

"I know it," she said firmly. "Anything that don't kill you will make you stronger. Just look at my Calvin."

I couldn't look at her Calvin, who was away at college, but I appreciated her sentiment. "Thanks, Mrs. Buck." I wiped my eyes with the hankie I'd pulled from my pocket.

"Cheer up, Mercy. Mrs. Buck's right," said Lulu. "You'll feel like you've died and gone to heaven when you get back to Ernie and us."

"I sure hope so," said I.

"You will," said Caroline and Susan in a sweet duet.

Mr. Buck entered the living room, picked up my two suitcases as I retrieved Buttercup from Lulu's lap, and everyone headed out to the driveway where sat my lovely 1924 blue Moon

Roadster. Chloe had given me the machine when Harvey'd bought her a brand new Rolls Royce Silver Ghost and a chauffeur to drive her and the baby—unborn as yet—around. He didn't want to take any chances with his precious wife and infant. Harvey was a good man. Maybe he and Chloe would have Christmas at their place. That notion brightened me for a second before I realized my parents would probably be there, too. But at least I could escape from Chloe's place. I couldn't escape from my parents for an entire week, because my mother intended to hold me captive.

Luckily for me, the Roadster didn't require a crank but had a self-starter. Ungainly or unfortunate people were always breaking their arms when the crank got away from them and whipped around to unwind itself. And I'd probably have been one of the ungainly or unlucky ones if I'd had to crank an auto.

Mr. Buck stowed my luggage in the tonneau, and Mrs. Buck placed the picnic basket on the floor on the passenger's side. I turned to say goodbye to my friends, who'd gathered to wave me off. I felt like crying again but sucked in a deep breath and said, " 'Bye, everyone. Have fun without me."

"Oh, Mercy, it'll be all right." Lulu rushed up to hug me. So did Caroline and Mrs. Buck. Susan was already on her way to work. Mr. Buck shook my hand.

"You take care of yourself, Miss Mercy. We'll take good care of the house while you're away. And it won't be too bad. At least you'll have your sweet little doggie with you. An' your sister will be there. She's a fine lady. A fine lady."

"Yes, she is. Thank you, Mr. Buck."

Then I placed Buttercup gently in the passenger's seat, plunked my handbag next to the picnic basket on the floor in front of the dog, climbed behind the wheel, and tried to remember how to back out of my driveway. I'd only been driving for a few weeks, after all. Ernie had taught me, and he was a very good teacher.

"You sure you remember how to work this thing?" asked Lulu, who'd gone adventuring with me one dark night. That was the night we'd been picked up for streetwalking, but that's another story entirely.

"Yes. I think so."

I shut my eyes, recalled all the things Ernie had taught me about operating my motorcar, turned the key, pressed the starter button, and the engine roared to life. A little too loudly. I eased my foot off the clutch and the gas pedal. Then I put the gearshift into reverse, again remembering to press my foot on the clutch as I did so. I didn't want to start my journey with a hideous clashing of gears, after all. The machine slowly but surely backed toward the street. Once I got to the street, I looked both ways—I also didn't want to have a smash-up right in front of my house—and carefully backed into the street, depressed the clutch once more, shifted into gear, and took off toward Broadway.

Ernie had given me a set of instructions on how to get to Pasadena, which I'd dutifully written down and memorized. Broadway would take me all the way to Pasadena Avenue, which went on for a while and then stopped. At that point I'd navigate through the complex of avenues and streets that led back to Pasadena Avenue. From there I'd hang a left on Fair Oaks Avenue, then turn right on San Pasqual Street and drive to the 1400 block. The drive would have been much easier if Pasadena Avenue had just continued, but I figured nothing about dealing with my parents was easy. There I'd find my parents' home. I was kind of surprised they'd not bought a home on Orange Grove Boulevard, since it was known by those in the know as "millionaire's row." Then again, perhaps that was too blatant a cognomen for my haughty Boston parents, who preferred not to advertise their wealth aloud.

The drive was nice. Buttercup and I traveled past a lot of

pleasant scenery and some that was not so pleasant. But for the most part, the drive was a pretty one, and I pretended I was driving somewhere I wanted to go instead of to my parents' house.

After about a half hour, I saw the park Ernie and I had seen on my first visit to Pasadena. I pulled off the road and fetched the picnic basket Mrs. Buck had been kind enough to pack for me. Buttercup and I enjoyed a roast beef sandwich each, an apple—well, I ate the apple—and a couple of oatmeal cookies. Buttercup was particularly fond of oatmeal cookies.

Then, after packing up all my luncheon items, throwing Buttercup's ball for her a few times, and making sure she did her duty as a dog, we climbed back into the automobile and drove off to meet our doom. I mean to my parents' house.

A little more than a half hour later, I pulled into the drive of my parents' palatial winter home. I sat in my machine and contemplated the structure for a while. It beat me why they needed so huge a place if they aimed only to spend three months a year there. I got a foreboding of things to come, should my father decide to retire one of these days. Then I prayed my brother George hadn't come with them.

But no. George was a junior partner in our father's bank, and he'd certainly have stayed in Boston to run things. George, in case anyone wonders, is *precisely* like my parents. In other words, he's stuffy, starchy, judgmental, and generally horrid. Chloe and I detest him.

Anyhow, as I contemplated the wrought-iron gate and wondered how to get in, it began to open before my very eyes. Good Lord. Did they have someone guarding the gate? Glancing around, I didn't see a gatehouse, but what did I know?

Gathering my courage in both hands and steeling my nerves—and probably performing several other clichés, only I can't think of them right now—I propelled my little Moon

Roadster up the drive to the enormous house.

I had to admit the place was pretty. Chloe'd told me it was in the Italian Renaissance style, whatever that was. Two stories high, it had a tall, elegant front door that looked as if it were made out of some very expensive wood and was carved to a fare-thee-well. Two arched windows flanked the door, and there were windows on the second floor with little balconies in front of them. I guess everyone got his or her own balcony upon which to stand and watch the stars at night. Or from which to leap to one's death.

No, no, no. I had to stop thinking things like that. *It's only for a week,* I reminded myself. *It's only for a week.* And Chloe would be there.

Speaking of whom, as soon as I pulled my Roadster to a stop in front of the huge front door—there was no porch to speak of—the door burst open, and Chloe ran outside to greet me. Her precipitate exit evidently startled the uniformed maidservant who'd opened the door, but she didn't seem to mind. In fact, I saw her smile as I jumped out of the car and hugged my sister. Buttercup did likewise. Well, she didn't hug Chloe, but she yipped and jumped, wanting some attention, too.

Bless Chloe's heart, she let me go and knelt to welcome Buttercup. "Oh, I'm so glad you brought her, Mercy. Mother will be livid."

"Good."

"Good afternoon, Mercy. Glad to see you here."

I looked over Chloe's shoulder to see Harvey, who was grinning broadly. He had a pipe in one hand and held the other out for me to shake.

"Oh, nuts, Harvey," I said, and I gave him a hug, too. He laughed and hugged me back. He was *such* a nice man. And *such* a departure from our parents.

Chloe finally left off greeting Buttercup and, while Buttercup trotted off to sniff (and mark) the formal plantings, Chloe, Harvey and I all took in the full beauty of the winter home of Mr. and Mrs. Albert Monteith Allcutt.

"Big place, isn't it?" said Harvey.

"No bigger than our home in Beverly Hills," said Chloe.

"Yes, but you have tons of friends and actors and directors who go to parties and meetings and so forth at your house. Mother and Father are only here three months out of the year."

"You hope. I'm afraid they're going to move out here permanently," said Chloe ominously.

"No. Please tell me you're joking."

"Wish I could. But Father's talking about building a branch bank out here, and then he'd come here to run it."

"Oh, Lord, no." I bowed my head. "Please tell me George isn't moving out here, too."

"Oh, no. That's the one good thing about it," said Chloe. "George would stay in Boston and run things there."

"Well, that's something, anyway."

"I suppose so."

But Chloe didn't like Father's plans any more than I did. I could tell.

With a large-sized sigh, Chloe took my arm. "You'd better come and meet the parents. They're on their high horses, of course."

"Of course." I turned and called to my dog. "Here, Buttercup. Brace yourself."

Harvey laughed again. "I'll send someone out to carry in your bags and move your auto to the stables."

"The stables?"

"Used to be stables. Now they're used as garages."

"Hmm." Such a thing wasn't uncommon. I was only surprised that my parents had converted stables to garages. How modern of them.

"The house is packed with servants," said Chloe in an undertone. "God alone knows why they need so many of them. I only brought my maid with me, and Harvey said he can dress himself, thank you."

"I feel the same way."

Chloe cast a disparaging glance at my simple winter suit. "Yes, well, the way you dress, I don't suppose you *do* need any help dressing, do you?"

"No, I don't," I said emphatically. "But I brought dinner dresses enough to last the whole stupid week, so you needn't worry about me looking dowdy."

"Sweetheart, you look dowdy right now."

As she led me to the front door, I looked down at my traveling costume. *I* thought it was tasteful and even rather pretty, being a sage green woolen coat trimmed with fur, under which I had on a sage green jersey dress with a bow at the neck and a belt at my hips. I had on a very nice brown velvet hat and carried a brown velvet handbag. The costume had cost a fortune, for Pete's sake! "What's wrong with this?"

Chloe giggled. "Nothing really, sweetie. I just like to rag you. Truly, you're dressing much better than you used to."

I sniffed. "I have to look professional for my job, you know."

"Ernie wouldn't care if you wore tatters. You know that."

True. Ernie wouldn't care if I wore nothing at all. In fact, he might prefer it.

Or maybe that was wishful thinking on my part.

Good Lord! I didn't mean that! Truly, I didn't. I blushed anyway, curse it.

As Chloe led me into the inner reaches of the palace my parents called their "winter home," she smiled cheekily. "Why the pink cheeks, Mercy? Have you and Ernie been doing anything you shouldn't?"

"No!"

"I'm so sorry. I think Ernie's just the fellow for you, you know."

"No, I don't know that. And he certainly isn't!"

Very well, so I'd entertained the occasional fantasy about Ernie and me. Still and all, there was nothing but a professional relationship between us, and I resented Chloe's sly hints.

"Please don't say anything of the kind to our parents. I'd never hear the end of it."

"Don't worry, Mercy. I'd never do that to you. We're our only consolation for this infernal week. Well, you and Harvey are mine. I expect you can borrow Harvey when you're feeling low, too."

"Thanks a lot."

"Anyhow, you have Buttercup. But buck up, Mercy. They're in here," said Chloe as we headed through a wood-paneled hallway with a twisty staircase, complete with elaborate wrought-iron railings leading to the upper story. "This is the great room." And with that, Chloe pushed one side of the pocket doors aside.

There, sitting and standing in state, were my mother (sitting) and father (standing). Frowning at us.

They would be.

CHAPTER THREE

"I see you finally got here. I suppose you drove that dangerous automobile. And is that your *dog* I see?"

"Good afternoon, Mother," I said as I dutifully went to the sofa and kissed her powdered cheek. For such a soft-feeling woman, she was solid steel at her core. I didn't respond to the rest of her statement, understanding from past experience that it wouldn't be worth the spit it took to say the words. Pardon me for saying spit.

Buttercup, cowed by the atmosphere, crept beside me and didn't even try to greet Mother. Smart dog, Buttercup. Anyhow, they'd met before. Mother deplored Buttercup almost as much as she deplored me. Buttercup returned her sentiments, and for much better reason.

"I see you're dressed appropriately at least," said my loving mater.

With an inner sigh, I didn't respond to this nasty riposte either, but straightened and went to my father, who stood before the massive fireplace, his arm resting on the mantel, a pipe in his hand, looking not unlike a statue of Napoleon in his emperor days only without a hand in his smoking jacket. "How do you do, Father?"

He nodded stiffly and held out his hand, which I shook. I could imagine Lulu saying, "You shook *hands*? Doesn't anybody in your family ever hug each other?"

The answer to that as-yet unasked question is no. Except for

25

Chloe and me. We hug each other.

"I'm well, Mercedes Louise. I see you're in health."

"Indeed I am, sir, and I hope you're the same." My inner Lulu said, "You call him *sir*?"

Can you wonder why I'm reluctant to visit my parents? Why I don't even call them my folks? "Folks" is much too easygoing a word to apply to those two.

"I'm fine, thank you, Mercedes Louise."

I hated my name. Of course it wasn't as bad as Chloe's, which was Clovilla Adelaide, but it was plenty bad enough.

"Um . . . shall I take my things to the room you've assigned to me?" I asked, thinking the question would surely draw ire from one of the two people responsible for my being alive on this earth, not to mention there at the moment where I didn't want to be.

"Don't be ridiculous, Mercedes Louise," said Mother from her perch on the sofa. "I'll ring for the houseboy." She frowned at me some more. "I'm sure you didn't bring your own maid with you to help you dress."

I couldn't suppress a sigh. "I don't have a maid, Mother. I don't *need* a maid. I'm a working girl, and I can put my own clothes on without help from another person."

"If you please, young woman, do not mention that so-called job of yours while you're a guest under my roof," said Mother in her Bostonian best voice.

I almost said I wasn't a guest but a prisoner, but I held my tongue. Fortunately for me, Chloe was there, and she touched my arm.

"Don't bother ringing, Mother. I'll go with you to fetch the houseboy, Mercy. He'll take your things upstairs. Your room is next to Harvey's and mine." She leaned closer and whispered in my ear. "And in the wing farthest from Mother and Father."

I turned and walked away with Chloe, holding on to her arm

like a lifeline. "Thank God for that."

"You betcha."

As soon as we left the frosty confines of the great room—not frosty in terms of physical heat, but frosty in terms of atmosphere—we both loosened up, looked at each other, and began to laugh.

"Oh, Mercy, I'm *so* glad you're here. These last two days with only Harvey for company have been miserable. Although I did meet a colleague of Harvey's who's a swell fellow. You'll meet him soon, because Mother is planning to hold a séance—"

"A *séance?* Our mother? Good Lord on high, whatever possessed her to do such a thing? The only other time she ever went to a séance, as far as I know, was with me, and somebody committed a murder during it!"

Chloe giggled—not because of the murder, which had been pretty icky, but because it was difficult to imagine our starchy mother succumbing to the blandishments of a spiritualist.

"I know. But this fellow, Harold Kincaid, is a costumier for Harvey's studio, and he knows a spiritualist with a reputation for being absolutely legitimate. Besides, Mother met Harold's mother, who uses this person all the time. She's the one who told Mother about this spiritualist. You'll never guess what her name is, either."

"Mr. Kincaid's mother? It must be—"

"No, silly, the spiritualist's name! And if you were thinking Harold's mother is Mrs. Kincaid, you'd be dead wrong. Her name is Mrs. Algernon Pinkerton. Her first husband, Mr. Eustace Kincaid, Harold's father, is a criminal who's spending a long term in San Quentin. I think he escaped once, but he's back in the clink for good now."

"Good heavens!"

"Indeed. I'm surprised Mother allowed the poor woman into her house, although I doubt she knows the story. Anyhow, this supposedly wonderful spiritualist is named—wait for it—Desdemona Majesty!"

"Desdemona? Majesty? You're kidding me, right?"

"Am not."

"Harold said she made up the Desdemona part when she was a little girl and started playing with a Ouija board, but her last name really is Majesty."

"That should sit well with Mother."

"Oh, it does. And Harold says she's brilliant at her work, too."

"Well, the séance should be interesting, at any rate."

"I can hardly wait myself." Chloe giggled like a schoolgirl.

Eyeing my sister critically, I said, "You don't seem to be showing, Chloe. Have you gained any weight? Shouldn't you be getting lumpy? After all, you're supposed to be eating for two, you know."

Chloe playfully slapped my arm. "Of all the nerve! Actually, I am growing, but these delicious Chinese pajama things do wonders for covering up a woman's condition. Mother hates them, of course. In *her* day, women hid away from the world when they were 'with child,' but I'm not about to do that."

"I should hope not," said I, ever the loyal sister.

Harvey greeted us at the foot of the magnificent staircase, a young Asian man at his side. "Ready to see your room, Mercy?"

"Yes. I've braved the gauntlet and lived through it." I gazed up at the curving staircase. "My goodness, but this is a lovely home, isn't it?"

"Doesn't hold a candle to our Beverly Hills house," said Chloe with a sniff.

"True, but you live in your home all year long. This is merely a winter residence."

"You hope," said Chloe, again sounding doubtful.

"I hope," I repeated, also doubtful. "But even if Father started a branch bank in Pasadena, Mother would never forsake Boston for good, would she? I mean, whom could she lord it over in little old Pasadena?"

"There are tons of millionaires here, too, Mercy."

"But aren't they mostly moving-picture people? Mother hates them almost as much as she hates me, doesn't she?"

"I think she's reconciled herself to Harvey," said Chloe, giving her husband a peck on the cheek. He smiled lovingly at her. I did envy them their happy marriage.

"Yes, your parents treat me quite well, considering my occupation," he said.

"And your money," I added dourly.

With a chuckle, Harvey said, "Riki Saito—that's R-I-K-I—here will take one of your bags upstairs, and I'll carry the other for you, Mercy. Won't you join us, my dear?"

"I sure will," said Chloe, who didn't guard her tongue with Harvey and me as she did with our parents. "This place is really gorgeous, Mercy. The room you'll be staying in is fit for a princess, at least."

"Well, that will be nice," I said, not meaning it. But as long as I had Buttercup and Chloe on hand, I prayed things wouldn't be too hard for me. "Come along, Buttercup, and then I'll take you for a nice walk and see all the other pretty houses on the street."

"There are lots of them in Pasadena," said Chloe. "Mrs. Pinkerton lives on Orange Grove Boulevard."

"That's the one they call Millionaire's Row, isn't it?"

"It is," answered Harvey. "But San Pasqual isn't precisely shabby."

Riki loped up the long staircase as if he carried heavy luggage upstairs every day of his life. Which he might, for all I knew. I also knew nothing about Japanese names, but Riki seemed a trifle incongruous. Then again, I knew beans about Japan, except what little I'd learned when I saw *The Mikado* in Boston, and I do believe Messrs. Gilbert and Sullivan took liberties.

"Here is where the parents live," said Chloe when we got to the top of the staircase.

I peeked inside the room to which she'd motioned. "Good grief, it's a whole entire apartment. Kind of like in the house on Bunker Hill."

"And then some. Father even has an office up here."

"Oh, dear. Maybe they really *are* going to open a branch bank in Pasadena."

"Appalling thought," said Chloe, "but I'm afraid they well might be."

I groaned a bit. Not too loudly. But can you blame me?

"Here we are," said Harvey as Riki opened the door to a room and stood aside for the three of us to enter.

"Goodness, it's very pretty. Did Mother decorate it herself?" I asked Chloe.

"Lord, no. She hired some decorator to do it for her."

"I didn't know there were such people."

"There are people who do everything, if you're willing to pay them enough," Harvey told me.

"I'm particularly glad we have a cook for our home," said Chloe.

"Me, too," I said, thinking, not for the first time, that cooking was something I really needed to learn how to do if I honestly planned to be of the people. So to speak. I'd have to ask Mrs. Buck to give me lessons. I could even offer to pay her for them.

My Thanksgiving quarters, like those of my parents, consisted of an apartment complete with sitting room, bedroom, dressing room, and bathroom. The walls were a soft green, and there were quite lovely landscapes hanging here and there. Evidently the bed looked inviting to Buttercup, because she bounded right over to it and leaped up on the counterpane, which was a darker green than the walls, was chenille and had a ruffle. Pillows were stacked two high on both sides of the bed, with little green and pink throw pillows dotted here and there. A rocking chair with a ruffled cushion sat in a corner, along with a footstool.

"At least they didn't plant me in the slaves' quarters," I muttered as I took in the full glory of the room.

"Even the servants' quarters are nice here," said Chloe. "Aren't they, Riki?"

"Yes, ma'am," said Riki, gently placing my suitcase on a stand in the dressing room.

Harvey plopped the other suitcase in front of the bed.

"Would you like me to ring for a maid to unpack for you?" asked Chloe.

"Good Lord, no!" I stared at my sister. "I thought you said you brought your own maid with you."

"Of course I did, darling. But there are other maids in the house. You can use one of those."

"I don't need a maid," I said grumpily.

"Well, I can't get in and out of my evening clothes as easily as you can. That's because your clothes are—"

"If you're going to tell me my evening clothes are dowdy, Chloe Nash, I'll take severe exception. I'll have you know, I had my duds expressly fitted so that I can get into them and out of them without anyone else's help, thank you very much."

Holding her hands up in a mock I-give-up gesture, Chloe said, "Sorry, dear. Didn't mean to ruffle your feathers."

"Speaking of ruffles," I said, glancing again around the room, "I'm surprised to see ruffles in any home occupied by Mother."

"The decorator talked her into them. Said they're all the fashion, and Mother, who felt a keen desire to be looked upon with respect and awe by her new acquaintances, acquiesced."

"My goodness. I can't recall another time when Mother

acquiesced to anything at all, much less a ruffle."

"Me neither. But unpack your stuff, and let's take Buttercup for a walk. I need to get out and move around some."

"You?" I stared at my usually indolent sister, goggle-eyed.

"Yes. Me. I like to walk, and the doctor said gentle walks are good for both the baby and for me. So you needn't look at me like that, Miss Smarty Pants."

"All right. I'll unpack in a jiffy."

"I see you're already wearing sensible shoes," said Chloe with something of a sniff.

"I *always* wear sensible shoes. You know that."

"Yes." She sighed. "I do."

"Will you be needing anything else, Miss Allcutt?" asked Riki politely, probably sick to death of listening to us blabber.

"No. Thank you very much, Riki. By the way, is Riki a common Japanese name?"

"Mercy!" cried Chloe, shocked at my bold question.

"I only just wondered. Hope I didn't offend you, Riki."

"Not at all, ma'am," said the houseboy with a grin. "My whole name is Rikiichi, but it's easier to say Riki."

"Oh, my. I like Rikiichi. Does it mean anything?"

"The strong one," said he. "My brother Keiji is a houseboy for a lady named Mrs. Bissel, who lives in a grand house in Altadena."

"Altadena? Is that the little community north of Pasadena?" said I, not completely clear on my geography.

"Yes, it is."

"I see. Well, thank you very much for your help, Riki."

"You're most welcome, Miss Allcutt."

And he took off.

"My goodness, he's a very polite young man, isn't he?" I said as Riki bustled away.

"Very polite, and smart as a whip. He's going to the local

community college and aims to attend the university when he's through there. I believe the brother of whom he spoke is now in medical school when he's not working for Mrs. Bissel."

"My word. Good for both of them. Are they local boys? I can't remember meeting any Japanese people before."

"He was born in Hawaii," said Chloe. "I asked him. He said there are lots of Chinese and Japanese people in Hawaii."

"Hawaii." I said the name with reverence. "I've read about Hawaii in the *National Geographic,* and in a Charlie Chan book. It sounds like heaven on earth. Wonder why they left Hawaii to come to the United States."

"Hawaii belongs to the United States, Mercy," said Harvey. "And it is lovely. Warm and muggy, but gorgeous."

"I didn't know that. About Hawaii belonging to the U.S., I mean."

"Few people do. We Americans don't pay much attention to geography as a rule."

I went into the dressing room and opened the suitcase Riki had deposited on the stool. As I flapped wrinkles out of my clothes and hung them in the closet provided, I queried Harvey. "Why were you in Hawaii, Harvey?"

"Made a couple of pictures there. As I said, it's beautiful, and the beaches are gorgeous. After the baby comes, I aim to take Chloe there for a rest. With the baby, of course."

"And a nurse," said Chloe, who liked the idea of motherhood but didn't want to clean up all the messes entailed thereby. Can't say as I blamed her.

"And a nurse," agreed Harvey with a chuckle.

After I'd unpacked the one suitcase, Harvey brought the other one from the bedroom to the dressing room, and I disemboweled that one next. Chloe eyed my wardrobe with a sardonic eye.

"What?" I asked. "Don't you approve?"

"I'm not sure yet. That blue thing looks passable. And that cream-colored gown with the lace overlay looks quite pretty. I'll have to pass judgment when I see them on you."

"They're nice. Lulu helped me pick them out—"

"*Lulu!* Oh, my Gawd! Whatever made you use Lulu as a fashion consultant? Did you lose your mind?"

Chloe had met Lulu several times, and Lulu's eye-popping sense of style had engendered more than one startled comment from Chloe. Not to Lulu, because Chloe is too nice for that, but to me.

"Lulu knew precisely what I wanted, and she helped me a whole lot. And I had everything altered so that I could get in and out of my clothing with no help from anyone." I spoke firmly, although my insides were a little quivery. Chloe herself was a pattern card of fashion, and she'd often scoffed at my "sensible" office attire. But I really had tried to select a wardrobe our mother wouldn't scorn. She scorned me enough already.

"If you say so," said Chloe doubtfully.

"You'll see."

"Guess I'll have to."

"Chloe, darling, I need to make some telephone calls. Are you and Mercy really going to take the dog for a walk?" Harvey had been hovering in the background, shifting from one foot to the other, and I could tell he was bored with our girl talk.

"Yes, we are, darling. As soon as Mercy finishes hanging everything up."

"Very well. I'll see you for dinner. I'll be stashed away in our suite until then."

With another buss on Chloe's cheek, Harvey left us to our own devices.

I grinned. "So not even Harvey wants to hang out with the parents, eh?"

"Lord, no. He's too sensible for that."

We both laughed. Then I dug in my handbag for Buttercup's leash, causing her to bound off the bed and race up to me, her tiny tail wagging a hundred miles an hour.

And we walked the dog.

CHAPTER FOUR

Chloe was right about San Pasqual. The houses on that street were fabulous, each one a masterpiece of architecture and garden maintenance. One of the nice things about living in Southern California is that you can have flowers blooming all year long. In Boston, autumn and winter can be mighty bare months. Not Pasadena. Why, even some of the rosebushes were in full bloom, and Thanksgiving was coming up that very week.

The Throop College of Technology had changed its name to the California Institute of Technology a few years earlier, and it shared space on San Pasqual Street, too, although I think its address said it was on California Boulevard, the next street south. You'd think a university would sully the neighborhood, but its grounds were manicured to perfection, and the students who went there, according to Chloe, were all too intellectual to cut up larks. I supposed that was a good thing, although if a couple of college pranks annoyed my parents enough, they might move back to Boston full time. But that was too much for which to hope.

"Golly, this is beautiful," I said once or twice as we moseyed along the sidewalk. Chloe, who was inclined to dawdle, made Buttercup and me walk much less briskly than we usually did. But I didn't mind. The weather was crisp and clear, and, as already mentioned, the surroundings were fabulous.

"The Castleton estate is not too far away. According to Harold Kincaid, it's like a palace."

"I've heard of Mr. Castleton. Wasn't he one of those railroad magnates who made a fortune on the backs of the poor Chinese and Irish immigrants who worked on his railroads?"

"You and your socialist ideas, Mercy. I swear, it's no wonder Mother despairs of you."

"I'm not a socialist, and Mother despaired of me before I became aware that our society treats some people better than it treats others. Why, only a few weeks ago, Mr. and Mrs. Buck's son was slammed in the clink for a murder he didn't commit! Only because his skin is dark."

"I remember, sweetie. How could I ever forget? You housed the murderess right under your own roof."

"Yes, well, I didn't know she was a murderess at the time," I muttered, annoyed that Chloe had remembered that one tiny mistake on my part. "Anyhow, she only killed men."

"That excuses her. I see." Chloe laughed, a tinkly sound that made me glad even as her words irked me.

"Darn it, there is no excuse for murder, Chloe! I know that as well as you do."

"Of course there isn't, Mercy. I'm only joking."

"Hmm. Well, I now have another girl renting rooms from me, and she's about as far from being a murderer as you and I are."

"I don't know," Chloe said, and rather darkly, too. "Sometimes I think it wouldn't be such a bad thing if a bad guy were to bump off Mother."

This time it was I who laughed, only my laugh didn't tinkle like Chloe's did. "That goes without saying."

Buttercup was in her glory, trotting along, her tiny tail held high and her nose stuck into every bush we passed as we strolled upon many park-like lawns. She also watered those same lawns quite often. Dogs know no shame, I guess.

Too soon, we had to turn back toward our parents' house.

"Mother would have a conniption fit if we were late to dinner or weren't clad impeccably."

"I'd like to peck her," I grumbled, feeling crabby. At *my* house, my tenants and I didn't bother to dress for dinner, a silly, antiquated custom that belonged to the Dark Ages or maybe Victorian England. "How many working stiffs do you suppose *dress for dinner* every day?" I asked my sister. Silly question, I know, but I couldn't seem to help myself.

There we were, two girls from a wealthy Boston family, walking with a purebred French poodle in a haven of wealth and magnificence, when only a few miles away people lived in poverty. Well, since we were at the moment in Pasadena, probably not abject poverty, but in circumstances not nearly as swell as ours. Mind you, I didn't want to give all my money away, but surely there must be *some* way to even things out a little bit, mustn't there? For instance, we could cease blaming everything on people who had skin a different color from ours or hire them only to be servants. That didn't sound awfully darned drastic to me. And don't get me started on how men were considered brave and smart and women fainting and stupid.

"Don't ask Mother that," Chloe advised, getting back to the dressing-for-dinner issue. "She'll think you've sold yourself to the commies."

"Nonsense. I'm no more a communist than I am a socialist, but I do think it wouldn't be a bad thing to spread the wealth around a little. Or at least make things fair for everyone."

"Mercy, you're a daydreamer. I've always liked that about you, but I think I'm the only one in the family who does."

"I suppose so." How disheartening. "Well, at least George isn't here."

"That's a bright note upon which to end our walk," said Chloe, laughing again.

So Chloe, Buttercup and I turned from the sidewalk and trudged the long, long path to the front door of our parents' mansion, and I returned to the room I'd been assigned for my stay. Oh, and I'd figured out how that gate had opened so opportunely when I drove my Roadster up to it. Evidently, Chloe had seen me and asked the houseboy to press the electrical button that operated the gate. The wonders of modern-day technology were evident everywhere, even in my old-fashioned parents' home.

That evening I wore a tubular, sleeveless, V-neck gown with a low waistline and an uneven hemline. A gown that I just had to slip over my head to get on. See? Who needs a maid when you have clothes like that? Anyhow, the gown was beautiful, beaded all over with metallic gray sequins, and with hem, neckline, and low waist picked out in gold and bronze beads. With it I wore some amber earrings Chloe had given me for my birthday and that dangled dangerously. I'm not sure my neck is long enough to successfully carry off the dangles, but I felt daring that evening, and I wore 'em anyway. I brushed my short hair behind my ears, and if I hadn't known better, I'd have thought I was one of the Bright Young Things people were talking about all over the place.

Oh, I also wore a waist-length elasticized cotton bust-flattener. Its adjustable straps couldn't be seen under my gown, and I attached my flesh-colored stockings to the support straps hanging from the girdle. The things I went through simply to spare me the vicious tongue of my mother. I couldn't wait to get back to my own home, where I *never* wore a girdle. I'd only been in Pasadena for a few hours, and already I was in a girdle. What's worse, I feared things wouldn't improve much with time. The idea that I had to face an entire *week* of girdles and bust-flatteners nearly made me weep.

Chloe tapped on my door as I was buckling my black shoes with their low Louis heels. It wasn't easy to bend over in that stupid girdle, believe me. "C'm in," I called.

"I thought I'd better visit you before you descend to make sure you're not going to incur the parental wrath. Harold and his mother are coming to dine with us tonight, so you'll get to meet him. He's a lovely fellow, although his mother is rather a silly creature."

Standing up, I held out my arms and turned slowly in front of my sister. "Well? What do you think?"

"I'm shocked and amazed. I didn't know you could look that good," said Chloe, not precisely flattering me.

"Gee whiz, Chloe, you'd think I was a kid from the docks or something, the way you talk about me."

"Not really, Mercy. You look grand. I love that dress."

"Thank you. Lulu and I sewed every single one of these stupid sequins on the thing."

"Golly, you did? Why didn't you get a dressmaker to sew it up for you?"

"I didn't want to spend money on anything as useless to me as a dinner gown."

"Mercy, you'd better not talk like that at the dinner table."

"For heaven's sake, Chloe, I know better than that." I eyed my sister, who was clad in a baby-blue two-piece gown that not only went smashingly with her eyes and blond shingles, but also hid her growing midsection. Chloe was much prettier than I, and she had the fashion sense of a queen. Or a French seamstress. Anyway, she always looked gorgeous. "You look marvelous, as usual." I didn't resent my sister for her beauty, although I wouldn't have minded having some of my own.

Not that I'm ugly or anything, but Chloe was . . . well, beautiful. I have a relatively pretty face, but my brown hair and blue eyes are just your normal brown and blue. I was nowhere near the ethereal creature Chloe was.

"Thank you. Harold made this for me."

"Harold? You mean Harold Kincaid?" I asked, slightly shocked.

"I told you he was a costumier for Harvey's studio, like Francis Easthope." Mr. Francis Easthope was perhaps the most handsome man in the known universe, and a very nice one, too. It was at his house where the prior, horrible séance had taken place. "Mr. Kincaid knows his stuff."

"I guess he does."

"Well, suck in a big breath, because we must descend into the parental maw now."

"I can't suck in a deep breath with this stupid girdle on," I groused.

Chloe only laughed. She probably didn't *need* a girdle. Unfortunately, my body didn't conform to the bustless, hipless, straight-up-and-down model required by the clothing manufacturers of the so-called roaring twenties. Hence, the bust-flattener and girdle. I'd have made a smashing Victorian. Oh, well.

Chloe and I descended the magnificent spiral stairs arm in arm. Harvey stood at the foot of the staircase, gazing upon his wife with adoring eyes. He nodded when he saw I, too, looked spiffy and winked at me. Harvey is a great guy.

"Harold and Mr. and Mrs. Pinkerton are here," said he, taking Chloe's other arm in his. "And Mrs. Hanratty and her son have arrived, too."

We walked like that, hooked together via our elbows, into the drawing room. At a glance, I saw our mother, clad in an alarming shade of purple, chatting with a plump woman of about Mother's age, who wore a long-sleeved green number. They looked like an eggplant and a large cucumber, animated and gabbing. I don't believe I'd ever seen my mother unbend so much as to chat with another human being. What did this mean?

"She's acting like a person," I whispered to Chloe.

"Astonishing, isn't it?" she replied. "Maybe it's the California

41

air or something."

"It's definitely something, all right."

And then a youngish man rose from the sofa and hurried toward us. Of average height and a little plump, he had a smile a mile wide on his face. "Chloe! You look charming, my dear. And is this your sister? Mercy, isn't it?"

I held out my hand for him to shake, which he did with vigor. "Yes, I'm Mercy Allcutt. And you must be Mr. Kincaid."

"Harold, my dear. Please call me Harold. Everybody does." He eyed me up and down with appreciation. "What a gorgeous gown. Is it Dior?"

"Um . . . no. It's me. I mean, my friend Miss LaBelle and I found it on a rack at the Broadway, and we spiffed it up a bit with sequins and beads."

"Oh, my! Well, you did a brilliant job. I can't wait until you meet Daisy. You and she will get along very well, if what Chloe's told me about you is correct."

"It's correct," said Chloe, kissing Harold's cheek.

Confused, I asked, "Who's Daisy?" The only Daisy I could think of was the woman in Mr. F. Scott Fitzgerald's *The Great Gatsby*, a book that confirmed my view of my own social set in Boston as being frivolous, wasteful and insincere.

"Desdemona Majesty, my dear Miss Allcutt. You'll meet her at the séance on Tuesday. But I shan't tell you anything about her. You'll have to find out for yourself."

"Oh. She's the spiritualist? Is Daisy short for Desdemona?"

This time Harold winked at *me*. I was slightly taken aback, not being accustomed to men winking at me. "You'll see," he said enigmatically.

I guess he was right about that, because I couldn't conceive of any way to get out of attending the stupid séance. It was difficult for me to believe that my mother—*my mother*—was actually going to have a séance performed in her very own home.

My mother, who considered it beneath the dignity of a woman from the Allcutt clan even to work for a living, was pandering to a spiritualist, of all things. I wondered what my father thought about it but didn't even consider asking his opinion. One didn't ask my father anything at all if one valued one's life.

Gee, I'm making my parents out to be monsters, but I don't suppose they were any worse than anyone else from back in Bean Town. My mother would kill me if she heard me speak of my birthplace as Bean Town, so please don't tell her.

Mother and the cucumber turned to glance at us, mother at first with disapproval—she invariably expected me to look unfashionable—and then with surprise. Ha! I'd show the old bat I could dress well when I wanted to. Well . . . I didn't really *want* to, but I'd do it in order to keep the peace.

"Good evening, Mercedes Louise. You look respectable for once, I see."

I'd have rolled my eyes, except that would have given Mother another reason to snipe at me. "Thank you, Mother," I said with faint sarcasm. Chloe pinched my arm. She didn't want to see me smashed like a bug, I expect.

"And Clovilla, that's a lovely color on you."

"Thank you, Mother," said Chloe, wincing only slightly when Mother called her Clovilla.

"Chloe is always lovely," said the loving and loyal Harvey.

"Yes," said Mother repressively. "But please allow me to introduce you to my daughters, Madeline. Mercedes Louise, come here and say how-do-you-do to Mrs. Pinkerton."

I did as commanded, giving Mrs. Pinkerton a little bow. "How do you do, Mrs. Pinkerton?"

"I'm very well, thank you. And you're so very pretty, my dear. Honoria gave me to believe you were the plain sister, but I see she clearly exaggerated."

I shot my mother a sour look and wanted to say, "Thanks a

lot, Mother dear," but naturally, I didn't. "Why, thank you, Mrs. Pinkerton," I said instead. And sweetly, too, darn it.

"I've already had the pleasure of meeting Chloe," said Mrs. Pinkerton. "It's good to see you again, my dear."

"Thank you, Mrs. Pinkerton. I hope you're well this evening."

"Oh, my, yes. Thank you for asking. You're such a sweet thing." She gestured at a man, who stood chatting with our father. "Oh, Algie, please come here and meet the young Miss Allcutt. Algie is my husband, you see," she whispered at Chloe and Harvey and me.

Algie Pinkerton? Goodness gracious.

A pink-faced, rotund gentleman made his way over to us. He seemed very pleasant, and I relaxed slightly. So far, it looked as if the only two stiff sticks in the room were Mother and Father. Everyone else appeared to be nice.

"Algie, darling, please say good evening to Chloe and Mercy, Honoria and Albert's two daughters."

"Charmed, charmed," said the jovial Mr. Pinkerton, shaking first Chloe's hand and then mine. "What a pleasure to meet two such lovely ladies."

I smiled at him, unable to stop myself. He really did seem like a good guy. Actually, Mrs. Pinkerton seemed nice, too, even if she was friends with Mother.

Chloe and I were introduced to another couple of people, one Mrs. Pansy Hanratty and her son, Monty Mountjoy. If I hadn't become accustomed to meeting moving-picture folks at Chloe and Harvey's parties, I might well have suffered a spasm on the spot when introduced to Mr. Mountjoy, because he was the current cinematic heartthrob. In fact, since Rudolph Valentino's untimely death earlier in the year, Mr. Mountjoy was the nation's leading man. He also seemed quite nice. Chloe, who had met him before, had told me he was.

I was about to ask Chloe what had possessed our parents to

invite movie people to dinner, but a stiffly erect butler entered the room at that moment and said, "Dinner is served," and I wasn't able to. We all trooped off to the dining room, which was down the hall from the great room. Both the great room and the dining room had sliding pocket doors made of some dark, shiny wood that gleamed like anything. I could imagine a maid polishing those panels every day or so, poor thing.

The dining room, like the rest of the house, was large and elegant, with a banquet-sized table, from which, I presume, a couple of leaves had been removed, because we weren't spaced so far apart as to prevent table chat. Candles lit the scene, and an Irish lace tablecloth had been spread atop a plain white one. It looked to me as though Mother had brought her complete Dawlish pattern Wedgwood china from Boston to Pasadena. There must be eighty-five or a hundred pieces in the set, which made my heart sink a little. This was Mother's favorite china pattern and added more weight to the notion the parents might be on the verge of moving to Pasadena permanently.

The thought of my parents living only twenty-two miles from me was nowhere near as comforting as knowing they were a couple of thousand miles away. Maybe I could move back to Boston.

But no. I loved living in Los Angeles in my pretty home on Bunker Hill. And I loved my job with Ernie Templeton. Besides, I'd miss all my L.A. friends and tenants.

Oh, bother my parents!

CHAPTER FIVE

Fortunately for me, I was placed between Harold Kincaid and Harvey at the table that evening, so I didn't have to duck any barbed comments from either of my parents. Poor Chloe sat next to Father at the head of the table, with Mr. Pinkerton on her other side. That was all right. Father didn't talk much during meals, and so far Mr. Pinkerton appeared to be a nice fellow.

Next to Mr. Pinkerton sat Mrs. Hanratty, and next to her sat her son. I don't suppose that was totally correct, putting a mother and her son together, but Mother sat at the foot of the table, and her word was law, so no one complained. Anyhow, I got to gaze my fill at the ultra-handsome Monty Mountjoy whenever I liked because the center table decoration wasn't very tall, consisting as it did of a cornucopia, with fruits, nuts, and vegetables spilling therefrom. Most suitable for the season.

Father said a brief prayer before the houseboy and butler began serving us, beginning with a tolerable clear soup. I made sure my manners were impeccable because, even though Mother wasn't near me, I could occasionally feel her piercing gaze upon me.

"Mmm," said Harold Kincaid at my side. "Brown Windsor soup. Tasty."

"Is that what this is? I don't believe I've ever had it before."

"Yes. As you can tell, I enjoy my food." He patted his tummy and laughed, a sound so pleasant—and so seldom heard at my parents' dinner table—that I joined in.

"Mercedes Louise," came Mother's stentorian voice from the foot of the table. "What are you laughing about with Mr. Kincaid?"

Bother. "Nothing, Mother. We were complimenting your cook on the delicious soup."

"And that's what you were laughing about?" Mother sounded displeased, but then, she always did.

"No, no, Mrs. Allcutt. It's my fault. I was telling Miss Allcutt about how much I enjoyed good food. She did nothing untoward."

"Hmph," said Mother, and her frigid gaze left me.

I felt my shoulders sag with relief. "Thanks, Harold."

"Not a problem, my girl. Your mother is a formidable woman, isn't she?"

"More than formidable," I said, barely repressing a shudder. "She's like an avalanche."

"Mercy always gets the brunt of her disapproval," said Harvey on my other side. "I have no idea why, but it's true."

"I think she disapproves of me because I left the ancestral home in Boston, came West all by myself, and got a *job*, of all unspeakable things."

"Goodness, she doesn't like it that you're a productive member of society?" Harold asked, clearly puzzled at so odd a reaction from my maternal parent.

"Precisely." I smiled at him, grateful that someone besides me understood my ambition to earn the space I took up on this green earth and not have it handed to me, gratis, on a silver platter.

"That sounds positively antediluvian," said Harold.

"It is," I agreed.

Harvey only chuckled. Mother didn't call him on the carpet for it, which just goes to show you how unfair to me she was.

But I incurred no further wrath for the remainder of the dinner, which was extremely tasty. After the soup, we had some kind of fish dish that was quite good, then a roast beef with Yorkshire pudding and various vegetables. Quite the feast. I decided to visit the kitchen and tell the cook how much I appreciated her efforts on our behalf. I felt fairly certain Mother and Father never bothered to praise her.

After the last course was served, a baked Alaska, which had a meringue that melted on the tongue, Mother rose like a statue from her seat at the foot of the table.

"Ladies," she commanded, "let us leave the gentlemen to their cigars and retire to the drawing room."

Oh, boy, if ever there was a custom as antiquated as dressing for dinner, this was it. However, Mother was Mother, so we ladies all complied with her demand, Chloe catching up with me as we left the dining room.

"I see she's brought Boston to Pasadena," I whispered as we left the men to their various smokes and followed Mother, who led us to the drawing room like a general leading his soldiers into battle. In the olden days, before Prohibition, the men would have had port with their cigars, but my parents were nothing if not law-abiding, so there was no liquor in their home.

Mrs. Hanratty, who had a voice like a particularly loud foghorn, came up to me as soon as we entered the drawing room. "Miss Allcutt, it's such a pleasure to meet you. I've enjoyed getting to know your sister these past few days."

"Thank you, Mrs. Hanratty. It's a pleasure to meet you, too." That wasn't quite true, since I hadn't pegged her yet, but she seemed pleasant and friendly.

However, she then went on to seal herself in my esteem by saying, "I can't believe your mother sticks to the custom of ladies withdrawing so the gentlemen can blather. Of course, my own mother is from the deep South, and she does the same thing. I guess some folks stick to the old ways, come hell or high water."

"Indeed they do," I said, appreciating her very much. "Mother and the Olden Days are as tight as twins."

Chloe, still at my side, said, "Mrs. Hanratty teaches dog obedience classes, Mercy. If you lived closer, you could take Buttercup to one of her classes."

"Oh, my, really? What an interesting thing to do."

"What kind of dog is your Buttercup, Miss Allcutt?"

"Oh, please call me Mercy, Mrs. Hanratty. Everyone does. And Buttercup is a toy French poodle. She's an apricot color and the apple of my eye. If you don't mind me mixing my fruits."

Mrs. Hanratty gave out with a honking laugh, which brought Mrs. Pinkerton over to us.

"What are you laughing about, my dears? Is Pansy cutting jokes?"

"Oh, no, Mrs. Pinkerton. We were discussing dogs."

"My, yes. Pansy and her dogs. You can hardly get her to leave them at home when you invite her to dinner."

"My dogs and my son are my passions in life," said Mrs. Hanratty.

"I understand completely," said I. "Well, about the dogs, anyway. I have no children because I'm not married, but I do love my Buttercup."

"She's a very smart pooch, too," said Chloe, bless her.

"Poodles are extremely intelligent animals," Mrs. Hanratty said with a nod of agreement. "But any dog can be trained as long as its owner is willing to take the time to do it. Why, Mrs. Majesty even took her dachshund to one of my classes, and he graduated at the top of his class. Dachshunds aren't known for their following dispositions, but tend to be stubborn. However, Mrs. Majesty's Spike will do almost anything for food, and Mrs. Majesty spent every day with him a few summers ago, teaching him how to behave."

"My goodness. Mrs. Majesty is the spiritualist, isn't she?"

"She is indeed," said Mrs. Pinkerton with a light of fervor in her eyes. "She's the most wonderful spiritualist you'll ever meet. Why, she's helped me *so* much over these past few years, which have been rather difficult at times. Well, and they have been for her, too, what with her husband's death and all."

"Her husband's death?" I asked, slightly shocked. I didn't know any widows, not that my circle of acquaintances was large. I'd only just moved to Los Angeles in June, after all, and the girls I'd known in Boston were schoolchildren.

"Yes." Mrs. Pinkerton lowered her voice to a dramatic whisper. "He was a casualty of the War, don't you know."

"Oh, how awful for her." Poor Mrs. Majesty! I couldn't imagine such a thing, although the Lord knew, thousands of our boys had been killed over there. I'd been a little young to understand it all while the war was progressing.

"It was devastating," said Mrs. Pinkerton while Mrs. Hanratty nodded her agreement. "The poor thing had only been married for a couple of months before her Billy was sent off to war, where he was shot and gassed."

"Good heavens," said Chloe. "That's dreadful."

"Indeed," said Mrs. Pinkerton.

The conversation had taken a depressing turn, so I reverted to dogs. "And she has a dachshund? Aren't those the dogs that look like animated sausages?"

"Those are dachshunds, all right," said Mrs. Hanratty with another laugh. Every time she laughed, I jumped a little. Her voice was *very* loud.

"Are you talking about Daisy's Spike?" asked a male voice. I turned to see Harold Kincaid, Monty Mountjoy at his side, stroll into the drawing room.

"I'm sure she is, Harold. You know my mother and dogs,"

said Mr. Mountjoy, giving his mother a loving glance that darned near made me cry.

Why couldn't Chloe and I have a mother who loved us as Mrs. Hanratty loved her son? And vice versa? Well, nobody ever said life was fair.

"Monty, you bad boy," said his fond mother. "If it weren't for my dogs, I'd have to live with *Mother,* and you know how we rub against each other."

Thank God I wasn't the only one.

"What is this?" asked my mother, coming to the party and frowning at me. Of course.

"We were discussing our dogs, Mother," I said. "Mrs. Hanratty teaches dog-obedience classes."

"Yes, I know," said Mother. "You should take that poodle of yours to one of her classes so it won't jump up on people every time they come to your house." She sniffed. She didn't approve of Buttercup any more than she approved of me buying Chloe and Harvey's house, either. She considered independence a dreadful thing in a daughter.

"Buttercup is pretty well trained," I said in defense of my darling pooch. "I've taught her how to shake hands and heel and lots of things. And she doesn't jump up on people every time they enter the house! I've trained her not to do that. You haven't seen her recently." So there, Mother.

Mother sniffed. "Dogs are so dirty," said she after her sniff.

"Buttercup isn't dirty, either. I bathe her every week or so."

"You mustn't bathe dogs too often," said Mrs. Hanratty. "It will dry out their skin and make them itch. If you bathe her every week, you should use some kind of soothing oil on her coat."

"What do you recommend?" I asked politely, hoping to stave off more of Mother's nasty comments about Buttercup.

"Coconut oil is very good for a dog's coat. And if you can get

51

hold of some oatmeal soap, that is good for them, too."

"Goodness, I didn't know that. Where does one come by coconut oil and oatmeal soap?" I asked, genuinely interested.

With a nod to her son, Mrs. Hanratty said, "Monty and I will be happy to take you to Priscilla's Pets. It's on Lake Avenue, near Washington. You'll drive us there, won't you, Monty? On Tuesday, perhaps?"

"Happy to," said her dutiful son, but with such a charming smile, I knew he didn't mind carting her around.

I wouldn't mind being in his company some more either. Maybe this week wouldn't be so terribly awful after all.

The evening wore on more pleasantly than I had anticipated. Both Harold Kincaid and Monty Mountjoy were swell fellows, with good senses of humor and with a lot of interesting anecdotes about the actors they worked with.

"Oh, my," I said at one point. "I didn't realize Lola de la Monica was so difficult to work with."

"She's a spiteful witch," said Harold, not mincing his words. "But she's not long for the picture world. She's getting a reputation as being *too* difficult. In truth, I'm surprised she's still around. I thought for sure they'd can her after *The Fire at Sunset.*"

"Oh, I loved that picture," I said.

"The picture was all right, but Lola nearly ruined the thing."

"Really? What did she do?"

"She threw temperament fits right and left. I'm surprised Daisy survived. Well, she almost didn't," Harold said darkly.

"Daisy? What did she have to do with the picture?" I had to admit I was getting more and more interested in meeting the spiritualist.

"Lola hired her to be her spiritual consultant during the filming of the picture."

"My goodness." What a fascinating job! It sounded almost

more interesting than my own employment as a private investigator. I mean as secretary to a private investigator.

"Anyhow, with half the population of Southern California longing to get work in the pictures, I'm sure Harvey or one of the other studio chiefs will replace Lola soon with a new face."

"Boy, I'd hate to have my livelihood depend on my looks and behavior," I said, glad to be working for Ernie Templeton, who didn't give a hang what anyone did as long as they left him alone.

"It's not merely looks," said Chloe, who kept chatting with us as we moseyed over to a long sofa against a back wall. "You know yourself, Mercy, that how one comes across on the screen is what matters. Why, there are tons of gorgeous women out there who'd fade into nothing on the big screen."

"I wonder if Lulu will ever be discovered," I muttered musingly.

"Lulu LaBelle?" Chloe gave one of her tinkling laughs that sounded like cherubs singing. Not that I've ever personally heard a cherub sing, but you know what I mean. "I don't know. It would be a kick to see her on the screen, though."

"I've never heard of Lulu LaBelle," said Harold. "Is she new?"

"Oh, no. She's the receptionist at the Figueroa Building, where I work."

"Ah," said Harold.

"But I know what you mean, Chloe. I remember thinking when I met Miss Jacqueline Lloyd that, while she was a lovely woman, she truly came to life on the silver screen. Not everyone has that . . . what do you call it? Stage presence?"

"I guess," said Chloe with a shrug.

"Oh, my, you knew *her*?" exclaimed Harold. "The murderess? How fascinating!"

I nodded. "Yes, and I met her equally murderous sister. In fact, the sister tried to kill me."

"You lead an exciting life, young woman," said Harold as if he approved, which was a novel experience for me.

"Oh, Lord, since Mercy's gone to work for that private detective, she's been in all sorts of scrapes and messes," said Chloe, laughing.

"You work for a private investigator?" Harold exclaimed, eyeing me with, if possible, even more approval.

"Yes, I do." I said it proudly, too, shooting a malevolent glance at my mother, who was lording it over Mrs. Pinkerton and Mrs. Hanratty at the other end of the room. She didn't see me, which is probably just as well.

"Fascinating," said Monty Mountjoy.

"She even rented a room in her house to another murderess," said Chloe. I wish she hadn't.

"My God, Mercy! You really *do* lead an exciting life!" said Harold.

"That was a mistake," I admitted, squinting at Chloe in an effort to stave off further information about the various tight spots I'd been in since I went to work for Ernie.

With a laugh, Chloe said, "Don't worry, sweetie, I won't reveal any more of your secrets."

"Thank you," I said drily. "But the fact is that both Mother and I met Miss Jacqueline Lloyd at a séance, which makes Mother's present interest in séances quite baffling to me."

"That," said Harold in an ominous voice, "is my mother's doing. She's an idiot, you know, but she positively *loves* Daisy Majesty. Claims she's saved her life more than once."

"My goodness. What do you think of Mrs. Majesty, Harold?" I asked, genuinely interested. Only later did I remember that he'd called his own mother an idiot. I should have been paying more attention. Oh, well.

"We're best friends," said Harold. "And I shan't say another word about Daisy. You'll meet her for yourself."

At that moment, Mother clapped her hands, and we all jumped and turned to face her. I feared for my life until I realized she only wanted to ask if anyone would like to join her for a rubber or two of bridge. As Chloe and I had very cleverly failed to learn how to play bridge, we didn't have to obey this summons.

Father, Mrs. Pinkerton and Monty Mountjoy were cajoled into participating, so he left our happy group. I was sorry to see him go.

"Don't look so downhearted, Mercy," advised Harold. "He's a very compliant fellow, and always does what people ask of him."

"Goodness. Doesn't he dislike always doing other people's bidding?"

"Not really," Harold said with a shrug. "He aims to please."

Very well, I decided I wasn't going to marry Mr. Monty Mountjoy, no matter *how* handsome and pleasant he was. Darned if I'd marry anyone who'd meekly follow Mother's commands.

Mrs. Hanratty wandered over to our group. "I hate bridge," she announced in a whisper that probably carried as well as her speaking voice. "But I'd love to meet your dog, Mercy."

"Oh, would you? I'd love to introduce her to you!"

So I trotted upstairs, freed Buttercup from her confinement, clipped on her leash, and led her downstairs to meet Mrs. Hanratty.

The two of them and Harold got along swimmingly. Mrs. Hanratty, Chloe, Harold and I even took Buttercup outside, so I could show Mrs. Hanratty what a good doggie she was.

Overall, I counted the evening a success.

Unfortunately, as was its wont, the evening drew to a close, all the people who weren't members of the family went home, and the family went to bed.

And then came Sunday.

CHAPTER SIX

We partook of Sunday breakfast in the breakfast room, where Riki Saito served us grapefruit halves, sausages, scrambled eggs, toast, and coffee. I reminded myself to chat with the cook and compliment her on her cooking skills.

"We shall attend church services at eleven," said Mother in a voice that brooked no nonsense. "I expect to see you two girls suitably attired and ready to leave by ten-thirty."

"Yes, Mother," Chloe and I chorused as one.

"Will you be joining us, Harvey?" Mother sent Harvey a look that would make a fainter soul than Harvey quake in his boots.

"Of course, I shall," said the ever-genial Harvey.

"Very good." Mother sniffed as if she'd managed to bridle a particularly troublesome colt, which Harvey definitely was not.

"I'll have Roberts bring the machine around," said Father.

I looked up from my eggs in astonishment. "You have an *automobile*?" My parents, when they lived in Boston, didn't own an auto. Father took taxis everywhere, and Mother never left the throne room if she didn't have to.

Mother glared at me, and I regretted my moment of impetuosity. "For heaven's sake, Mercedes Louise, there's no need to shout at the breakfast table."

"That's all right, Honoria," said Father, surprising me. He didn't generally come to my defense. "Yes, Mercedes, I decided that, since this area of the world is more spread out than Boston is, I should secure my own means of transportation."

"I see. And you have a chauffeur, too?"

"Indeed we do. Roberts has proved most competent, and he takes excellent care of the Imperial."

"The Imperial?" asked Chloe, bless her heart. I'd have asked, but Mother would probably have leapt upon me and crushed me flat. "I've never heard of an Imperial."

"Is it a Chrysler Imperial, sir?" asked Harvey with interest.

"Yes, it is. A Chrysler Imperial five-passenger phaeton. It's basically a touring car."

"My goodness, I can't wait to see it," said Harvey.

I couldn't either, but I didn't dare say so.

"We shall all see it after we finish breakfast and tidy up for church," said Mother at her most overbearing. "This morning, we need to possess our souls in peaceful contemplation so that we can receive the message Father Clark will deliver."

From this speech, I deduced that the parents were continuing the custom of attending the Episcopal Church, and I wondered where it might be. Chloe clued me in when she and I went upstairs to change into our church clothing.

Let me interrupt the narrative to say something here. Living with our mother was a trying ordeal. Not only was she an unpleasant and commanding woman to begin with, but we were forever having to change our clothes. We had to go down to breakfast in one outfit, change into another for church, then change into something else for lunch and the afternoon, and then change *again* into dinner attire. It was simply idiotic, and any self-respecting working girl could never keep up such an imbecilic routine. On the other hand, Mother refused to accept that her younger daughter *was* a working girl.

Maybe I should move to Hawaii. That's a U.S. territory, isn't it? According to Harvey and Riki Saito, it is.

Never mind.

Anyhow, Chloe said, "They attend St. Mark's in Altadena.

The church is directly across the street from another of Mother's new acquaintances, Mrs. Bissel."

"Good Lord, she seems to have made a lot of friends in a very short period of time."

Chloe eyed me slantways. "I wouldn't call them *friends*. You know Mother."

"Yes. *Associates* is probably closer to the mark."

"Yes. She's surrounded herself with all the rich people she could accumulate in her short stay in Pasadena. There are lots of them from which to choose."

I only sighed and went into my rooms to dress for church.

We all traipsed out the front door after we were appropriately clad for our visit to St. Mark's. I wore a rust-colored, flowered rayon day dress with a bow at the low boat neck and another at the hip-length waist. The skirt had an uneven hem, as my prior night's evening gown had boasted. With it, I wore a coat I'd borrowed from Chloe. It was light yellow with brown fur trim. What with my brown felt cloche hat and brown leather heels, not even Mother could complain about my grooming.

That didn't stop her from trying. "Mercedes Louise, I'm glad to see you're taking more care with your clothes these days. Why, when I visited last August, you looked quite frumpish."

"I wear clothes suitable for my occupation, Mother," I said stiffly.

"Your *occupation*, indeed." She sniffed.

"Leave Mercy alone, Mother. She looks wonderful today." God bless my sister. Chloe always tried to divert Mother's attention.

Of course, Chloe herself was a vision of loveliness in her dark blue day dress and fur coat. She'd probably had the dress made for her by the seamstress she patronized. Nothing off-the-rack for Chloe.

A loud noise prevented Mother from further berating me. As

we stood on the—well, it wasn't a porch, precisely. It was more like a paved space that curved from the tiny front porch to the drive. Anyhow, as we stood there an enormous motorcar swung into view. Good gracious! Father hadn't merely bought an automobile; he'd bought a gigantic *red* automobile! Astonished didn't half describe my emotions upon first glimpsing that monster car. I sneaked a quick peek at our mother's face, and saw her grimace with disapproval before she tamed her feelings. Not for the world would she allow anyone to discern her dislike of anything our father did. The two of them presented a united front, no matter what the circumstances. Well, there had been one exception to that rule, but that's another story entirely.

However, she sure didn't like that car. Inside, I smiled. I know, how evil of me. But really, do you blame me?

The chauffeur, a young, good-looking man with white-blond hair and clad in a sober livery, descended from the automobile and opened the back door. Mother, Chloe, and I got into the backseat. Father and Harvey took the seat behind the chauffeur, Roberts reentered the machine, and we were off to church. Since I'm not familiar with Pasadena, I can't tell you our route, but the church was uphill from San Pasqual. It was also lovely once we got there.

Across the street from it loomed a gigantic mansion situated amidst fields and fields of pasture. Chloe whispered in my ear, "That's Mrs. Bissel's house. She's the acquaintance of Mother's I told you about."

"There's no need to whisper, Clovilla," said Mother. "I'm sure Mercedes Louise is interested in our new friends, and she will have the opportunity to meet them during the week."

Oh, joy. I could hardly wait.

But the church was pretty, and smiling ushers met us at the door as we trooped in. I'm not sure where Roberts went; probably to park the car. I didn't see him again until the service ended. Then, as we left the church, a large woman bustled up to Mother.

"Honoria! Is this your other daughter? How lovely to meet you!" And whoever she was, she held out her hand for me to shake.

Well, this was interesting. And welcome. Mother's Boston friends weren't nearly as friendly as this woman.

"Yes, Griselda. This is our younger daughter, Mercedes Louise," said Mother in her frosty voice.

"Everyone calls me Mercy," I told Griselda, whose last name I had yet to learn.

She took my hand and shook it cordially. "So very glad to meet you, my dear. I'm Griselda Bissel, and I live right across the street." She waved an arm in the direction of the mansion across the street, which was Foothill Boulevard, if anyone cares.

"Yes, my sister told me. You have a good deal of property. Are those horses I see?"

"Yes, indeed, I have three horses, although I no longer ride myself. But my children loved their horses until they left for school. Used to ride up in the foothills all the time."

"That sounds wonderful," I told her, meaning it. What a pleasant life for a child, to be able to jump on her own horse and ride for miles up in the hills.

"You and your sister and mother and father must come to dinner one of these days, my dear."

"We're not sure what our schedule will be for this week, Griselda," said Mother in a quelling voice. "Mercedes Louise is only here for a week." She gazed at me. With disapproval, I'm sure I need not add.

"I'm sorry to hear it. But you can visit me some morning or afternoon, my dear. I'll show you my dogs. Do you like dogs, Mercy?"

"Indeed I do. I have a toy French poodle."

"Poodles are nice dogs. However, *I* breed dachshunds. Naturally, I consider the dachshund to be the perfect dog."

I blinked. "Oh, are you the one from whom Mrs. Majesty got her dachshund?"

She beamed at me. "Why, yes! I gave Daisy her doggy, Spike, after she exorcised a ghost from my basement."

My mouth fell open for a second, but no sound escaped therefrom, so I shut it again. Desdemona Majesty had exorcised a *ghost* from this woman's *basement*? I could scarcely wait to meet Mrs. Majesty, who seemed to possess magical properties. Maybe she could teach me how to make Mother disappear.

Mrs. Bissel evidently noticed my state of startlement (if that's a word) because she laughed softly. "I know it sounds very strange, but it's true. The woman is a wonder." She turned to Mother, who was glaring impartially at everyone in her vicinity. "But you're holding a séance, aren't you, Honoria? Your daughters will get to meet Mrs. Majesty then."

"Yes. But shall we go to the coffee hour in the Community Hall? Let's not stand here jabbering," said Mother.

"Oh, yes, let's," said Mrs. Bissel, clearly not cowed by Mother's description of her conversational style.

So Mother led the way to a big room behind the church where coffee and cookies were laid out. Several people approached Chloe, Harvey and me and introduced themselves in the casual manner so many people in Southern California seemed to possess. Nobody in Boston would approach a person without a proper introduction. I *so* appreciated my new home!

Dinner was ready when we got home a little past one o'clock, so Chloe and I had to dash upstairs to change clothes yet again. I wore a simple day dress and steeled myself to withstand Mother's stern objections.

Oddly enough, she didn't object. In fact, she yawned once or twice during the meal, which again was served to us in the breakfast room by Riki. Yankee pot roast today, according to Mother. You couldn't prove it by me. It tasted like any other pot roast I'd ever eaten in my life.

After dinner, Mother went upstairs where she aimed "to contemplate today's sermon." In other words, she wanted to take a nap, which sounded like a good idea to me.

First, though, I took Buttercup for a walk around the neighborhood again. Chloe didn't join us this time, as she, too, decided to rest. The houses on San Pasqual Street in Pasadena, California, were absolutely spectacular. As much as I loved my home on Bunker Hill, it didn't hold a candle to those grand estates.

But neither Buttercup nor I repined. Rather, we had a very nice walk and then retired to my suite of rooms, where I rested a bit, and then wrote some of the book I'd begun in June. I'd thought about bringing my typewriter to the parents' house, but opted not to, certain Mother would complain about not merely the noise from the typewriting machine, but also the fact that I'd ignored family tradition and learned to type. Whoopee. I'd also learned Pitman Shorthand. What's more, I'd then used my skills to get a *job*. So there.

Once during the afternoon I heard the telephone ring. Nobody came to get me, so I presumed the call wasn't for me, which was moderately depressing.

Not that I expected any of my friends to telephone. Both Lulu and Ernie, the two people I'd most like to hear from, had met my mother, and neither one of them would bother her on a lazy Sunday afternoon unless my house was burning down or something. The call had probably been for Harvey, who was always in touch with other people in the picture industry.

Along about five o'clock, a tiny tap came at my door. I managed to grab Buttercup and clap a hand over her muzzle before she could bark and annoy Mother. I spoke sweet nothings to her as I walked to the door and opened it. She didn't bark when I removed my hand to do so, bless her.

"Chloe! I'm so glad you came to see me. I'm bored and lonely."

"You've only been here a day, Mercy. If you're already bored and lonely, what are you going to do for the rest of the week?"

"I don't know," I said, gesturing for her to come in and sit down. "Suffer a lot and go nuts, I guess. I miss my friends."

"Poor Mercy. But Mrs. Hanratty telephoned a while ago, and asked if you and I would like to go to Priscilla's Pets with her and Monty on Tuesday."

"Oh, my, yes! I'd love to. Monty Mountjoy is dreamy, isn't he?"

"Don't get your hopes up, Mercy. Monty isn't your type."

Rather indignantly, I said, "Oh? And why, precisely, is that?"

"Don't get your feathers all ruffled, sweetie. It's not you. It's him. Monty's one of those men who don't go for the girls."

I looked at my sister, puzzled. "What does that mean?"

Chloe rolled her eyes, something she seldom did. "Oh, dear. You're so innocent, aren't you?"

"Am I?" Chloe wasn't one to ridicule another person, so I knew she didn't mean her comment as an insult.

"Well . . . yes. In this case, yes, you're innocent."

"Explain, please," I said, hoping for enlightenment.

"Well, you know Francis Easthope."

"Of course, I know him. He's another handsome man, and he's also a very nice one."

"Yes, he is. You see, there are some men in the world—and some women, too—who don't feel attracted to people of the opposite sex. They prefer people of their own."

I stared at her, trying to understand what she was saying. Then it hit me. I gaped at my lovely sister. "You mean . . ."

"Yes. Both Francis and Monty—and Harold, too, actually—

63

are homosexuals. That doesn't mean they aren't wonderful people, no matter what people of our mother's stamp might say. It just means . . . well . . ."

"I shouldn't hold out any hopes that any of them will ever ask me to marry them. Right?"

"Right. And, believe me, Mercy, men like that make the *best* friends."

"Do they?"

"Yes. Perhaps because that nasty thing, sex, never lifts its ugly head. They can just be friends. Good friends. Without any expectations of anything else."

"I see. My goodness, I'd never even thought about people like that, although I've heard of them."

"You needn't speak of Monty, Francis and Harold as if they were members of some exotic species, Mercy Allcutt." I don't believe I'd ever heard Chloe sound so astringent.

"I didn't mean to," I said, feeling humble. Far be it from me, Mercedes Louise Allcutt, whose own mother detested her, to dislike another person for being . . . different. "Truly I didn't, Chloe."

"Oh, I know it, sweetheart. It's just that so many people consider people like Monty and Francis evil for being what they are. And they can't help it. Francis told me so, and I believe him."

"Like Oscar Wilde," I said, suddenly recalling reading about the famous author and his trials and tribulations.

"Yes. Like Oscar Wilde."

"I see. Well, that's all right then."

Chloe and I smiled at each other, and all seemed well with the world again.

I ought to have known it wouldn't last.

CHAPTER SEVEN

I'm not altogether sure how I survived Monday at my parents' house, but it probably helped that Chloe made me go with her to downtown Pasadena, where there were lots and lots of shops. I'm not much of a shopper as a rule, but Chloe and I had fun. We also ate luncheon at a pretty little restaurant, and didn't get home until the late afternoon.

Mother carped at me for having been gone all day when I was supposed to be visiting with her and Father, but she only did so because she hated me. She really didn't want me around.

That evening, Mr. and Mrs. Pinkerton visited again, and they and Father and Mother played bridge again. Mrs. Pinkerton's son didn't come with his mother, so I ultimately retired to my bedroom and read for a while. You can bet I was ready for bed when Monday finally ended.

However, Tuesday began pleasantly enough once breakfast was over and Mother went away. Mother spent the breakfast hour deploring Mrs. Pinkerton's skill, or lack thereof, at the bridge table. "The woman's a nitwit," she proclaimed.

"That's not very kind, Mother," said Chloe. I stared at her in astonishment. I agreed with her, but would never say so.

Mother sniffed. "It's the truth."

So much for Mrs. Pinkerton.

Anyhow, Monty Mountjoy and Mrs. Hanratty came over to pick us up in a sporty Stutz Bearcat at ten o'clock. Monty's car, I'm sure.

"Don't be too long," Mother told Chloe and me as we headed out the front door to freedom. I mean to Priscilla's Pets. "Tonight is the séance, remember, and I want everything to be in order."

"We remember, Mother," Chloe called over her shoulder.

"How could we forget?" I muttered under my breath.

"We're taking your daughters out to luncheon," said Monty Mountjoy, much to my delight.

Mother didn't respond. I'm sure she humphed, however. She always did when her younger daughter was offered a treat.

"Your mother reminds me *so* much of my own," said Mrs. Hanratty after we'd settled in the automobile.

I looked at her in surprise. "Really? I'm so sorry." As soon as I said it, I wished the words unsaid, but Monty, Mrs. Hanratty and Chloe all laughed, so it was all right, I reckon.

"I'm fortunate in my own mother," said Monty. "She's a peach."

Mrs. Hanratty patted his cheek.

"Our mother's a sour apple," said Chloe, and we all laughed again.

"And mine is a wilted magnolia blossom," said Mrs. Hanratty. This time our laughter sounded more like a roar, and we all had to dry our eyes, we laughed so hard.

For some reason, probably because Mother and Father together are enough to stifle the liveliest spirit, I felt *free* as I stepped into that snazzy car and Monty roared us off to a pet store in Pasadena.

Priscilla's Pets sat on Lake Avenue, near Washington Boulevard, and it was a nice place. Priscilla, whoever she was, had stocked the store with an amazing array of collars, leashes, dog and cat food, and shampoos, etc., for one's dog, cat, parrot, or rodent. My nose wrinkled at the notion of having a rodent as a pet, but Chloe said, "Don't sneer, Mercy. Mrs. Dearing's daughter, Mary Lou, has white mice. She loves them."

"Who's Mrs. Dearing?" I asked my sister.

"The Dearings live across the street from Mrs. Bissel."

"I thought St. Mark's Episcopal Church was across the street from Mrs. Bissel." I was getting confused.

"In the other direction. Across Maiden Lane, not Foothill."

"Oh." I had noticed that Mrs. Bissel's property extended an entire block, from Lake Avenue on the west to Maiden Lane on the east. "That's another gigantic home."

"Yes, it is. Oh, but look, Mercy! Look at the parrot over here."

A striking red and blue bird sat on a perch, surveying us with interest. I moved closer to the bird carefully. I'd heard that some parrots bite, and I didn't want this one's sharp beak taking one of my fingers off. "Hello, bird," I said.

"Hello," it said back, much to Chloe's and my delight.

"Polly want a cracker?" said Chloe.

"Cracker, cracker. Hee-hee-hee," chirped the parrot.

"His name is Rufus," said a voice from behind the counter.

Chloe and I turned to see the pet store clerk, smiling at us. We smiled back.

"Would you like to give him a cracker?" asked the clerk, whose name, according to the embroidery on his blue coat, was Chester Withers.

"Will he bite?" I asked uneasily.

"Rufus? Heavens, no. He's a peaceable bird, aren't you, Rufus?"

"Peace," squawked Rufus. "Peace! Peace! Peace!"

I decided parrots were entirely too noisy to be companion animals to a struggling authoress. That didn't stop me from accepting a cracker from Mr. Withers and holding it out to Rufus, who snapped it right up, making me glad I'd held the cracker by its end. Otherwise, Rufus might have enjoyed a bit of finger with his cracker.

I'm not sure how long we stayed at the pet store, but it was fully long enough for Mr. Withers and me to decide the best dog I could get for a newborn baby was some kind of spaniel.

"I'd suggest an English toy spaniel," said Mr. Withers with certainty.

"Really? Why?"

"They're friendly, and they like children. They're also smart and easy to train."

"My poodle is a wizard," I said, leaping to defend Buttercup's reputation as one of the smarter breeds of dog.

"Poodles are fine," said Mr. Withers. "But they can be snappish. An English toy spaniel will never bite."

"Buttercup wouldn't bite anyone," I said.

Mr. Withers smiled at me. "Buttercup is your poodle, I suspect."

"Yes, she is."

"Well then, let me say that *some* poodles can be snappish. The English toy spaniel won't need to be groomed nearly as often as a poodle, either."

"Go with the English whatever, Mercy," said Chloe, standing behind me. "We certainly won't need to groom a dog every day along with everything else that comes along with a baby."

"Not that you'll be doing the grooming," I reminded her.

"Don't be nasty, dear."

"I'm not being nasty! But you have to admit that you'd have a servant groom your dog, no matter what breed I got the baby." I turned back to Mr. Withers. "Do these English toy spaniels have any sort of exciting history to them?"

"Oh, my, yes! Why, if you look at any painting of King Charles the Second of England, you'll almost invariably find an English spaniel with him. Today's English toy spaniels are the direct descendents of Charles the Second's dogs."

"A dog with a history! How fun!" cried Chloe. "Oh, Mercy,

you must get one of them for the little tyke." She looked at Mr. Withers. "Where does one find an English toy spaniel if one wants one?"

"You'll have to purchase one from a breeder," said he.

Chloe and I glanced at each other. As far as I knew, neither of us knew any dog breeders—well, except for Mrs. Bissell, and she bred dachshunds.

"Well, never mind," I said. "I'll bet Mrs. Hanratty will know. Thank you very much, Mr. Withers."

"You're more than welcome," he said with a smile.

So I paid for shampoo and conditioner, as well as a pretty pink collar and leash I'd snagged for Buttercup, and we all left Priscilla's Pets.

"Don't you think pink will clash with her apricot coat?" Chloe asked.

"I hope not. If it does, I'll . . . think of something to do with it."

"You can get us a lady dog, and I'll use them for her," she suggested.

"Brilliant idea."

With that settled, Monty and Mrs. Hanratty, who had been present during the whole dog conversation, took Chloe and me to lunch at the Hotel Castleton. And what a fabulous place *that* was.

However, as it has a habit of doing, time passed, and shortly after lunch, Monty sped us back to our parents' house on San Pasqual.

"Won't you come in for a while?" I asked with faint hope.

"Oh, no, dear. You know as well as I do that your mother will be in a perfect taking about the séance tonight. Monty and I don't want to add to her burdens."

Darn.

"Well," I said. "Thank you ever so much for taking us out and about today. I had a wonderful time."

"So did I," said Chloe.

As Mrs. Hanratty had predicted, Mother was all abustle when we returned to our parents' new home.

Not that Mother's bustle approached that of anyone else you might meet. Think of a stately ship on a turbulent ocean. That was Mother. None of the hurrying around that one associates with the word *bustle* for her, thank you. She ordered things done, and things were done.

After I'd put away all my purchases and taken Buttercup outside to piddle and poop—not that I'd ever tell Mother she'd done so—I braved going down that fabulous curving stairway.

It looked to me as though our mother were preparing for a veritable feast day. The dining room table had already been set for twenty people. I stared at it for a long time, wondering if all twenty of us were going to participate in the proposed séance. Twenty sounded like a rather unwieldy number, not that I knew much about séances.

Lucky for me, Chloe met me at the foot of the stairs. I gestured for her to join me in the sun porch. We sat in a couple of wicker chairs and gazed out onto an enormous patio lined with rosebushes, some of which were still abloom this late in November.

"I saw the table set for twenty. Are all those people going to attend Mrs. Majesty's séance?" I asked my sister.

With a shrug, Chloe said, "I have no idea."

"When Mother and I went to a séance before, the spiritualist had only six or eight of us in the room. Twenty sounds like a lot of people for a séance."

"I wouldn't know." Chloe yawned.

I decided she didn't care one way or another about the

séance, so I changed the topic of conversation. "I wonder what Father paid for this place."

"Don't know. A bundle, I'm sure."

"I'm sure it was, too." I heaved a sigh. "Oh, I wish this week were over and I could go home again!"

"It's all right, Mercy. You've already spent Saturday, Sunday, and Monday here. And today's Tuesday. A few more days, and you'll be released from durance vile."

"Not soon enough for me."

"At least you have Harvey and me with you."

"That's true. I can't imagine having to be with Mother and Father for a whole week without you along to shield me."

"I wonder why she picks on you so much."

I peered at my sister, wondering why she was wondering about something so obvious. "Because I refused to allow her to rule my life, of course. If I'd stayed in Boston, or only come out here to visit you, she probably wouldn't be so hard on me. But I came out here and got a *job*. And not merely a *job*, but a job with a *private investigator*. Small wonder she's in such a fuss."

"You're right, of course," said Chloe. Then she yawned again. "I'm so tired all the time," she complained. "Don't ever get pregnant, Mercy. It's an exhausting experience."

"I'll consider your advice," said I. And I would. So far, Chloe had endured weeks of morning sickness, now she was tired all the time, and eventually she'd go through extreme pain and possibly worse in order to bring a new Nash into the world. I wasn't altogether sure I wanted to go through all that.

"Girls," came a commanding voice at our back, and Chloe and I both stiffened. Mother.

Bravely daring, I turned and smiled at her. "Yes, Mother?"

"It's time for you two to get dressed. Our guests will arrive shortly for dinner. I want dinner to be over with by the time Mrs. Majesty and the rest of the party arrive."

Chloe and I rose from our basket chairs. "You're having guests for dinner and more guests for a party?" I asked our mother, still daring—you never knew how Mother would react to a question. "Will all those people attend the séance?"

"Don't be ridiculous, Mercedes Louise. Surely you recall that when we went to a séance at that young man's house, only six or eight of us were allowed to attend the séance. Mrs. Majesty never allows more than eight people to attend her séances."

"I see," I said.

"Well, get moving. I don't want you dilly-dallying. Chloe, how are you feeling, dear?"

Hmph. Mother never asked how *I* was feeling, and she never, ever, called me *dear*. Of course, I wasn't going to have a baby, either.

"I'm well, Mother. Thank you."

"Go on, Mercedes Louise. Since you don't have a maid with you, I'm sure it will take you a long time to get ready."

I could have protested, but to do so would have been pointless. I merely smiled again, left the sun porch, and headed upstairs. There I petted Buttercup for a few minutes before going to the dressing room and deciding what I should wear to dinner and a séance.

It didn't take me long. Black was the answer, and I had the perfect dress. Embroidered net over a black silk georgette gown. Worn with dark silk stockings and my black Louis heels, and with a black band in my shingled locks, I'd either look like a witch or a séance participant. The blasted dress had cost almost twenty dollars, for pity's sake! And all because my mother had made me come to Pasadena for Thanksgiving. I'd never be able to live on the wages I earned as Ernie's secretary at this rate. I'd known it all along, but this sealed my opinion: my mother was bad for me!

But never mind. This evening's gown, too, was one I merely

had to pull over my head to get on, so I did. Pulled it, I mean. Buttercup tried to help.

"No!" I yelled at my adorable doggie.

Buttercup, startled and alarmed, flattened herself on the pretty floral carpeting. Totally ashamed of myself, and furious that I'd allowed Mother to influence my purchase of a too-expensive evening frock, I knelt before my dog.

"Oh, Buttercup, I'm so very sorry. I didn't mean to snap at you!"

I darn near cried, I was so appalled at my behavior.

Darling Buttercup forgave me at once. Unfortunately, her forgiveness came with putting her paws on my lap, from the embroidered net of which I disentangled her little sharp claws very gently. "Oh, dear. I knew this dress was a mistake."

I heard a tap at the door, and then Chloe's, "What was a mistake?"

Making sure I was totally free from Buttercup's little puppy paws, I stood. "This dress," I said darkly—at least as darkly as the dress itself.

"I think it's pretty. You look sophisticated and alluring in it. I didn't know you had such a gown in your wardrobe."

"I didn't until Mother insisted I come here for Thanksgiving. Then I spent far too much money on it, and I'm ashamed of myself."

"Why?" asked my sister, annoying me.

"Why? Because I only bought it to deflect criticism from Mother. I should be above such petty things."

"Nuts. Nobody's above trying to deflect criticism from that source."

"Well . . . maybe you're right."

"You know I am," said Chloe firmly.

I glanced at her evening costume, a lovely rose-colored, two-piece evening frock. This one, too, concealed Chloe's interesting condition. "You look smashing, as usual," I told her.

"Thank you. I had to find a new dressmaker when we moved to Beverly Hills. I think I found the right one, don't you?"

Surveying her gown more closely, I said, "I certainly do. That's just beautiful."

She twirled in front of me, sending her gored gown sailing out around her. I was impressed. My own gown had a gored skirt. At its hemline, at five or six places, the embroidered overlay split apart and the shiny silk georgette flared out. It truly was a stunning gown. And it might even have been worth the twenty bucks I paid for it, although I couldn't imagine ever wearing it anyplace other than the parents' house.

No. It had been a stupid, impulsive buy, and I was ashamed of myself.

So as not to dwell on my many shortcomings, I asked Chloe, "Will you help me put this stupid ribbon in my hair?"

"Sure, sweetie." I dangled the ribbon in front of her. "Oh, black satin. How classy."

"Black silk georgette," I corrected her. "It came with the gown. Sort of."

"Sort of?" Chloe took the ribbon and eyed me for a second.

I heaved a sigh. "I had to get the stupid dress fitted, and the dressmaker I used had some of the black georgette left over, so I had her make a hair band for me."

"You always were a smart cookie, Mercy."

"If I'm so smart, why am I here?" I asked bleakly.

"Because you didn't want to leave me alone in our parents' clutches."

"Nonsense. You have Harvey."

"I do indeed," said my sister smugly.

Speaking of Harvey, he showed up in the doorway just then, and we all headed out of my room and to the grand staircase.

"I love this staircase," I said, surprising myself. I didn't want to admit my parents had good taste.

"It's grand, all right," said Harvey.

"It's steep," said Chloe, clearly not appreciating its gracious qualities.

With that, we got to the bottom of the twisty stairs, and headed toward the drawing room. I sucked in a deep breath for courage.

CHAPTER EIGHT

I didn't need the deep breath, mainly because the first person I saw when I entered the drawing room was Harold Kincaid, who rushed over to us.

"Oh, my, Miss Allcutt, you look utterly stunning tonight."

I glanced at Chloe, remembered she was Mrs. Nash, and instantly felt my face heat. How embarrassing. "Thank you very much, Harold. And please, do call me Mercy."

He took my hand and eyed me up and down as if I were a mannequin in a store window. I tried to keep in mind that this fellow was a costumier, that he wasn't interested in women, and that his scrutiny was professional in nature.

"Don't tell me you got this creation off the rack," he said.

"Well . . . no, I didn't. But I have to admit it wasn't made for me. And I did have to have it altered."

"Where did you get it, Mercy?" Chloe asked me.

My cheeks caught fire. "At a Chinatown shop. It carries lots of merchandise that, I think, are given to the owners on consignment."

"A consignment shop?" Chloe said, aghast.

"But I had a dressmaker alter it for me," I repeated, feeling silly.

"You're a wise woman, Mercy," said Harold. "I knew I'd seen this number before. It looked wonderful on Renee Adoree, and it looks wonderful on you."

"Renee Adoree?" I stared at Harold in astonishment, then

peered down at my gown, for which I suddenly had a good deal more respect. "You mean, I fit into a dress once worn by Renee Adoree? My goodness!"

"Both you and Miss Adoree have excellent taste," said Harvey. He was trying not to laugh; I could tell.

"Mercedes Louise!" came my mother's commanding voice from the front of the room, near the fireplace, which was blazing away. Father stood nearby, looking stern and disapproving. In other words, he looked like he always did.

My head snapped up. What had I done to get on the wicked witch's bad side now? Rather than ask such a provoking question, I smiled at her and walked over to join her. She stood with Mrs. Pinkerton, who this evening, looked like a plump asparagus stalk. Really, rotund women shouldn't try to wear the straight up-and-down gowns popular at the time. Our mother, on the other hand, wore black, as did I, although not a speck of embroidery marred her stern Boston style.

"Yes, Mother?" I asked sweetly as I came within her aura. Her aura, by the way, was as black as her dress. I nodded at Mrs. Pinkerton. "How do you do, Mrs. Pinkerton?"

"I'm fine, dear. That is a perfectly gorgeous gown."

"Thank you." Harold's mother might well be a nitwit, but at least she was nice.

"Indeed. You are looking well this evening, Mercedes Louise." Mother said it ruefully, as if she regretted not being given an opportunity to snipe at me.

"Thank you, Mother."

"She looks gorgeous," said Harold, who'd come over with me to his mother and mine.

I hoped to heck he wasn't going to let on that I'd purchased my evening wear at a consignment shop. My mother would faint.

Hmm. On the other hand, maybe he *should* mention the fact.

But no. That wasn't kind, and I truly didn't want to be in any way like my mother, who was generally unkind.

"And, Chloe, you are charming, as usual," said Mother.

"Thank you, Mother."

Hmph. Chloe looked charming, and I looked well. I supposed I could stand it.

"But come along, girls. Dinner is almost ready to be served. You came downstairs just in time."

"The butler hasn't announced dinner yet, has he?"

"That has nothing to do with anything," said Mother. Naturally. "He will do so any minute now."

She was right. About a second after she made her announcement, the butler came in and announced the meal.

So we all wandered dining-room-wards. Harold escorted me into the room. I actually wished then that Chloe and I had descended the grand staircase earlier, so that I could have met the other guests attending dinner that night.

As I gazed around the table, I saw a few people I knew. There was Pansy Hanratty and her son. Monty Mountjoy smiled at me from across the table, and I smiled back. Next to him was an elderly woman with white hair, marcelled to perfection, who wore a rather alarming rose-colored taffeta number that looked as if it belonged on a southern plantation before the Civil War. Mrs. Hanratty's mother? Might well be. I was curious to meet the woman who had as deleterious an effect on her daughter as my mother had on me.

Harold sat next to me on my left, and another fellow, whose name I didn't know yet, sat on my right. I smiled at him, and he smiled back.

"Miss Allcutt?"

"Yes. Mercy. And you are?"

"Delbert Mann. I'm Mrs. Winkworth's secretary."

"Oh. Um, Mrs. Winkworth? I'm not sure I know who she is."

"The little southern lady across the table from us."

"Oh, yes. She's Mrs. Hanratty's mother, I believe?"

"Indeed she is."

He didn't sound too happy about it, although I didn't know if his distaste sprang from Mrs. Hanratty or Mrs. Winkworth. My money would be on Winkworth, if I were asked to make a bet.

"I'm a secretary, too," I told him. I said it proudly, too, by gum.

"Really? For whom do you work?"

"Ernest Templeton, P.I.," I said, still proud.

"You work for a private investigator? My goodness. That must be interesting work."

"Sometimes. Other times it's boring."

"I hope your employer is good to work for."

Mr. Mann shot a gloomy glance across the table, and I judged his employer was not good to work for.

"He is. He's very good to work for. I enjoy my job ever so much."

"How nice for you."

Riki served our soup, and I lifted my spoon, praying I wouldn't spill any. I wished I could ask Mr. Mann why he found his own employment so distasteful, but I didn't. It wasn't my business, even if I am naturally nosy. As I sipped my soup, I gazed upon the little white-haired woman across the table from me, and thought she had a sweet face. Of course, that might well be a façade behind which she hid her deplorable tendencies. And that, actually, might make her more of a pain in the neck even than my mother, who didn't bother to disguise her contempt for those whom she considered beneath her. Like me, for instance.

"How long have you worked for Mrs. Winkworth?" I asked after I'd swallowed some soup.

A heavy sigh preceded Mr. Mann's, "Four months. It will be four months this week."

"You don't sound as though you enjoy your job much."

Mr. Mann slid me a sideways glance. "It's all right. It's better than nothing. And the surroundings are lovely."

"Really? Do you work at Mrs. Winkworth's home then?"

"Yes. It's just down the street from this house."

"Is it? My goodness. Which house is it? I've enjoyed walking my dog past the lovely homes on this block."

"It's fifteen thirty. A huge estate. Gated and guarded."

"Is it the one with the big gate covered in ivy?"

"That's it, all right. It's a huge property. Mr. Mountjoy bought it for his grandmother. There are three houses on the grounds. Mrs. Winkworth lives in one, Mrs. Hanratty in another, and Mr. Mountjoy keeps one for himself. For when he's not on a picture location."

"My goodness. That's a gigantic property, all right. It must be nice for them all to be together, yet separate. If you know what I mean."

Mr. Mann gave me a thin smile. "Yes. I'm sure they enjoy being able to be apart or together, depending on what they want at any given time."

"Although," I said, "I'm not sure I'd like to live that close to my parents."

"Mercedes Louise."

Oh, dear. The old cow hadn't heard me, had she? I glanced at the foot of the table and found my mother frowning at me. No surprise there. I gulped. "Yes, Mother?"

"What are you and Mr. Mann talking about so seriously?"

Well, of all the nerve!

"We're just discussing our jobs. Mr. Mann is a secretary, too."

"And a very good one," came from across the table.

When I looked, I saw it was Monty Mountjoy who had spoken. I glanced at his grandmother. She didn't appear at all pleased. Hmm.

"Your jobs, indeed," said Mother. Fortunately, she didn't go on to condemn me out loud, but turned instead to her table mate, a small, middle-aged man to whom I hadn't yet been introduced.

"Your mother doesn't approve of you working?" guessed Mr. Mann.

"She hates the very idea."

"Out of curiosity, why *do* you work? If you don't mind my asking. It's really none of my business, but—"

"No. That's all right. I came to Los Angeles in order to get away from Boston and its stuffy confines. I had no idea Boston would follow me here. I wanted to get a job and work like so many young women these days, because I wanted the experience of being . . . well, of the people."

After gazing at me in silence for a couple of tense seconds, Mr. Mann said, "You do know that millions of young women would gladly trade places with you, don't you?"

"Of course, I know that," I said snappishly. "I'm not taking food from anyone's mouth, Mr. Mann. My job was advertised in the *Los Angeles Times*. I was the one whom my employer chose to hire. Any other young woman—or young man, for that matter—might have applied for the position."

"Of course. I didn't mean to imply anything."

"Sorry. I'm a little sensitive on the subject of my employment. My mother disapproves. So does my father. And so does everyone else in the family, except Chloe and Harvey."

"Chloe is your sister?"

"Yes."

"Mr. Mountjoy likes working for Mr. Nash. Says he's very human, unlike many of the big studio heads."

"Harvey is a wonderful man," I said, happy to have my opinion of my brother-in-law confirmed.

"Indeed," said Mr. Mann. Then he went back to his soup.

Very well, so much for that. I turned to find Harold scraping up the very last spoonful of his own soup. He glanced at me and smiled as he swallowed.

"Good soup," said he.

"Yes. It was, wasn't it?"

"I listened in to your conversation. Can't help myself. I'm incurably nosy. I heard Mann fill you in on his job with Mrs. Winkworth."

"Yes. He doesn't seem too pleased with his employment."

"Have you met the woman?"

"No, not yet."

"You'll understand once you meet her."

"Oh, dear. Another miserable mother." I shot a glance to the foot of the table, regretting my choice of words instantly and hoping Mother hadn't heard me. She hadn't. She continued to chat with the gentleman next to her. "Well, Mrs. Hanratty had told us as much."

"She didn't hear you," said Harold with a chuckle.

"Thank God."

"Or Doc Benjamin."

"Oh, is that Dr. Benjamin to whom she's speaking?"

"The very same. Great guy, Dr. Benjamin. That's his wife next to your father at the other end of the table, near my stepfather."

I glanced at the head of the table and saw a pretty, trim, middle-aged woman seated at my father's side. She wore a benevolent smile and appeared ever so much nicer than my mother. "She looks like a nice person."

"She is. They both are."

"My parents seem to be collecting a lot of nice people.

Wonder how that happened."

Harold burst out laughing, and I could have kicked myself. Surreptitiously, I glanced again at my mother. She'd begun scowling at me again. It figured.

"What *are* you two chatting about?" asked Mother in a cutting voice.

How rude of her! Fortunately, before I could tell her so, Harold spoke up.

"Mercy is just telling me about her dog, Mrs. Allcutt."

"That dog. Hmph."

"Thanks, Harold," I whispered out of the side of my mouth.

"Not a problem, sweetie. At least your mother, unlike poor Monty's grandmother, doesn't 'smile and smile and be a villain.' "

"Oh, my, is she as bad as all that?"

"She's kind of a snake," said Harold. "You won't be expecting anything, and then she'll strike. Poisonous, that woman."

"Well, at least my mother doesn't try to hide her true colors. She's a frosty Bostonian, no matter what."

"At least you know when to duck."

"Good point. I tend to duck every time I see her. It's safer that way."

The rest of the meal proceeded apace. It was a very good dinner, and I renewed my vow to tell the cook how much I appreciated her.

And then the ladies withdrew to the drawing room, and I finally got to meet Pansy Hanratty's mother.

CHAPTER NINE

First of all, let me say that the physical contrast between Mrs. Beauregard "Lurlene" Winkworth and my own austere and regal mother couldn't have been more pronounced.

While Mother presented an indomitable façade to the world, Mrs. Winkworth seemed like a fragile magnolia blossom. Small, slender, dressed in a gown that would have done her ancestral acres proud—she was from South Carolina—she had a soft voice with an accent so thick, it might have been soaked in honey before the words left her lips.

"It's a pleasure to meet you," I said to the woman as soon as Mrs. Hanratty introduced us. As yet, I didn't know if I'd just lied or not.

"How do you do, Miss Allcutt?"

"I'm well, thank you. I understand you live nearby."

She heaved a sigh a good deal larger than she was. "Yes, indeed. My grandson bought the place for his mother and me."

"How nice of him."

"Well, he makes a good deal of money in the pictures." She sniffed. "Scandalous profession. The least he can do is take care of his family."

Oh, my. "It sounds as if he's doing that very thing."

"I very much fear that Pasadena," the elderly woman said, her voice still sweet as molasses, "is *not* what I'm accustomed to."

"It's a lovely town," I ventured.

"Do you think so?"

"Well, yes. I've only visited Pasadena a couple of times, but I think it's a very pretty little city."

"Alas, I fear your horizons are limited, my dear. Although I suppose you can't help yourself." She gave me a pitying smile, and my hackles began to rise.

"Oh? And why do you say my horizons are limited?"

"From what I've heard, your family hails from Boston, Massachusetts."

"Yes. Generations of Allcutts hail from Boston."

"Then you wouldn't understand how very much I miss the gentility of my youthful home, Miss Allcutt. I'm sure you can't help yourself."

"And you're from South Carolina, Mrs. Winkworth. Is that correct?"

"Yes, indeed. Lovely South Carolina. So genteel. So special." She sighed again, mournfully. "You can't imagine what I lost when Monty made me come out to this rough place."

I glanced around. "Rough" didn't capture the ambience for me. Elegant, yes. Wealthy, certainly. Grand, even.

"But surely your grandson only meant the best when he bought that . . . that compound for you and his mother."

"Monty," said she with a sad mien, "is an actor."

"And a very good one." Not to mention a fabulously wealthy one who, according to everything I'd heard, had rescued his impoverished elderly grandmother from dire circumstances. "Don't you think you're being a little hard on him? It seems he's doing his best to take good care of you."

She gave me a pitying smile. "Ah, my dear. You just don't understand, do you?"

"I guess not," I admitted.

"Then perhaps you ought to keep your opinions to yourself, if you don't know what you're talking about. A young woman

who broke her mother's heart shouldn't argue with her betters."
And with that pithy shot, she turned and walked away.

Well, really! Deciding that sticking my tongue out at the
miserable female would be counterproductive, I envisioned stab-
bing her in the back instead. I'd broken my mother's heart, had
I? If my mother possessed a heart, she'd kept it well hidden
from her children for lo, these many years.

"It's no good getting upset with the woman, Mercy," said
Chloe softly at my side. "She's a ghastly person. Doesn't appreciate a single thing anyone ever does for her. She's probably
worse than you-know-who."

"Hmm. Yes, that's what Harold told me. At least you-know-
who doesn't try to pretend she's anything but a witch from
hell."

Chloe chuckled softly. "True."

The men straggled in about then, and I found Harold Kincaid. "You were right about Monty's granny," I told him. "She's
horrible."

"You have no idea," he said. "She even sent Monty poison-
pen letters a year or so ago. Trying to get him to quit the
pictures. As if he hadn't used the money he'd made to take care
of her. And does she appreciate it? Not on your life."

"Are you talking about Mother?" asked Mrs. Hanratty, joining us. "She's a miserable old coot. Monty's done everything
humanly possible for her, and she absolutely loathes him for it.
Poor Monty."

"At least you appreciate him," I said, smiling upon Monty's
mother with affection. I really did like her.

"You bet I do. He's one in a million, my Monty."

Just then a flurry at the drawing room door made us all turn
and see who had entered.

"*Monty!*" a woman in white screamed.

"Good Lord, who's that?" I asked as the woman streaked

across the floor, her black hair streaming behind her, eventually throwing herself into Monty Mountjoy's arms.

"That, my dear, is Lola de la Monica, Hollywoodland's number-one menace," said Harold.

"My goodness, I had no idea the parents would invite her to their home."

"They probably didn't. Lola invites herself wherever she wants to go."

My eyes widened. "Honestly? You mean she really crashes parties?"

"All the time. No manners, our Lola."

Poor Monty seemed to be having trouble fending the woman off. From what folks had told me about him, I expected he was attempting to be polite, which probably wouldn't work with a woman like that. I felt sorry for him. "Do you think we should try to rescue him?" I asked Harold.

"Couldn't hurt, I guess. She's hard to handle. Daisy's going to have a fit when she discovers her here."

"Oh, yes, I remember you said they'd met."

"That's a kind word for it." Harold grinned, took my arm, and guided me toward Monty and Lola.

"Really, Lola, please let me go," I heard Monty say as we approached him and the clinging woman.

"But *Monty*! I'm so *glad* to see you here!"

Lola de la Monica had a thick accent, although I couldn't quite place it. I think I'd read somewhere that she was from Spain. She was a beautiful woman, despite her personality, with long, wavy black hair, skin as white as porcelain, and a trim figure.

I blinked at said figure. She clearly wore no undergarments. I sneaked a peek at my parents and saw them standing stiffly before the fireplace, glaring at the spectacle Lola had created. Oh, dear. In order to prevent murder, I decided to be bold.

"Miss de la Monica," I said loudly. "How nice to meet you in person." I grabbed one of her arms and jerked. She came free of Monty and whirled around, her claws bared and her teeth flashing. I flinched back, and Harold grabbed her arms.

"Here now, Lola. None of that. You don't want to injure a daughter of the house."

"A daughter?" she said. "Who is this person, Harold?"

I stuck my hand out to her. "Mercy Allcutt, Miss de la Monica. I've enjoyed seeing you in the pictures. I particularly loved *The Fire at Sunset.*"

My words seemed to mollify her. With one hand, she swept up her flowing tresses and let them fall through her fingers. The other hand she held out to me. Her hands reminded me of Lulu LaBelle's, the nails were such a brilliant red.

"Charmed, I'm sure," she said. Out of the corner of my eye, I saw Monty Mountjoy pull his suit coat into place. He stepped back several paces until Mr. Mann stood between him and the actress. "I came to see Monty."

"Yes, I gathered that. Have you met my parents?"

"Parents? You have parents here?"

"This is their home."

"Ah. Well, no, I needn't meet your parents. I shall—*Daisy!*"

She bellowed the name, and I winced.

Harold muttered, "Oh, Lord," and grabbed Lola, who was poised to attack another guest.

Already intrigued by Mrs. Majesty, by reputation, I turned and saw a woman about my size, but spectacularly pale and interesting, clad in a perfectly stunning evening dress of white with lashings of red beads. She'd paused at the door to the drawing room and looked to see who had bellowed her name. I'm pretty sure I saw her take a step back when she spotted Lola.

"Mercy, could you please introduce yourself to Mrs. Majesty?

I'll hold off Lola for as long as I can."

"Certainly," said I, and I hurried up to the newcomer.

She looked at me uncertainly.

I said, "Mrs. Majesty?"

"Yes." She had a deep, smooth voice, quite lovely, although she sounded a trace uncertain at the moment. Can't say as I blamed her.

"Let me take you to my parents, Mr. and Mrs. Allcutt. I'm Mercy Allcutt. Harold Kincaid is attempting to thwart Lola's pursuit of you." I took her arm and started to steer her toward the fireplace and Mother and Father, who still looked disapproving. Then again, they pretty much always did.

"Oh, my. Thank you. I . . . I didn't know Lola would be here."

"I don't think my parents knew it either."

"Gracious! She just barged in?"

"Something like that."

"Well . . . I suppose that's something she would do."

"Mrs. Majesty, how lovely to see you again." And Mrs. Winkworth stepped in front of us.

"How do you do, Mrs. Winkworth? It's good to see you again."

"Daisy!" And there was Mrs. Pinkerton, all aflutter.

"Good evening, Mrs. Pinkerton."

"So very glad you're here, dear," said Mrs. Pinkerton.

"Daisy! How is dear Spike?"

"Mrs. Hanratty. How nice to see you, too."

I was impressed at the way the spiritualist handled all these women coming up to her and demanding her attention. I doubt I'd have remained as unruffled as she. Then again, she was a spiritualist. Maybe they have to be unflappable. Anyhow, she'd probably had lots of practice.

"Daisy!" said Harold, hurrying up to us. "I got rid of Lola for the time being."

"Thank you, Harold. I didn't anticipate seeing her here tonight."

"No one did. Excuse us, ladies." Harold, smiling at his mother and the rest of the feminine mob, took Mrs. Majesty's other arm, and we finished the trek to the fireplace as a linked trio.

As we walked away, I heard Mrs. Winkworth's sugary voice. "Delbert, have you finished those letters?"

"Not quite, ma'am," said Mr. Mann. His voice was strained.

"Then I believe it's time for you to do so."

"Yes, ma'am."

"And this time, try not to make so many mistakes."

I heard nothing from Delbert Mann, so I presume he hied himself away from the party to do his employer's business. Why she'd brought him—and work—to the party, I have no idea, but I felt sorry for him.

Mrs. Majesty spoke then, and I forgot all about the Winkworth witch. "Thank you for intercepting me and subduing Miss de la Monica, Miss Allcutt, and Harold. I appreciate being spared an emotional scene."

"I sent her upstairs to powder her nose," said Harold. "I told her she had a smudge on it."

"Harold! You didn't!" Mrs. Majesty laughed.

"Did so. But let's not think about her. With luck, we'll all be in the séance when she appears again."

"I sincerely hope so," said Mrs. Majesty.

"Me, too," said I.

We'd reached the fireplace.

"What was all that commotion?" Mother asked. She frowned at me as she did so, as if she considered me at fault somehow.

"Lola de la Monica was the one who hollered, Mother. Did you invite her to the séance or the party?"

"I have no idea who Lola de la Whatsis is," said Mother. "I'm sorry your entrance was attended by such a hubbub, Mrs. Majesty."

"It certainly wasn't your fault, Mrs. Allcutt," said Mrs. Majesty holding out her hand for Mother to shake.

"No, but I don't know how that woman got in," said Mother. "I shall speak to Riki."

"I'm sure it wasn't his fault," said the spiritualist. "I've met Lola before. She's rather a force of nature, and she's almost impossible to stop once she gets going."

"Harrumph."

Mrs. Majesty turned to Father. "Good evening, Mr. Allcutt. I must say your daughter rescued me in the nick of time."

"Did she," said my loving father, as if he didn't want to give me credit for anything at all, much less a timely rescue.

"Yes, she did. She and Harold saved me from what might otherwise have been a painful encounter." In a lowered voice, Mrs. Majesty continued, "I've had dealings with Miss de la Monica before."

"I understand she hired you to be her spiritual advisor during the shooting of a picture," I said, wanting to know all about it.

"Oh, did Harold tell you about that? Yes, it was one of the more ghastly times of my life, for that and other reasons."

"Don't even think about it, Daisy," advised Harold. "That's all over and done with."

"Yes. Yes, it is."

But I noticed a bleak expression cross her face. Now I was really curious as to what had happened during the filming of that picture.

"I think it would be a good idea to get Daisy and the rest of the séance attendees into the séance room," said Harold. "Before Lola escapes and busts in on us."

Mrs. Pinkerton giggled. It was an incongruously girlish sound coming from the large green asparagus stalk.

"Yes, that's an excellent idea, Mr. Kincaid. Come along, Mercedes Louise. Clovilla, I expect you to join us, too."

"Yes, Mother," said Chloe, winking at me.

So Mother, Mrs. Majesty, Chloe, Harold, Mr. and Mrs. Pinkerton, Mrs. Bissel—whom I hadn't noticed before—and I all trooped to the breakfast room, which had been set up for the séance. Riki was there, too, stationed at the light switch, ready, I presumed, to turn off the lights when Mrs. Majesty gave the signal.

The table was bare except for one cranberry-glass candle-holder in the middle of the table. The set-up was great. The room already appeared mysterious. I expect Mrs. Majesty had arranged the mood. So far, it seemed Harold was right, and she was a mistress of her art, if art it was and not a true calling. I can't say that I believed in spiritualism myself.

Mrs. Majesty sat at the table's head, and the rest of us parked ourselves in the other chairs. I noticed there were only eight of us at the table. It looked to me as if Mrs. Majesty held firm sway over her domain. I approved. Not that she needed my approval, but it was nice to see that my mother hadn't cowed her into altering her arrangements.

"Everyone, please take hands," she said after we were all seated. I sat between Chloe and Harold. Mother sat next to Mrs. Majesty.

We all took hands.

Mrs. Majesty then smiled at Riki and nodded. The lights went out, and I heard the door to the kitchen close.

"Please be silent," Mrs. Majesty told us.

We obeyed.

Then we sat there in silence for what seemed like forever, but probably wasn't more than a couple of minutes. Then I heard a sigh from the table's head, and the fun began.

It really was fun. Mrs. Majesty conjured up the spirit of a Scottish gent named Raleigh or Rolly or something, and he, her supposed spirit control, told us all sorts of stuff about our dearly departed. Not that I personally had any dearly departeds, but Rolly chatted about Mother's aunt, who'd ruled the social set in Boston during the 'eighties and 'nineties. Then he told us that Mrs. Bissel's late husband was happy on the Other Side and expected Mrs. Bissel to be happy on this one until she joined him naturally. I guess if you're a spiritualist, you have a duty, of sorts, to keep people happy. It would be a shame if someone were so eager to join his or her late relations that he or she decided to commit suicide in order to join them.

Anyway, the séance proceeded apace. Nothing spectacular happened, and I was still unwilling to believe in spirit-conjuring when it came to a conclusion. We knew it was the conclusion when Mrs. Majesty sighed heavily and slumped in her chair.

Someone whispered (I think it was Mrs. Bissel), "We must remain quiet until Mrs. Majesty recovers from her swoon."

"Absolutely." I knew that was Harold, because I sat next to him. "We wouldn't want Daisy floating around in the nether reaches forevermore, would we?"

"Harold," said Mrs. Pinkerton, "that won't happen. Daisy knows what she's doing."

"Of course, Mother." But Harold was smiling; I could tell.

Anyway, we were all quiet for several seconds until Mrs. Majesty "recovered" from her spirit-induced spell, sat up straight in her chair and sighed once more. Then we stood, someone turned on the lights, and the ladies began chatting animatedly with Mrs. Majesty. We left the breakfast room in a clump and walked out into the hall where the great staircase loomed.

And then, reminding me of a fairy, a vision in rose-colored taffeta uttered a shriek of hellacious fright, fluttered over the high balcony, and fell to the parquet floor with a sickening splat.

CHAPTER TEN

I don't know about anyone else, but I stood riveted to the spot, aghast. I couldn't quite take in what had happened.

Suddenly, Harold broke the trance we were under. "Mrs. Winkworth!" cried he, and rushed to the rose-colored figure on the shining parquet floor.

"Good God, is it Mrs. Winkworth?" said somebody.

"Daisy! Mercy! Come here!" Harold beckoned to the both of us, and we hurried over to him.

I looked down and nearly gagged. I don't know if you've ever seen a person who's fallen from a high place onto a hard surface, but the sight isn't one you'd look at on purpose if you could avoid it.

"Good Lord, what happened?" asked Mrs. Majesty, although it seemed fairly obvious to me.

"She fell over the staircase railing," I said.

Mrs. Majesty lifted her head and gazed at the staircase. "How did she do that? She'd have had to climb over it, wouldn't she?"

I glanced up and realized the spiritualist was right. The wrought-iron railing, in all its perfect fanciness, was a high barrier. It was also one over which Riki Saito now peered, his eyes wide, looking frightened. Good heavens, had *he* heaved Mrs. Winkworth over the railing? I couldn't quite believe it.

"Somebody get Doc Benjamin," Harold ordered. "And Daisy, call Sam."

"Yes," she said, sounding rattled—and I didn't blame her—

94

"of course, I'll call Sam."

"Who's Sam?" I asked.

"My fiancé. He's a detective with the Pasadena Police Department."

"Oh, Lord, Mother and Father are going to love that," I muttered.

"What is going on here?"

And, as if by magic, my mother appeared. I'd been leaning over the body, wishing it weren't leaking quite so much blood, but I glanced up at her. For the first time I could remember, she didn't look stodgy and stuffy. She looked horrified.

"It's Mrs. Winkworth. Somehow she fell over the staircase railing from the upstairs hallway."

"Is she . . . is she . . . ?"

"Can someone get me a sheet or something?" asked Harold.

"Yes, she's deceased."

Mother actually staggered a bit. I was shocked. Fortunately, Chloe was there, and she took Mother's arm and began leading her toward the drawing room.

Mrs. Pinkerton, who appeared to be edging toward hysterics, cried, "Oh, Daisy! Oh, whatever has happened?" Mr. Pinkerton took her arm as if to hold her up. As she was a good deal larger than he, this might have been a problem had she actually fainted.

"It's all right, Mrs. Pinkerton," said Mrs. Majesty in a calm voice. "It was an accident. Why don't you and your husband and Mrs. Bissel go along to the drawing room? I need to use the telephone."

"Oh, Daisy!" Mrs. Pinkerton cried again.

Mrs. Majesty gave Mrs. Bissel a quelling look, and she came up and helped Mrs. Majesty and Mr. Pinkerton cart Mrs. Pinkerton off. I was impressed with the power Mrs. Majesty seemed to wield over her subjects.

People who'd spent the séance time in the drawing room

began to arrive on the scene. I wasn't sure how to prevent them from viewing the late Mrs. Winkworth, but Mrs. Majesty took it upon herself to herd them back to where they'd come from. I guess her skill at training dogs helped her in other situations, too. The rest of us huddled in a tight knot surrounding the body, unwilling to allow others to view the spectacle.

Riki, appearing pale and shaky, came up with a sheet, and he and Harold covered the body. I heaved a sigh of relief.

"Did you see what happened, Riki?" I asked, not sounding accusatory, but wanting to know. He'd been at or near the spot, after all.

"I didn't see anything. I heard a scream and came running."

"Where were you when you heard the scream?" I asked.

"I'd been putting things to rights in the bedrooms. I always do that before the family and guests go to bed at night."

Hmm. Maybe so. But he'd been awfully convenient when the woman went overboard. On the other hand, what reason would Riki Saito have to heave Mrs. Winkworth over a stair railing? Unless, of course, she'd managed to get on his nerves. She seemed to do that to everyone she encountered.

Just then a clatter sounded on the staircase, and Mr. Delbert Mann fairly leaped into the room. "What happened? Where's Mrs. Winkworth? We were talking, and then she left, and then I heard some people talking, and then I heard a scream and—" And then he ran out of breath.

"You were upstairs, too?" I asked, thinking the suspect pool was growing by leaps and bounds. So to speak.

He held a hand over a probably palpitating heart. "Yes. I . . . I was going over some letters with her, but then she saw something in the hallway, said 'Oh, my,' and left the room. Then I heard what sounded like a loud argument that went on for only a couple of seconds, and then I heard the scream."

Hmm. Over dinner, I'd received the distinct impression he

didn't care for his employer, and she'd treated him pretty badly right before the séance. Something to think about, and I'd rather believe Mr. Mann a murderer than Riki Saito.

Good heavens, I didn't mean that!

"What's going on?"

Oh, dear, I'd know that honk anywhere. My thoughts instantly stopped counting suspects, and I turned and intercepted Mrs. Hanratty. Monty Mountjoy held her arm, and they both appeared pale and alarmed.

"Is that Grandmother?" asked Monty.

"I'm afraid it is, old chap," said Harold, rising to his feet with something of a grunt and a definite couple of creaks.

"Good heavens." Mrs. Hanratty slapped a hand over her mouth, and tears sprang to her eyes. "She was an awful old woman, but . . . but . . ."

"No one wanted her to die," Harold finished for her. "Yes, I know." He turned to me. "Mercy, could you help Daisy find the telephone? I really do think we need to get Sam here as soon as possible."

"Do you truly believe we need to telephone the police?" I asked Harold, dreading what my parents would say to this usurpation of their home ownership.

"She couldn't have fallen over that railing, Mercy. Certainly you see that," said Harold, sounding edgy.

Again I glanced up to the spot from which Mrs. Winkworth fell. "Yes," I said. "Yes, of course. I'll show her to the telephone room right this instant." And I began scooting off to find Mrs. Majesty, casting a glance back at Mrs. Hanratty and Monty, who held on to each other. Mrs. Hanratty was weeping on her son's shoulder, and Monty was attempting to comfort her. I felt bad for the both of them.

I barely noticed when Harvey came down the staircase until he spoke. Then I turned abruptly and stared at him.

"I heard a racket. What—" He stopped speaking and stared at the sheet-covered form on the floor. "Good Lord. What happened?"

"It's Mrs. Winkworth," Harold said. "Somebody heaved her over the staircase railing."

"Is she—" Again he abruptly stopped talking.

"She's dead," said Harold.

"Good God. I must find Chloe!" And Harvey rushed off to the drawing room. Lucky Chloe. But what had Harvey been doing upstairs? My head had started aching by that time, and I didn't want even to think about adding Harvey to my list of suspects.

When I entered the drawing room, everyone turned to stare at me. Mrs. Majesty had eased Mrs. Pinkerton down onto one of the sofas and was attempting to soothe her. Mrs. Bissel and Mr. Pinkerton had joined her in this endeavor. The middle-aged man who'd been pointed out to me as Dr. Benjamin was leaving the room, headed for the hallway. I presumed Mrs. Majesty had made a detour in his direction before she'd returned to take Mrs. Pinkerton in tow.

Chloe and Harvey clung together in a corner. I thought Chloe might have been crying, but didn't know for sure. All I knew was that they made a practically perfect couple.

"Mercedes Louise," Mother called to me in her most magisterial tones. "Come here at once."

"Just a minute, Mother. I need to show Mrs. Majesty to the . . ." Oh, Lord, Mother would have a conniption if I told her I was leading the spiritualist to the telephone so she could call the coppers.

"To the what?" Mother asked sternly.

Feeling a little desperate, I hurried over to my parents, who'd gone back to the fireplace. "Listen, Mother and Father. Mrs. Winkworth couldn't have fallen from that balcony. She had to

have had help, and Harold needs Mrs. Majesty to telephone her
. . . uh, friend at the police station."

"The *police*?" Mother demanded. "The *police*!"

"Yes. The police." I'd had about enough of this interrogation.
"Listen, I'll explain it all later. Right now I need to get Mrs.
Majesty to the telephone." And I hustled myself away from my
disapproving parents and over to where Mrs. Pinkerton lay
prostrate.

"Mrs. Majesty," I whispered when I got there. "Harold asked
me to take you to the telephone. Come with me, please."

"Thank you, Miss Allcutt." She glanced at Mrs. Bissel. "Can
you take care of her from now on, Mrs. Bissel?"

"Yes, dear."

"As can I," said Mr. Pinkerton in a shaky voice.

"Do go and telephone that nice policeman of yours," Mrs.
Bissel added.

Mrs. Majesty rose from the sofa rolling her eyes. When she
saw me watching her, she colored a bit, but her frustration with
the fainting Mrs. Pinkerton and with Mrs. Bissel's description
of her policeman friend only made her seem more human to
me. I smiled at her and said, "This way."

"Mercedes Louise! Stop this minute!"

"Good Lord, now what?" Mrs. Majesty and I paused, and I
turned toward the fireplace, from whence cameth my mother's
command. "Yes, Mother?" Darn it, I was impatient to do
something useful.

"Telephone that fellow you work for. Mr. Templeforth. Tell
him to come here and take care of this."

"Templeton, Mother. His name is Ernest Templeton. You
want me to telephone him?" Astounded doesn't half cover my
reaction to my mother's order.

"That's his job, isn't it? If you're going to disobey your
parents and *work* for a living, you can at least have him come

here and solve this problem."

She wanted me to telephone Ernie and invite him to her home to solve the murder of Mrs. Winkworth. Would wonders never cease? "Very well, Mother." It would be a comfort to me to have Ernie here, even if he'd hate every minute of it. I turned and resumed walking toward the telephone room.

"Who's Mr. Templeton?" asked Mrs. Majesty.

"My boss. He's a private investigator."

"Oh, my, you work for a private eye?" Mrs. Majesty sounded fascinated.

"Yes, much to my parents' dismay. But you'd better call your policeman first, Mrs. Majesty."

"Oh, please call me Daisy. Harold has told me all about your sister and brother-in-law, and he's taken quite a fancy to you, too," she said. "It must have taken a good deal of courage to fly in the face of your family and get a job. Not that every woman in my own family doesn't have to work for a living. But we're not wealthy like your family is."

"Actually, it was kind of easy at first, because the parents were in Boston and couldn't scold me except by post. Things are different now that they've bought a winter home here in Pasadena." I didn't appreciate it one little bit, either.

"I'm glad my family is plain old middle class, I guess," said Mrs. Majesty. I mean Daisy. "We seem to cope with things ever so much better than most of my clients, almost all of whom have more money than brainpower." She shot me a worried glance. "I didn't mean to say that. I'm sorry. Please don't repeat it."

"No, feel free," I said, heartened by her attitude. "I couldn't agree more."

"Well, I shouldn't say things like that. I make a good deal of money in my line of work, and I really ought to refer to my clients with more respect. Only . . . well, I've been doing this for more than half my life, and it's difficult to take people seriously who actually believe in spirits and such."

"You mean you don't?" Again, my sense of astonishment soared.

"Oh, dear, I shouldn't have said that either. Please pay no attention to me. I'm not used to seeing people fall from balconies and perish on parquet floors." She lifted a white hand to her white brow, and I noticed that her hand trembled. I guess she really was shaken up, poor thing.

Well, I was too, of course, but my own experiences since I'd gone to work for Ernie had made me . . . not indifferent or inured to tragedy, but not as shocked as Daisy seemed to be. It occurred to me that I'd packed a whole lot of know-how in the few months I'd lived in California. I was darned proud of myself for it.

"Here's the telephone room. Why don't you call . . . who is it you're going to telephone?"

"Sam Rotondo. He's a detective at the Pasadena Police Department, and he often investigates homicides. We recently became engaged."

"Congratulations," I said dutifully.

"Hmm. Yes, I guess so."

That didn't sound like a ringing endorsement of her beloved, but what did I know? "Do you think he'll be annoyed if I obey my mother and telephone Ernie?"

She shook her head, which made her shingled hair shine in the light. She had pretty hair. Dark red. Maybe auburn is the right word. Not plain old brown like mine, at any rate. "I'm sure Sam will be peeved, but I think you ought to do as your mother said. I sure wouldn't want to have her breathing down my neck if I disobeyed a direct command."

"Ha! You seem to have pegged her right off," I said with admiration.

101

"It's my job," she said simply, and lifted the receiver. Turning to me, she said, "Do your parents have a party line, do you know?"

"I . . . I don't know. I've never asked them."

"Well, I'll take care of it," she said.

And she did. She picked up the receiver, rattled the depresser thing, and said, "Is this Medora? Yes, it's Daisy Majesty. Medora, will you please connect me with my home? It's Colorado thirteen forty-five. Thank you." She covered the receiver and whispered, "Medora Cox is an old friend of mine from high school. She's worked at the telephone exchange ever since we graduated."

"That's nice," I said, uncertain how to respond to her confidence. "Is, um, your intended at your house at the moment?" I think I was shocked, although I didn't want to show it to Daisy, who was quite blasé about telephoning a man to whom she wasn't yet married at her own home.

She smiled at me. "He and my father play gin rummy all the time." She sighed. "They used to play with my late husband, but now it's only the two of them. I'm sure he's there now."

"Oh, I see." For some reason her explanation relieved my mind. I didn't want to think of this nice woman who had such an interesting profession as being less than moral.

"Ma? Yes, it's Daisy. Listen, is Sam there?" She remained silent as the person on the other end of the wire said something. "Yes, please get him. Thanks." Again she turned to me. "He's there." She sounded at least as relieved as I'd been with her explanation of why he was there. "Sam, you need to come to the Allcutts' home." She paused for a moment. "Yes, on San Pasqual." Another pause. "Yes, I mean it." She frowned as she paused this time. "No, I don't want you to sit in on the séance. A woman was pushed over the balcony." Pause. "Yes, she's dead." Pause. "No, she couldn't have committed suicide." Her face became grim. "Her name is Mrs. Winkworth." Pause. "Yes, the same Winkworth who owns the property on San Pasqual. Or the property Monty Mountjoy owns, I mean. In fact, this house is right down the street from hers." Pause. "Darn you, Sam Rotondo, this isn't my fault!"

CHAPTER ELEVEN

"Darn it!" Daisy slammed the receiver back onto the cradle. "He drives me crazy."

"Is he coming?" I asked, a little worried.

"Oh, yes, he's coming. Drat the man. He thinks it's my fault that these things happen around me."

"I know *just* what you mean!" I cried. "Ernie is the same way about me."

"Is he?" She gave me a huge smile, and I could see she was reassured. "Men are so unfair. But I don't feel so alone now."

"I guess I'd better telephone Ernie. He's going to yell at me."

"I know the feeling."

Taking a bracing breath, I picked up the receiver and asked the operator, whom I didn't know, so I didn't call her Medora, to connect me to a Los Angeles exchange. This took several minutes, but eventually I heard the telephone ring on the other end of the wire. And it rang. And rang.

I was getting desperate when Ernie's voice rasped in my ear, "Templeton."

"Oh, Ernie, I'm so glad you're there!"

Silence. Then, "Mercy? What the devil are you calling me for? Did you snap and kill your mother?"

"No, but someone else went 'round the bend and killed a guest in her house. Flung her over the stair railing from the second floor."

"Yeah?"

"Yeah. I mean, yes. And Mother told me to telephone you and get you to come here and solve the murder."

A rather long silence ensued. I wondered if our connection had been interrupted.

"Ernie? Are you there?"

"Yeah. I'm here. She wants me to drive to Pasadena and solve the murder of a guest in her home? A guest who was pushed over a stair railing?"

"Precisely," I said, glad he'd comprehended at last.

"Is she nuts? She should telephone the police."

"The police have been called, Ernie. But Mother told me to call you, so I'm calling you."

"Good God."

"Something like that. Will you come? Please? It's going to be bad enough around here already. If you refuse her command, I'll really be in for it."

"Shit."

It wasn't the first time I'd heard that word issue from Ernie's mouth, but I was still taken aback.

"Why do these things always happen to you?" he asked, sounding frustrated.

"That's not fair, Ernie!" I cried, reminding myself of Daisy. "This isn't my fault. And Mother told me to telephone you. If you won't come—"

"No, no. I'll come. Give me the address. If I leave now, I'll be there in about an hour, give or take. I should imagine the police will still be investigating and interviewing people by the time I get there. How many people were in the house when the woman fell?"

"Lord, I don't know. A lot. There were twenty of us at dinner, and more arrived afterwards. I expect about thirty or thirty-five people are here and were here at the time Mrs. Winkworth fell."

"Ah, shoot. Well, tell 'em not to go anywhere until after the police get there and can take everyone's name and address. I don't suppose you have a clue who pushed the broad overboard."

The *broad*? I presumed that was a euphemism for a woman, but I didn't appreciate it. "I have no idea who pushed the feeble old woman," I said pointedly. "But the houseboy was nearby. I saw him staring over the balcony after the woman fell. Or was pushed, I should say. And so was the dead woman's secretary." I didn't mention that Harvey, too, had been upstairs at the time of the murder.

"Do you think one of them did it?"

"I have no idea. I shouldn't think so." My patience snapped like a dried twig. "Oh, for heaven's sake, Ernie, hang up the stupid telephone and drive to Pasadena! I can't tell you anything over the telephone! You need to investigate for yourself."

"Sure, sure, Mercy. Don't get snippy. I'll be there as soon as I can be, provided the Studebaker makes it."

Oh, dear, that was right. Ernie drove the most disreputable old Studebaker I'd ever seen. It had driven us to Pasadena in July, but it was several months older by this time. "Well, try, all right? I'll make sure no one leaves the house before the police arrive. However, I don't know if I can make them wait for you."

"Criminy."

And with that, Ernie hung up the receiver on his end of the wire. I frowned at the telephone, which sat on a desk in the telephone room. Darn him, anyway!

"Is he coming?" asked Daisy.

"Yes. It'll take him more than an hour, I suppose. He has to drive from Los Angeles. And his car is a . . . well, it's not new."

"I hope for your sake he makes it," said Daisy. "I'd hate to have to face your mother after failing to perform one of the tasks she'd set for me."

106

"You have her pegged to a tee," I told her. "But I suppose we have to go back into the lion's den. Somehow, I have to convince everyone they need to wait until the police arrive."

"I'll help you. And I'm sure Harold and Doc Benjamin will help, too. They should be very effective at crowd control."

That made me feel better. Daisy and I walked together back to the drawing room, where we were met by silence and a herd of blank faces. It looked to me as if everyone was so appalled by the happenings that they didn't know what to do or what to say. I didn't either, but I took a stab at it.

"The police have been summoned. And I've been asked to keep everyone here until they arrive and are able to take everyone's statements." Very well, so I hadn't been asked to do that by a policeman, but Ernie had told me to do it, and I knew what was required in a case like this.

"Did you telephone that man?" demanded my mother.

"Yes, Mother. He'll be here as soon as he can be. I expect it will take him an hour or so to drive from Los Angeles."

"Hmph. And did you telephone your friend on the police force, Mrs. Majesty?"

Now why was it, I wondered, that Mother could sound polite when she spoke to everyone in the world except me? But I really shouldn't wonder. She disapproved of me, and she didn't disapprove of Daisy. And this, in spite of the fact that Daisy Majesty also worked for a living—and at a profession even she didn't believe in. Well, I'd already learned never to expect fairness from my maternal parent. Or my paternal one, either, for that matter.

"What do you mean, we can't leave?" shouted Lola de la Monica, who'd reappeared from wherever she'd been when the tragedy occurred.

Hmm. Where *had* she been? Harold had told us he'd shooed her upstairs. Could she . . . ? But why would she shove Mrs.

Winkworth over the stair railing? She'd probably been talking to Harvey, although I couldn't think of a good reason for her to do that either.

Nuts. No answers occurred to me. Neither did a polite response to Miss de la Monica's question. However, the suspects in this case were piling up rather too fast for my liking.

Fortunately, Daisy didn't suffer from my muteness.

"It's a rule, Miss de la Monica," she said. "Any time there is a death at a party or anything like it, all the guests need to remain until the police can take their names and addresses."

"Indeed," said my mother, for once on the side of the angels. Or the spiritualists, anyhow. "Everyone must remain here until the authorities give you leave to . . . leave."

From this muddled speech, I could tell she was still upset. Well, who wouldn't be? For once, I acquitted my mother of being aloof. In actual fact, when I glanced over to her, I saw that she had a death grip on my father's arm. Boy, you didn't see those two entangled much these days. I guess the blush had faded from that particular rose a long time ago, if it had ever been there to begin with.

People started whispering among themselves. Mrs. Pinkerton, I noted, still lay sprawled on the sofa. Her son wasn't with her, so I assumed he was still with the body and Monty and Mrs. Hanratty. Because I didn't want to remain in that room with a bunch of strangers and my parents, I decided to join them.

Mrs. Hanratty had stopped crying. She sat in a chair someone had brought into the hall, and Monty stood with her, his hand on her shoulder. They both appeared drawn and frightened.

Dr. Benjamin rose to his feet right after I entered the hall. "She's gone, all right, and I can't see how she could have climbed that railing by herself," he said. He glanced around and saw me. "Miss Allcutt?"

"Yes?"

"I'm sorry we haven't been properly introduced, but you were pointed out to me. Have the police been called?"

"Yes. Daisy called the Pasadena Police Department, and Mr. . . . um, Sam is on his way. And my mother told me to telephone my employer, who's a private investigator, so I did and he's coming too, although he won't be here for a while because he has to drive from Los Angeles."

"Oh, boy, Sam's going to love that," muttered Harold.

"I know. I'm sorry. But Mother commanded, and I obeyed."

"Well, that's all right. Sam Rotondo is a sensible fellow," said the doctor. "I'm sure he'll understand."

"I hope he does. I've told everyone to remain in the house until the police say they can go."

"Excellent," said Dr. Benjamin, snapping his black bag shut. I don't know where it had been when he was summoned from the drawing room, but he had it with him now.

I looked at the sheet-covered lump on the floor. Blood had seeped through the sheet in a few places, and I couldn't help but think blood wasn't good for the flooring. "Um, may we move the body somewhere else? It's rather . . . conspicuous in the middle of the floor there."

"No can do," said Harold. "I'm no policeman, but I know enough to be sure Sam would have a fit if we moved anything before he got here and saw exactly how the body fell and from where."

"Oh." I glanced up and remembered Lola de la Monica. "Say, Harold, were you here when Miss de la Monica reappeared from whatever exile you sent her to?"

"Sure was. She descended the staircase shortly after you and Daisy left for the telephone."

"So she was upstairs at the time?"

"Yes, she was. So was Delbert Mann. For that matter, so was Harvey Nash."

So he'd noticed Harvey's descent from the upper floor too. I don't know why, but the knowledge troubled me. "And Riki Saito. Hmm."

I could almost picture Lola de la Monica lashing out at someone and flinging that person over the stair railing. And Mr. Mann hadn't seemed thrilled with his employment or his employer, but I couldn't really feature either one of them doing the evil deed. Still, they were both more probable than Riki Saito or Harvey Nash in my humble opinion. Poor Riki had appeared entirely too shaken and dismayed when he looked over that railing to the floor below. And Harvey had only wanted to find Chloe and give her aid and comfort.

Then again, what did I know? Not a darned thing, was what. Nuts.

Just then a knocking came at the front door. The butler, whose name, I had learned, was Hoskins, walked stiffly in, didn't glance once at the body, and opened the door. I was interested to see a tall man in a rather rumpled suit and two uniformed policemen standing there.

"Please come in," said Hoskins frigidly. I guess he didn't approve of murder in any house over which he held sway. Didn't blame him a bit.

"Thanks." The man, who I presumed to be Daisy's Sam, glanced at those of us surrounding the body. "Is that it?" he asked.

I decided to take control of the policemen, since I didn't want my parents to interfere with them until absolutely necessary. I strode over to the three men and said, "Yes. I'm Mercy Allcutt, and the victim is Mrs. Lurlene Winkworth. I understand from Harold Kincaid and Mrs. Majesty that you were acquainted with her, if you're Daisy's Sam." I felt my cheeks heat from the boldness of this speech.

Sam, whose last name I couldn't recall, eyed me coldly. "Yes.

I'm Detective Rotondo."

Rotondo! That was it. An Italian name. And he seemed to have an Eastern accent, too. My money was on New York City.

"If you'll please step over here, you'll see what happened. The result of what happened, I mean."

Still feeling foolish, I led all three men the few paces to the sheet-covered body.

Harold turned and held out his hand. "Howdy, Sam. Unfortunate that we have to meet this way."

Detective Rotondo shook Harold's hand, although he seemed oddly reluctant to do so. "Evening, Kincaid. So what's the story here?"

Harold looked at me, and I looked at Dr. Benjamin, who looked at Mrs. Hanratty and Monty. None of us spoke for a moment until Harold said, "Miss Allcutt is a daughter of the household, and she was on the scene. Perhaps she'd better describe what we saw."

That was all right by me. "Yes, I'll be happy to. Or, if not precisely happy, then—" Detective Rotondo commenced glaring at me, and I stopped dithering.

"Very well. We'd just endured—er, attended the séance, and when we walked out of the room in which it was held, we all heard a scream, looked up, and Mrs. Winkworth fell from the second floor, over the stair railing, and landed right in front of us." I remembered the peculiar *splat* her body had made when it connected with the floor and shuddered.

"You say 'we all heard the scream.' Who are 'we all'?" Detective Rotondo, I was interested to see, was not taking notes. One of his subordinates, however, had a pad and a pencil poised. I wanted to see if he used the same Pitman method of shorthand I used, but didn't think it would be wise to enquire at the moment.

"Um, let me see. Mrs. Majesty was there, of course, and

111

Harold Kincaid and Mrs. Pinkerton. Mrs. Hanratty and my mother also attended, as did my sister, Chloe Nash. And who else? Oh, yes! Mrs. Bissel also attended the séance. There are more people here, but not all of them were in the séance with the rest of us."

"I see," said Detective Rotondo. "And are all the guests who were here at the time of the incident still here?"

Incident. That was one word for it.

"Yes, they are. I told them they couldn't leave until you told them they might."

"Good. Let me see the body, and then I'll tackle the crowd."

I wondered why he didn't ask to see Daisy, but maybe he didn't want to insert personal matters into professional ones.

He knelt beside the body, lifted the sheet, and perused the body with a clinical air of detachment. Glancing up at Dr. Benjamin, he asked, "Was the fall the cause of death, Doctor?"

"Yes, it was. The old lady was quite frail, and she couldn't withstand the impact. Well, I don't suppose anyone could unless they were extremely lucky. This is a hard floor." He stamped on it to prove his point.

Detective Rotondo grunted. For some reason, although there was no earthly resemblance between the two men, he reminded me of Ernie in that moment. Same method of communication, I reckon.

"Did you check the body for other bruising? Say, if someone struggled with her and dragged her to the staircase?"

"I did, although I couldn't perform a thorough job. That will have to be done at the post-mortem examination. As much as I could determine, there didn't seem to be any extraneous bruising, although some might appear. It sometimes does, after death."

"Right. Thanks."

Rising to his feet, he turned to the doctor. "Can you get the coroner's wagon up here, Dr. Benjamin? I suspect the owners of the house would like to have the body removed, and I can't think of any reason to leave it lying around, since the cause of death is obvious. And if you didn't see any unusual bruising, there probably isn't any, although we'll find out for sure later."

"Be glad to, Sam," said the doctor, who then turned to me. "Miss Allcutt, can you direct me to the telephone?"

"Certainly. Come with me."

I led Dr. Benjamin to the telephone room, which was nearby under the staircase. So many people's telephone rooms were, I guess because otherwise the closet under the stairway would fill up with brooms and mops and so forth. It was also a fairly convenient place, being sort of in the middle of things.

"Thank you."

"You're more than welcome." And I left him there and hied myself off to the drawing room. I wanted to see if the Pasadena Police Department did things the same way the Los Angeles Police Department did. I also wondered if the PPD was as corrupt as the LAPD, but I didn't think I'd better ask, at least not until Ernie got there.

CHAPTER TWELVE

It looked to me as though things were getting ugly in the drawing room. Lola de la Monica took one look at Sam Rotondo and sent up a howl that would have shattered the windows had they been of poorer quality.

Then she cried, "No! Not *that man!*"

"Hush up, Lola," said Harold. He said it loudly and firmly, too, what's more, and he marched right over to Lola, took her by the arm, and shook her.

God bless Harold Kincaid! I'd wanted to do that at least three or four times since Lola de la Monica crashed my parents' party.

"Oh, but Harold!" she hollered. "It's *that man* again!" She pointed a blood-red fingernail at Sam Rotondo, who looked upon her with every evidence of loathing.

"Of course, he's here. He's a homicide detective. He's here to find out who . . . how Mrs. Winkworth fell over the railing."

"Oh!" the woman screamed again. Then she fainted, or pretended to, into Harold's unwilling arms.

"Criminy," said he. "Will someone help me get her to a sofa or a chair or something?"

Monty, who had escorted his mother into the drawing room, assisted Harold in this endeavor, eventually dumping Miss de la Monica into an overstuffed chair near Harold's still-prone mother.

Mrs. Pinkerton, however, was beginning to revive. This probably had something to do with the water Mrs. Bissel was sprinkling on her. It looked to me as if she got the water from a vase of flowers on the table next to the sofa.

"Oh!" Mrs. Pinkerton said feebly. "Oh, dear, what's happened? Oh, yes. I remember it all now." She sobbed a couple of times. "Poor Lurlene! Whatever possessed her to end it all in that horrible way?" And she subsided into tears. This time Mrs. Bissel didn't wait, but dribbled more water on her immediately. Mrs. Pinkerton spluttered and sat up. "Griselda! Please!"

"Well, you need to get hold of yourself, Madeline," said the practical Mrs. Bissel. "The police have to question all of us who witnessed the accident."

"Oh," said Mrs. Pinkerton, bringing a handkerchief into play as she wiped moisture from her face. "Did they determine it was an accident? I thought she must have done herself in, since I don't see how she could have fallen." As soon as she heard herself, she gasped. "Oh!" she cried again. "Could it have been . . . *murder?*"

"Mother," said Harold, hurrying over to her, "please don't say anything more. You don't want to upset people any more than they're already upset."

She grabbed Harold's hand and wouldn't let it go. "Oh, Harold, but—"

"Mother!" he said sternly. "That's enough. Please allow the authorities to question everyone. And you be quiet."

I didn't know he could be so firm with his silly mother. I was impressed.

"Indeed," said Daisy, wafting up to the two of them and Mrs. Bissel. "Please, Mrs. Pinkerton, allow the police to do their jobs. We may never know quite what happened, but it's their duty to clarify everything." She didn't sound at all pushy, but her words carried a good deal of steel.

"Yes," said Mrs. Pinkerton in a small voice. "Of course. Oh,

Daisy, I'm *so* glad you're here."

Daisy only smiled her spiritualist's smile and spoke no more. She did, however, take Mrs. Pinkerton's hand and exchange a glance with Harold, who cast his gaze to the ceiling for a second.

"All right, everyone, please let's have quiet." This command came from Sam Rotondo, who stood in the doorway, eyeing the crowd as if he wished they weren't there. Or maybe he wished he wasn't.

"Sam," said Daisy in her soft purring voice. "Thank you for coming so quickly."

He only nodded at her, but I thought his expression softened for a moment. I'm probably wrong about that.

"First of all," said he, "I need to talk to everyone who witnessed the incident. I'll take you one at a time. Officer Ross will take names and addresses of everyone else in the room."

Because I didn't want any of my particular suspects to vanish, I hurried up to him and spoke in a whisper. "Miss de la Monica, Mr. Mann, and Riki Saito were all upstairs when Mrs. Winkworth took her dive." That sounded callous. Oh, well. Then I added, because I thought I really should, "And Harvey was upstairs too."

He lifted an eyebrow at me. "Harvey?"

"Harvey Nash, my sister's husband."

"Thank you, Miss Allcutt. I'll talk to them right after I talk to the others." He again addressed the crowd. "I'll need to see Miss de la Monica, Mr. Mann, Mr. Nash, and Mr. Saito, too. Please make yourselves available to me. I'll speak with you as soon as I talk to the others."

Lola screamed again. This time it was Monty who grabbed and shook her. Detective Rotondo only looked sardonic. I had a feeling that was his natural expression.

"Mercedes Louise!"

My mother's voice came at me like a blow. I even jumped a bit.

"Yes, Mother?"

"Fetch Riki, please."

"Very well." I turned back to Detective Rotondo. "Is that all right, Detective? Shall I fetch Riki Saito, or do you want me to wait until after you talk to him?"

"Better get him in here," said Rotondo. "We don't want him leaving for any reason."

My goodness. It hadn't occurred to me that Riki might flee the scene. I still had a lot to learn about this detectival business. "Very well," I said meekly, and went off to search for Riki.

He wasn't hard to find. He sat in the kitchen, clutching a cup of tea and looking sick.

"How are you feeling, Riki?" I asked, concerned.

"I'm all right," he said, although he didn't look it. "I'm not used to seeing people . . . die."

"No. I'm sure that's true. Neither am I. It was awful." And my nerves took that instant to give out on me. Before I could fall, I grabbed another kitchen chair and plopped into it. "I'm feeling rather shaky myself."

"Oh, you poor dear thing," said the cook. She rushed to the counter where sat a flowery teapot and several teacups and commenced pouring tea.

I watched her and said, "I'm so sorry I haven't come in to your kitchen before. I've been wanting to tell you how very much I've enjoyed the meals you've prepared for us since I arrived. What is your name?"

"Mrs. Thorne, dear. That's T-H-O-R-N-E, with an E on the end. Here, have some tea. I put sugar and milk in it. Hot sweet tea is the ticket for disordered nerves."

"Thank you very much, Mrs. Thorne," I said, taking the proffered teacup. My hand shook. "I didn't realize how upset I was until a moment ago," I admitted.

"It was pretty awful," agreed Riki. "I've never seen anyone . . . dead before."

After taking a sip of tea, which was delicious, I told him, "The police will need to talk to you after they speak to my parents and the rest of us who were in the séance. We're the ones who saw the . . . accident."

"Was it really an accident?" asked Mrs. Thorne, sounding as though she wished it were.

I pondered whether to tell the truth and decided what the heck. "Actually, I don't believe it was. She was a small woman, and unless she climbed up that railing, which I can't picture her doing, someone must have lifted her up and flung her over." I shuddered again.

"My goodness," said Mrs. Thorne.

"Golly," said Riki. "In that case, I guess I'm a suspect, aren't I? I was upstairs, after all." He shivered. "But I didn't do anything, Miss Allcutt. Truly, I didn't. I came out of the bedroom I was preparing when I heard loud voices and then a scream, and I got to the railing right after she hit the floor."

"I believe you, Riki. But you and Miss de la Monica, Harvey, and Mr. Mann were upstairs when she went overboard, so you'll need to give a statement."

"Of course." He didn't appear very happy about it, though.

"Riki wouldn't hurt a fly," declared Mrs. Thorne. "He's a thoroughly good boy."

"Thanks, Mrs. Thorne," said Riki, sounding wretched.

"I'm sure he is. But Riki, as soon as you finish your tea, you'll need to come with me. Detective Rotondo asked me to bring you to the drawing room to wait for the police."

"I'm supposed to put up the dishes," he said, looking worried. "Mrs. Thorne and the two maids have done the washing up. One of my jobs is to put everything away again."

"Don't trouble yourself, Riki," said Mrs. Thorne. "I'm sure I don't mind doing that."

"But—"

"I'm awfully sorry, Riki, but the detective in charge asked me to get you, so I'd better do it."

He heaved a huge sigh. "Very well. I hope I don't lose my job over this."

"I don't see how you could," said the nice Mrs. Thorne. "If anyone complains, they'll have me to deal with."

Shooting her a tight smile, he said, "Thanks, Mrs. T."

"You're most welcome, Riki."

"They'll have to deal with me, too," I told him stoutly. I refrained from saying my parents never listened to or took advice from me.

"Thank you." He gave me a smile almost as sweet as the tea.

So, after swallowing the rest of our tea, Riki and I removed ourselves to the drawing room once again.

I was interested to note that the police had separated the guests into two groups: those who had witnessed Mrs. Wink-worth's fall, and everyone else. I saw that Sam had put Mr. Mann, Harvey, and Miss de la Monica in the latter group. A policeman was busily taking down the names and addresses of everyone in that group—at least I guess that's what he was doing.

As for Sam, he glanced up impatiently when Riki and I entered the room and said, "Good. You're back. Please have the boy take a seat over there." He pointed to the non-witness group. "And you, please come with me."

So I did. After a parting smile for Riki, who needed it, I joined Daisy and Harold, Chloe, Mrs. Bissel, and the rest of us who'd witnessed the fall, and we all headed to the dining room. Naturally, the maids had cleared away all evidence of dinner by this time.

Detective Sam Rotondo questioned the ladies first, although he didn't begin with his fiancée, I presume so as not to appear biased. One of the uniformed policemen, whose name was Officer Ludlow, according to the name on his badge, took notes as the questions and answers flew. Because I was a member of the household, I got to go first. Lucky me.

"Did you know Mrs. Winkworth before this evening?"

"No."

"So you know nothing about her?"

"I know she's Mrs. Hanratty's mother and Mr. Mountjoy's grandmother." And nobody liked her. I didn't add that part.

"Why was she invited to your home this evening?"

"First of all, it's not my home. I have no idea why Mother and Father invited her to dinner this evening. I'm shocked they invited anyone from the motion-picture industry, if you want to know the truth."

"But isn't your brother-in-law in the industry?"

I sighed. "Yes, but he's my sister's husband, so he doesn't count."

"He doesn't count?"

Detective Rotondo could use his stolidity to great advantage, I noticed. With the slightest lift of a dark eyebrow, he could make a person feel like a worm, which was approximately how I felt when I tried to explain myself. "What I mean is, Mother and Father have to recognize him, because he's my sister's husband. But my parents are from Boston, and I never before knew them to have anything to do with anyone connected with the pictures except for Harvey. They generally deplore the picture industry and those who work in it."

"I see. And you don't know who might have had a grudge against Mrs. Winkworth?"

Oh, dear. What to say? "Um . . . well, I got the impression no one much liked her."

"Indeed? Will you please give me names?"

Nuts. I'd hoped he wouldn't ask me for names.

I slid a glance to Daisy, who nodded and said, "Might as well tell him. He's like a dog with a bone, and he'll never let it go. Save yourself some misery and just spit it out." She sounded slightly disgruntled, as if she'd been through this before. I thought they made a curious couple, but I don't suppose anyone can help with whom he or she falls in love.

Detective Rotondo scowled at his fiancée but didn't speak.

"All right," I said, "I chatted with Mrs. Winkworth's secretary at dinner, and I could tell he was unhappy in his position as her secretary."

"Did he tell you so?"

"Not precisely, but he looked gloomy and cast her looks of . . . unhappiness, I guess you could call them. Mrs. Hanratty and Mr. Mountjoy also mentioned that she is—I mean was—a difficult woman."

"How so?"

Botheration! "Oh, I don't know. I spoke to her briefly, and that one short encounter was enough to make me want to shove her over the balcony." Instantly I wished I hadn't said that, although Daisy gave a brief laugh.

Detective Rotondo scowled at her again, and she spoke right up. No shrinking violet she. "You know it's true, Sam! Why, she even sent Monty and Lola those awful letters a couple of years ago."

"I'm interviewing Miss Allcutt now, Daisy," he said in a shut-up-and-stop-interrupting tone of voice.

"I heard about that," I said. "She was just a miserable old coot, basically."

The detective heaved a large sigh. "Yes. She was," he said, kind of surprising me until I remembered that he, too, had known the victim.

"Can you think of any reason anyone might have to hate her enough that he or she would throw her off the staircase?"

"Well, nobody liked her, but I don't suppose most of us go around killing people just because we don't like them."

"Very well. Thank you, Miss Allcutt. I may have to speak to you again later. You may rejoin your parents now."

"Thanks, but I think I'll go see Chloe and Harvey. My parents are as ghastly as Mrs. Winkworth."

I don't think I shocked Detective Rotondo, and I saw Daisy smile. I was glad to get out of that room and head to the drawing room. A ring of the doorbell made me detour toward the front door, since all the maids were busy cleaning up after the party and poor Riki was confined to the drawing room with everyone else.

Swinging the door open, I cried, "Ernie! How'd you get here so fast?"

He gave me a frown at least as black as the couple Detective Rotondo had flung at Daisy Majesty. "You telephoned me an hour and a half ago, for Pete's sake."

"Oh, my, has it been that long? I guess it took time for the police to sort everyone out."

"Fill me in on what's happened before I do anything about the situation. And, in case you wondered, I'm not happy to be here. This is a police matter, and the coppers don't generally like having P.I.s cluttering up their crime scenes."

"Your being here isn't my fault," I said resentfully. "My mother made me telephone you."

"Christ."

"Stop swearing and tell me what you want to see first."

"The scene of the crime."

"There are two parts to that. The top of the stairs and underneath, where she landed."

"Upstairs first," said Ernie.

"Very well. Come with me."

"Lead on, Macduff."

Good Lord. Now he was misquoting Shakespeare at me. He must be peeved. However, I led Ernie up the stairs to where Mrs. Winkworth had been shoved to her death and did as he asked. I filled him in on what had happened up until the time he knocked at the door. The story didn't take long in the telling.

CHAPTER THIRTEEN

After I'd filled Ernie in on all the details I knew (or remembered), he stood there, silent, rubbing his chin and glowering at me. I noticed he hadn't shaved. I also noticed he appeared tired and drawn.

"Are you feeling all right, Ernie? You look a little peaked."

His hand dropped, and he frowned down at me some more. "You woke me up in the middle of the night and made me drive to Pasadena. Small wonder I look *peaked*, whatever the hell that is."

"Darn you, Ernest Templeton, if you aren't the most irritating—"

"Mercedes Louise!"

Ernie and I both jumped a yard or so into the air. When I glanced over the stair railing, it was to perceive my mother's regal form staring up at me, looking most displeased. Well, darn it, I was displeased, too!

"What is it, Mother? I'm telling Mr. Templeton what happened this evening."

"Bring that man down here at once, Mercedes Louise. *I* shall speak to him."

"Cripes," said Ernie. Softly. "She'd better be paying me for my time, too."

"I forgot about your fee. You ought to clear that up before you begin investigating. If she doesn't aim to pay you, to heck

124

with her." I was extremely annoyed with my mother by that time.

"Why the hell didn't you find out if she expected to pay my fee before you called me?" demanded Ernie.

Good question. Wished I had a good answer. What I said was, "I . . . I was upset. I didn't think." When he opened his mouth, probably to tell me I never thought before I acted, I hurried to say, "For heaven's sake, Ernie, I'd just witnessed a woman fall from the second floor and die on the parquet flooring at my feet! She was seeping blood. It was awful. I was upset. I . . . I can't think of everything, can I?"

He said, "Hell," and commenced walking down the circular staircase.

Blast the man. The fact that he was correct and I ought to have made it clear to my overbearing parent that if she wanted his services, she'd have to pay for them, didn't make me feel any better about what had been an altogether horrid evening.

By the time I'd followed Ernie downstairs and into the drawing room, he was in deep conversation with Mother. Neither of them looked as if he or she were particularly happy to be speaking to each other. Greatly daring, I joined them.

"Well, what are your charges, young man, if you insist upon being paid?" Mother asked in quelling tones.

Unquelled, Ernie said, "Twenty-five dollars a day plus expenses—and if I have to hang around Pasadena for a couple of days or more, expenses will include a hotel room."

"There's no need for that," Mother declared. "You shall stay here."

"I shall, shall I?" said Ernie. "Where?"

"What do you mean, 'where'?"

"I'm not sleeping on the floor or in the servants' quarters or outside in the garage. I'll need a bedroom and appropriate facilities."

"What sorts of facilities?" demanded Mother.

I wanted to bury my face in my hands. Instead of doing anything so unproductive, I said, "Mother, you made him drive all the way out here to investigate this crime. He needs a bedroom and a bathroom, and he'll take his meals with the family."

Mother turned her basilisk stare upon me. It was all I could do not to wither into the crumpled remains of a daughter on the spot. But I'd had practice, and I remained upright and maintained my stern and unruffled demeanor. Never mind that my innards were roiling as if a tornado had picked them up, whirled them around, and dropped them, splat, like Mrs. Winkworth's body had splatted on the hall flooring.

"You demanded his presence, Mother. You may be able to command your children around and be obeyed, but Mr. Templeton's services are for hire." With a silent prayer that I wouldn't be struck down then and there, I added, "You *must* have known that when you ordered me to telephone him."

Mother sniffed. It was an indignant sniff, but Ernie and I had her stumped. I wasn't sure about Ernie, but I was pretty sure she'd get me for standing up to her later. Ernie could probably take care of himself.

"Very well. I shall have Riki prepare a room for you," said Mother, her voice indicating in no way whatsoever that she'd been bested by the pair of us.

"Riki can't prepare anything," I pointed out. "He's being held with everyone else for questioning."

Her stare, when she turned it upon me, was as hateful as it possibly could be. "Then whom do you expect to do the job, young woman?"

"Oh, for God's sake, Mother, *I'll* prepare the stupid bedroom!"

"Mercedes Louise—"

But I'd had enough. "And don't you 'Mercedes Louise' me, Mother. A woman was murdered in your home—a home, I might add, that could house a small city—and Ernie is here at your insistence. I'm sick of being 'Mercedes Louise'd by you! I'm going to prepare a room for Ernie, and then I'm going to introduce him to Detective Rotondo. And how Detective Rotondo is going to like *that*, I have no idea. But however he feels about having his job usurped by your hireling, it's your responsibility and no one else's."

Mother stared at me. So did Ernie. If I'd been outside my body, I'd have stared at me, too. Never, in all my twenty-one years, had I spoken to my formidable mother that way. I wanted to applaud my bravery, but I didn't. Rather, I turned on my heels and headed back to the staircase.

I hadn't gone far before Ernie caught up with me. He didn't take my arm, but he did say, "You did good, kiddo. It's about time you told off that old battleaxe."

"Thank you." My insides, which had not long earlier been hurled to the ground by that tornado, had been picked up again and were revolving nauseatingly inside me. "I think I'm going to be sick."

Ernie laughed. He would.

We both walked up that twisty staircase again. "Keep away from the staircase railing, please," said a uniformed officer. Another uniformed officer was dusting fingerprint powder on the railing. I wanted to watch, but Ernie grabbed my arm, as though he expected me to interfere with the officers in their duty. As if I'd do anything so idiotic!

Before I could say so, I noticed Ernie had paused at the place where Mrs. Winkworth had gone over and peered around. I peered around with him. "What are we looking for?" I asked.

"Anything. Nothing. I don't know yet, but I need to evaluate this area and see who might have been where and how whoever it was did the deed."

I thought I understood. "Oh."

"Do you know where anyone was about that time?"

My brain commenced pondering. "Hmm. Riki was up here getting the guest rooms ready for the guests. I don't know which room he was in when the deed was done. I expect Mr. Mann was with Mrs. Winkworth in the upstairs room my father uses as an office. Mrs. Winkworth lives just down the street, and I imagine he lives there, too, since I understand the place is vast. And Lola de la Monica was up here someplace, although I have no idea where. She made a scene downstairs, and Harold sent her upstairs by telling her she had a smear of something on her nose. Um . . . I'm not sure where Harvey was at the time."

"Do you suppose he might have had business with the de la Monica person?"

Lifting my shoulders in a shrug, I said, "I don't know. I . . . well, I'm not sure, but I think she belongs to his studio. Harold and Monty—"

Ernie interrupted me to say, "So he's *Monty* already, is he? You've come to know him pretty well in the two days you've been here."

Irritated, I barked, "What difference does that make? Anyhow, I don't really know him. He and his mother took Chloe and me to a pet store in Pasadena. Oh, and that reminds me! Ernie, do you remember telling me that I shouldn't get a French poodle for Chloe and Harvey's baby?"

He rolled his eyes. "What does that have to do with the murdered woman?"

"Well, nothing, I guess, but I talked to the fellow at the pet store, and we decided the perfect dog to get for a little child, boy or girl, would be an English toy spaniel. That's the kind of dog Charles the Second—or was it Charles the First? Well, I don't remember, but—"

Again Ernie interrupted. "Quit babbling, Mercy, and tell me what I need to know."

"You started it," I said, sounding like a petulant schoolgirl.

Another eye roll on Ernie's part. "To get back to the matter at hand, do you think Mr. Nash and Miss de la Monica might have had business to discuss?"

"How should I know? Ask them." Something occurred to me that might—or might not—be or become relevant. "I don't think Mother and Father invited her to the party, by the way. According to Harold, she barges in wherever and whenever she wants to. Oh, and according to Daisy—or was it Harold? Well, I don't suppose it matters "

"Dammit, Mercy, *will* you stop jabbering and give me the facts?"

"Darn you, Ernie Templeton, I *am* giving you the facts! I'm trying to get them straight. Anyhow, I don't remember exactly who told me this, but evidently Mrs. Winkworth wrote poison-pen letters to both Monty and Lola de la Monica a couple of years ago."

"She wrote nasty letters to her own grandson?" Ernie was definitely as confounded as I'd been when whoever it was had told me the same thing.

I nodded vigorously. "Yes. Unbelievable, isn't it?"

"If it happened, I guess it's not unbelievable, but it sure is odd."

"I'd say so."

"Do you know why she did it?"

"Not precisely. I think Harold told me—unless it was Mrs. Hanratty or Daisy—that she disapproves of acting as a profession, and was trying to scare him out of it. This, in spite of the fact that he rescued her from dire circumstances in whatever southern state she comes from. She despises him for being an actor." I added bitterly, "Although, it seems she doesn't mind taking the money he makes at it and using it for herself."

Ernie shook his head. "Did anyone give her hell for it? I don't honestly know if writing poison-pen letters is a crime, but she must have at least got her wrist slapped or something."

"I don't know. Daisy didn't say. Or maybe it was Harold who—" a glance at Ernie's countenance, which was beginning to assume the aspect of a thundercloud about to burst and rain all over me, made my mouth snap up. "Maybe you can ask Daisy. Or Harold. Or Monty."

"Thanks. I will."

"Good."

"Do you know if Lola de la Monica and Monty Mountjoy were an item?"

"An item? What do you mean?"

"Aw, hell. You have to enlarge your vocabulary, kiddo. Do you think they were in love with each other? Dated. Went out together. I seem to remember photos in the newspapers putting them together at some swanky restaurant or other."

All at once my cheeks felt hot. Ernie must have noticed, because he said, "Out with it, Mercy. What do you know about Lola and Monty?"

I pursed my lips, wondering how to say what I was pretty sure I had to say to my annoying employer. "I don't know anything about them being a couple." There. That was enough, wasn't it?

According to the perfectly astounding scowl on Ernie's face, I deduced it wasn't. I heaved a huge sigh. "Monty Mountjoy isn't a ladies' man."

"What does that mean?"

Darn Ernie Templeton anyhow! "He doesn't like women. In that way."

"You mean he's a fairy?"

A fairy. Isn't that what Ernie'd called the marvelously handsome Francis Easthope when I'd first met him? Men could be really mean to each other. Fairies, my left hind leg. "He's a homosexual," I announced out loud. Instantly, I slapped my hands to my cheeks. They felt as if they'd just caught fire.

"Huh. Well, there are lots of those running around Hollywood these days."

I thought about Monty, Francis and Harold and allowed as how Ernie might be right about that. I didn't speak because I was too humiliated by my blushes by that time.

"All right, so much for the thwarted-love theory. Can you think of a reason any of the people who were upstairs at the time of the murder might have had it in for the old lady?"

"Except for Mr. Delbert Mann, her secretary, whom I heard her scolding right before the séance, I don't have a clue. He doesn't seem a likely suspect to me, but who knows? And I surely can't imagine Harvey doing anything so vile, even if the woman was a troll. I don't know a thing about Riki Saito or Lola de la Monica, except that everyone's told me Lola's a pain in the neck, and from what I've seen of her, they're right. Oh, and Harold and Monty both said they were surprised she hadn't been fired from the studio a year or so ago, because she's so difficult to work with."

"Huh. Well, I suppose I'd better meet this copper friend of yours."

"He's not my friend! He's Daisy's fiancé."

Squinting at me, Ernie said, "Who is this Daisy person you keep talking about anyway? Is she a friend from way back, or did you just meet her when you met *Monty*?"

I didn't like the way he said Monty's name, but I didn't let on. "She's the spiritualist. She's the one who held the séance."

"Cripes. She's the *spiritualist*?"

"Yes."

With another of his characteristic eye rolls, Ernie said, "Why don't we just hold another séance and ask the Winkworth broad herself who did her in."

"That's not funny, Ernie."

"Gee, I thought it was."

My boss was perhaps the most impossible person on earth. Well, except for my mother, of course.

CHAPTER FOURTEEN

I led Ernie to the dining room, where I'd last seen Detective Rotondo with those of the party members who'd witnessed Mrs. Winkworth's fall. He didn't look as though he was enjoying himself. He had my sincere sympathy. Mother and Harvey were gone, so I presume he'd already questioned them, for all the good that probably did him. We'd all seen exactly the same thing, after all.

It was Chloe's turn on the rack, and I knew she wished Harvey were still there as soon as Ernie and I entered the room and she nearly broke her neck turning to see who'd come in.

Detective Rotondo frowned at the two of us. "What is it, Miss Allcutt? We're busy here."

"I know, and I'm sorry. My mother insisted I telephone my employer to come and . . . and help the police." The detective's thick eyebrows almost met over the bridge of his nose, he scowled so hard. "Mr. Sam Rotondo, please allow me to introduce Mr. Ernie Templeton, private investigator. Believe me, Detective Rotondo, it's not Ernie's fault he's here, and he won't cause you any trouble."

"Yeah," said Ernie. "I'm pretty tame."

"Why the devil did your mother insist you call in a P.I.?" asked the detective, not unreasonably.

"It isn't her fault, Sam," Daisy piped up, bless her. "You've met her mother, so you know why Mercy followed her orders."

"Huh," said Rotondo.

"I won't get in your way," said Ernie. "Promise. But I'm here, and I might as well earn my keep."

Detective Rotondo muttered something under his breath. I think, although I'm not sure, it was something quite rude. "Well, take a seat and keep quiet." He turned to me. "There's no need for you to remain, Miss Allcutt."

Darn him! I was about to protest, but Ernie beat me to it.

"I'd like her to stay and take notes, Detective. I know your men are taking notes, too, but Mercy and I have worked together for some time now, and she's good. Hell, she's even been useful once or twice."

My mouth fell open for a second before it snapped shut. I was good? I'd *even* been useful once or twice? "I saved you from the electric chair a month or so ago, darn you, Ernie Templeton!"

"Yeah, yeah. But get a pad and pencil, sit down, and take notes now, will you?"

"Listen, you two—" said Detective Rotondo, but Daisy interrupted him.

"Just let them stay, Sam. What harm will it do? Better a trained private detective than nobody. Besides, you've met her mother." She lifted her eyebrows in a significant way, which conveyed to me, if not to him, that his health would remain better if he did as Mother wanted.

"Mr. Templeton used to be a policeman," I added, trying to be helpful.

"Used to be?" Rotondo's sneer was a work of art.

"Yeah. Couldn't cope with the corruption," said Ernie, who had a rather good sneer of his own going on.

"Huh," said Rotondo.

I glanced over at Daisy, who glanced back at me, and we both shrugged. So I trotted upstairs, said a very short good evening to poor Buttercup, grabbed a secretarial pad and a few sharp pencils—I'm never without several sharpened pencils—and rushed back downstairs to the dining room, where Detective Rotondo hadn't stopped his questioning of witnesses on my account. When I entered the room, he looked up, frowned, and commenced ignoring both Ernie and me as he spoke to the others.

"Oh, Lord, I don't know," said Chloe. I could tell she was close to tears and wished I could comfort her. But I had to take notes. "It was awful. We were all walking to the drawing room through the hall, and I heard a scream, looked up and this . . . this pink . . . *thing* . . . came floating down from the second floor. I mean . . . I mean, she wasn't floating, she was falling, but her dress sort of flowed out around her, and . . . and then she . . . she landed." Chloe buried her face in her hands and began sobbing. I felt horrible for her.

"Detective Rotondo," I said sternly. "My sister is in the family way, and she doesn't need to go over that dreadful incident more fully. Surely you know *she* didn't shove that old bat over the stair railing. Question the rest of us, but leave Chloe alone!"

The whole darned population of the dining room swiveled their heads and stared at me. Then a babble of voices began.

"Oh, my dear, are you going to have a baby?" Mrs. Bissel asked, as if this were the most fascinating piece of information she'd ever heard.

"A baby!" cried Mrs. Pinkerton. "How wonderful for you." She clasped her hands to her bosom and stared at Chloe, beaming. Quite a change from her collapse on the drawing-room sofa.

"What the deuce does her being pregnant have to do with anything?" Rotondo asked. Well, truth to tell, he bellowed.

I winced and noticed Ernie, too, appeared irked with me. "I'm sorry. I just mentioned it because Chloe really doesn't need all this stress and strain," I said in a small voice.

"I'm only asking questions, Miss Allcutt. I'm not torturing your sister."

Chloe gulped, sniffled, and wiped her face with a handkerchief Harold handed her. "I'm sorry. I'm just . . . upset." She cast a wild glance around the room. "I'm sure we all are. Mercy was merely trying to help me." Giving me a quavery smile, she said, "Thanks, sweetie. I didn't mean to fall apart. I need H-Harvey!" She broke down again, and I laid my pad and pencil aside and went to her.

With a black scowl at Detective Rotondo, I said, "Come with me, Chloe. You may speak to her later, Detective." Meeting Ernie's frown, I returned it with one of my own and told him, "I'll be right back."

Harvey was so glad to see Chloe, leaning heavily against me, and me supporting her with an arm around her shoulder, he all but ran up to us. She fell into his arms, leaving me feeling slightly bereft. But I pulled myself together and hurried back to the dining room, where things were still proceeding apace. Blast! I didn't know how much I'd missed, but I instantly began taking notes again.

Detective Rotondo stopped speaking to Mrs. Pinkerton and turned to me. "Is your sister quite well again?" he asked. Sweetly. Kind of like curdled vanilla pudding, if you know what I mean.

Frowning, I said, "She's with her husband, and no, she's not *quite well.* She's exhausted and upset, as I'm sure anyone but a . . . an insensitive dolt would understand."

I thought I heard Daisy utter a small snort of a laugh, but I'm not sure. When I glanced at her, she grinned and nodded at me, so I guess she didn't hate me for what I'd said to her beloved.

"Thank you, Miss Allcutt." Rotondo returned to Mrs. Pinkerton, and I returned to my notes.

I don't know how long we were in that room, but by the time the detective had finished with us, we'd all pretty much told him the same thing. We'd left the séance room, started walking through the hallway to the drawing room, heard a piercing scream, looked up, and we'd seen Mrs. Winkworth fall to the parquet flooring. No one had anything else to add, and a couple of people—the men, naturally—hadn't even seen that much, because they'd been talking to each other.

We then went into the drawing room, and Detective Rotondo told all the persons whom he'd already interviewed that they could leave, either to go to their rooms or to head home. Chloe seemed to want to cling to Harvey, but Harvey gently suggested she go upstairs and lie down, telling her he'd be with her shortly. Harvey was a real gentleman.

"Will all the people who were upstairs at the time of Mrs. Winkworth's fall, please go with Officer Ludlow. He'll keep an eye on you until I can interview each of you."

I should have, but hadn't, expected Lola de la Monica to kick up a fuss about that, but she didn't get very far. Rotondo rounded on her with that special, eyebrow-lowered glower of his, and she sort of shrank into herself. Harvey stepped up, took her arm and said, "Come along with me, Lola."

She gazed upon him with adoring eyes. He clearly didn't find her adoration charming, but at least she went quietly, along with Riki Saito and Mr. Mann, who had a hangdog expression on his face.

I'd expected the throng from the drawing room to take a long time to sort through, but Detective Rotondo did it in a snap. He just asked if anyone had anything to say about the evening's doings, and if anyone knew why Mrs. Winkworth might have been shoved to her death.

Except for one or two people telling the detective that she'd been a hateful woman, no one had anything of a useful nature to provide. Mrs. Hanratty did say, "I don't know anyone who really liked her, but I never thought anyone would hate her enough to . . . to kill her." She started sniffling again, and Monty put his arm around her.

"It's all right, Mother. Everything will be all right."

I hoped he was right about that.

"Very well," said the detective. "You can all leave or do whatever you need to do." He turned a jaded eye upon Ernie and me. "You two, come with me."

"What about me, Sam?" asked Daisy. I got the impression she wanted to be in on the action as much as I did.

"You go home. You've already given your statement, and if I need to talk to you again, I know where to find you."

Not a precisely lover-like speech, and Daisy didn't appreciate it. "Darn you, Sam Rotondo, I want to listen! I know those people better than you do. I can probably help."

But Detective Rotondo was firm. "Go home, Daisy," he said in a measured voice.

I sensed a seething volcano underlying the words, however, and I guess Daisy did, too, because she huffed and said, "Oh, all right, but you'd better tell me everything the next time you come to dinner, Sam Rotondo."

Rolling his eyes very much as Ernie did, the detective said, "Fine." Then he turned his back on his fiancée and walked back to the dining room where the main suspects—at least in my mind—lurked.

When Ernie and I entered the room behind Detective Rotondo, we found Lola de la Monica having a perfect snit at poor Officer Ludlow. Harvey was attempting to subdue her; Mr. Mann stood in a corner of the room, looking on, appalled; and Riki Saito was futilely attempting to pull the crazed woman away from Ludlow. Ludlow, while trying to dodge her sharp, red fingernails without decking her, attempted to exert control. He lost.

Finally, Ernie and Rotondo each went to one side of the idiotic woman, grabbed an arm, and drew her bodily away from Officer Ludlow, whose countenance bore evidence of Lola's lethal fingernails.

"Sit," commanded Rotondo as he and Ernie wrestled her into a chair. "Stay."

He sounded as if he were giving commands to a dog. I regret to say my mind offered up the word "bitch" in reaction to his words, but I didn't let on.

"Want me to cuff her?" asked Officer Ludlow.

"*Cuff! Cuff?* What is this *cuff?* Don't hurt me! Stop! Stop!"

Interesting. Her accent seemed to be slipping some. Did I detect traces of New York in her tone as well as Detective Rotondo's? Might they have known each other back east? Could they possibly—I told myself to get a grip on my nerves. Rotondo and de la Monica hated each other; that much was obvious. And New York City's a big place. Hardly anyone there knows anyone else. I remember that much from when I lived in Boston, which isn't nearly as big as NYC, but the same anonymous conditions prevail there, too.

"Shut the hell up, you," said Ernie, loudly, not mincing his own words. "You're the one doing the hurting. You should be locked up for attacking an officer of the law." He pressed down hard on her shoulders. "Want me to tie her down, Detective?"

"*No!*" Lola screamed. Then she started sobbing as if someone had just cut off one of her ears or something. What a blooming idiot!

Harvey walked over to the chair in which she struggled, looking angrier than I'd ever seen him, Harvey being in general a mild-mannered fellow.

"Lola," he said. "This isn't helping anyone, least of all

yourself. Calm down, answer the policeman's questions, and you can go home."

She gazed up at Harvey with beseeching eyes. "Oh, but Mr. Nash. How can you be so cruel. My life is *ruined*!"

Ernie, Rotondo, and I all exchanged a glance and then turned our attention to Harvey, who still seemed irked.

"You're the only one who has control over your life, Lola. You chose to create a fuss, and you're reaping your rewards now. Don't blame anyone else if you think your life is ruined, because you're the only one to blame."

"Oh, no, no, no!" she whispered, and then she dissolved into tears once more.

Ernie and the detective still held on to her arms, in case she decided to fight again, but gradually they let up on her. I expected she'd have bruises in the morning, but they were no more than she deserved.

"Are you going to sit still and behave now?" asked Rotondo of the sobbing actress.

She only nodded and subsided more deeply into the chair, which was not overstuffed or anything, but rather a straight-backed dining room chair. She must have been uncomfortable, but at that point I didn't give a rap.

Then she lifted her head, and I realized she'd been putting on an act the entire time. Her eyes were as dry as mine, darn her! I had to admit, however, that she'd proved herself to be a good actress. When I glanced at Officer Ludlow and saw him dabbing at bleeding scratch marks with his handkerchief, my brief admiration for Miss Lola de la Monica's acting talents underwent a downward plunge.

"Why, you weren't even crying! You were faking it all the time!" I told her, truly angry.

She smirked at me. "I was frightened," she said, her Spanish accent back in place.

"Nuts! You're a maniac!"

Lola commenced pouting.

Giving her a furious glare, I went to Officer Ludlow and put a hand on his arm. "And look what you did to this poor man!" I asked him, "Would you like to wash those scratches with warm water and soap? I'm sure there's iodine in a medicine cabinet somewhere."

"Oh, for cripes' sake," muttered Ernie.

"Miss Allcutt, get away from my officer," growled Detective Rotondo.

I whirled around and blasted both men with my fiercest frown. "Not until this poor man takes care of his wounds. Why, I've read that human scratches are worse than cat scratches!" With what I hoped was an expression of supreme contempt, I added, "Although in this case, I doubt there's much difference."

Rotondo muttered, "Christ," reminding me—again—of Ernie.

"Better let her look after the officer, Detective. Once she gets the bit between her teeth, there's no stopping her."

"But there won't be anyone to take notes," Rotondo pointed out.

"They'll be back," said Ernie with his characteristic insouciance.

"Dammit—"

"It's not worth arguing with her," said Ernie, interrupting the detective.

Rigid with fury now, I said to both men, "That's right." I turned to Ludlow. "Come with me right this minute."

Ludlow cast a pleading look at his superior officer. Rotondo gave one curt nod. Ha! I'd known I'd prevail. Well . . . I'd hoped I'd prevail, at any rate.

Looking at Lola, I commanded, "And you stay right where you are. If you cut up any more stupid larks, Mr. Templeton will tie you to that chair."

I peeked at Ernie, hoping he wouldn't defy me.

He only shrugged. "Whatever you say."

How very . . . Ernie-like of him.

But at least poor Officer Ludlow got his wounds attended to.

CHAPTER FIFTEEN

It didn't take me more than ten minutes to haul the policeman to the kitchen, wash his wounds with warm sudsy water, and fetch the bottle of iodine kept in the downstairs bathroom. He looked sort of like a red-and-pink zebra when I was through with him, but at least he wouldn't catch any sort of vile infection from that awful woman's pointy red fingernails.

Huh. Lulu LaBelle had pointy red fingernails, too, but she'd never do anything so awful as scratch the face of another human being with them. Lola de la Monica had by that time shrunk to the rank of a couple of the more beastly criminals I'd met since I'd been hired to work for Ernie.

When I opened the dining room door, everyone turned to look at us. Ernie and Rotondo smirked, and I'm sorry to report that Ernie snickered.

"She got you good, huh?"

"If you're talking about *me*, Ernest Templeton, let me tell you that *I'm* the one who saved this poor man from possible infection from the wounds inflicted by *that* person." I cast a look of scorn upon Lola, who gave every indication that she didn't give half a whit what I thought of her.

"All right, all right," said Rotondo peevishly. "Let's get back to work here. Mr. Nash, why don't you tell us what you were doing upstairs at the time Mrs. Winkworth met her death."

Met her death, eh? It was more like she met the floor.

I forgot all about Mrs. Winkworth when Harvey didn't speak

at once. In actual fact, when I glanced up from my notebook and peered at him, he seemed rather put out and embarrassed by the detective's question. Well, well, what did this mean? I couldn't believe Harvey was a murderer, but there was clearly something he felt uncomfortable divulging to us.

After several fraught seconds, Harvey said, "I don't believe my actions would be of any assistance to you in the solution of this problem, Detective Rotondo."

Giving Harvey an exceptional imitation of my mother's most intimidating, imperious glare, Rotondo said, "The reason we ask questions and expect people to answer them honestly is that we're trained to sort the wheat from the chaff. If you don't choose to answer my questions here, I'll be glad to take you down to the station and continue your interrogation there."

Harvey glanced down at his feet, frowning. I could tell he was uncomfortable about telling everyone what he'd been doing while upstairs, and I couldn't account for his hesitancy. Which went to show that Rotondo was absolutely correct: one needed all the facts before one could reach a valid conclusion.

Because I couldn't seem to help myself, I said, "Please, Harvey. I know you weren't doing anything wrong, but if you'd just tell the detective what you *were* doing, we could move this questioning stuff along."

All three men in nominal charge of the proceedings—Rotondo, Ludlow, and Ernie—frowned at me.

"Keep your mouth shut and take notes, Mercy," said Ernie. "If you don't, the police are going to kick us both out of here, and then what do you think your mother would do to you?"

He had a good point. "I'm sorry," I said, although I still pleaded with Harvey, using my best begging glance.

With a gigantic sigh, Harvey said, "Very well. Although it has no bearing whatsoever on what happened to Mrs. Winkworth,

I'll tell you what I was doing. Miss de la Monica and I were . . . chatting."

Lola sat up suddenly in her chair and threw a chilling gaze at Harvey, who didn't seem to notice. My goodness, what did this mean?

"About what?" asked Rotondo, wasting no words.

"Now that," said Harvey, "truly has nothing to do with the matter at hand. I don't believe you need to know what we were talking about."

"Certainly not," said Lola, her tone as frosty as her expression.

"For God's sake, let *us* be the judges of that, will you?" bellowed Rotondo. "Can't you get it into your heads that we need all the facts? *All* of them? Not just the dribs and drabs *you* think might be pertinent? Now what the devil were the two of you talking about?"

I don't know about Harvey or Lola, but I'd have spilled the beans right then and there. Detective Rotondo could be quite formidable when he chose to be. I wondered how he and Daisy got along when there were no murder mysteries to solve. Quite well, I supposed, or they'd never have become an engaged couple. They certainly didn't seem to suit each other, at least not in my mind, but the scene of a murder was probably not the best place in which to observe normal human interactions.

"No," said Lola. "No, no, no. I will not tell anyone about our conversation."

Rotondo pinned her with his dark, dark eyes and growled, "I wasn't asking you." He turned back to Harvey. "However, you'd better tell me what your conversation involved, or you'll come down to the station until you do."

"Oh, for God's—All right, all right. We were discussing Lola's employment with the Nash Studio."

"The last time I was in Miss de la Monica's company, I

thought her days in the industry were numbered. Quite frankly, I was surprised to see her here tonight," said Rotondo.

I wanted to tell him we were all surprised to see her here tonight, but I held my tongue, mainly because I didn't want to be kicked out of the room. This was getting interesting.

"Yes," said Harvey. "That's what we were talking about. Miss de la Monica's services are no longer required by the Nash Studio. Her contract is not being renewed. When an actor or actress is under contract with a studio, he or she can't easily be dismissed from the contract. The most efficient way to get rid of a nuisance like Lola is not to renew her contract."

"*No!*" screeched Lola. "No, no, no, *no!* You can't fire me!"

"I just said that," muttered Harvey. "We're not firing you. We're not renewing your contract."

"You *must* renew my contract!" Lola screamed. "I'm a *star*! I'm *important*!"

"You're also a pain in the ass," said Rotondo bluntly. "Which is why nobody wants to work with you any longer, from everything I've gathered about your career. Not to mention what I saw on the set of *The Fire at Sunset.*"

"*Pig!*" cried Lola, leaping to her feet and heading at Rotondo with her claws bared.

Ernie, bless his heart, stuck out a foot and tripped her. She went sprawling onto the dining room carpet and commenced beating her fists on the floor and drumming her toes. I don't believe I'd ever seen an adult human being in a full-blown tantrum before. It was something to behold.

Because I felt like it, I lifted the roses out of a handy vase and dumped the water on to Lola's head. She leaped to her feet, spluttering and screeching.

"Oh, be quiet," I said, whapping her claw-like hand aside with the vase. She'd been going to rake my own personal face with those talons of hers, and I didn't feel like treating her with kid gloves. In fact, if I'd had a poker handy, I'd probably have bashed her head in with it. Violent, I know, but can you blame me?

Coming up from behind, Ernie put his arms around her and held her fast, pinning her own arms to her sides. She made a fairly dramatic spectacle, what with her eye makeup streaking her cheeks, her face flaming, and her hair in sopping disarray. She tried to kick Ernie's shins, but didn't have much luck, since she had to kick backward.

"That's enough of that," said Rotondo. He turned to Ludlow. "Cuff her and stick her in the patrol car. She can spend the night in a cell for attacking an officer of the law."

"*No!*" Lola screamed again.

"And if you have to," Rotondo said, watching Lola's attempts to cripple Ernie with the heels of her gorgeous shoes, "tie her feet, too."

"You can't lay a *finger* on me!" she howled, sounding like a banshee on an Irish moor. Not that I've ever heard a banshee. I have been on an Irish moor. But that's not pertinent to this case. I only mention it.

This time, however, no one paid her any mind. Ludlow, with Ernie's help, got her hands behind her back, and the officer clicked a pair of handcuffs on her. They'd been hanging from his belt before being put to such good use. Eyeing her feet, which were now doing more damage to Ernie's person because she'd managed to whirl around, Ludlow knelt, grabbed one aimed foot, and Lola went down for the second time that evening, this time with quite a *whump*. It must have knocked the breath out of her, because she quit screaming.

"Got anything to bind her legs together with?" Rotondo asked, aiming the question at me.

"A couple of napkins tied together should work," said I, and promptly acquired two such articles. Ludlow had managed to snag her other ankle and now held both of them firmly together and pressed to the dining room carpet. He made quick work of the knotted-together napkins I handed him, and Lola couldn't move.

Unfortunately, she could still scream, and as soon as she recovered her breath, she did. I covered my ears and looked around for another vase of flowers, but Ernie solved the Lola noise-making problem with his own handkerchief, which he tied around her head like a gag, so she could only gurgle.

Then Ludlow and Ernie had to carry her out to the waiting police vehicle, which had been parked before the front door. No one said a single word until the two men returned.

"Is there any way she can get out of the machine?" asked Rotondo of Ludlow.

"Nope. She's behind the screen, the doors are locked, her hands are cuffed, her feet are tied, and her mouth's gagged." He smiled with satisfaction.

"Good," said Rotondo.

"What a hellcat," muttered Ernie. Turning to me, he said, "I'm glad you're not like that, Mercy."

"I presume that was meant as a compliment," I said sourly.

"Yeah. It was." Ernie grinned at me.

"Back to business," Rotondo grumbled. He resumed questioning Harvey, who didn't have much more to say.

When asked how long he and Lola had "chatted," he thought for a moment and said, "I'm not sure. Probably ten or fifteen minutes. She didn't want to hear what I had to say, but she didn't pull any of her usual stunts. Her performance tonight will give you a fair idea of why we no longer want to put up with her antics. It's bad enough that moving picture actors are always being portrayed as drug fiends and dipsomaniacs in the newspapers. At least most of the drunks and drug-takers don't throw fits and disrupt filming."

"Where did your conversation with Miss de la Monica take place?"

"In Chloe's and my suite. She left in a huff, and I'm not sure where she went after that. I . . . used the facilities, and then heard a scream. When I went out the door to see what had happened, I saw a pink blob on the floor below. I know now that the blob was Mrs. Winkworth." Harvey shuddered. Most appropriately, I believe.

"You don't know where Miss de la Monica went when she left your suite?"

"No." Harvey shook his head. "Sorry. She was in quite a state, however. I doubt she'd have gone downstairs until she'd managed to assuage her temper on some helpless thing or being." He turned to me. "You might want to have one of the maids check the upstairs rooms for breakage."

"I will. Thanks, Harvey."

"Can you think of anything else that might be of help to us?" Rotondo asked, although I could tell he already knew the answer to his question.

He got it. "No," said Harvey.

"All right. You may go to your wife now," said the detective, and he instantly turned to Riki Saito, who winced slightly.

"Your name is . . ." Rotondo squinted at a piece of paper, upon which, I deduced, the names of his interviewees were written.

"Riki—that's R-I-K-I—Saito. S-A-I-T-O."

Rotondo frowned at him. "That's not what it says here." He flapped the piece of paper in the air.

"It probably says Rikiichi," said Riki, "but everyone calls me Riki."

Rotondo lifted an eyebrow at the houseboy. "Japanese?"

"Yes. My brother, Keiji, works for Mrs. Bissel."

"Ah. Of course. Your brother taught Mrs. Majesty how to use

chopsticks if I recall correctly."

With a tiny grin, as if he wasn't sure Rotondo appreciated Daisy's and his brother's ingenuity, Riki said, "Yes. He did."

"I remember it well," said Rotondo wryly. "Anyhow, where were you when the tragedy occurred?"

"I was upstairs, making the guestrooms presentable. The Allcutts require that there are fresh flowers in all the rooms, and that the beds are turned down. I also made sure there was a new cake of scented soap in each bathroom and fresh towels on the racks."

"Did you see Miss de la Monica during your tour of the rooms?"

"I . . . I'm not sure." Riki's brow wrinkled in, I presume, thought. "I . . . I think I heard a loud conversation, but I'm not sure where it was coming from. I try to stick to my duties and not get sidetracked. The Allcutts are pretty strict employers." He shot a glance at me. "Not that they're not nice or anything, but—"

"You needn't be polite on my account," I assured him. "My parents are crusty Bostonians, and there's no getting around that. Or them. They're both difficult, hard-nosed icicles." I hoped the detective wouldn't object to my interjecting that little piece of information into the procedure in an attempt to make Riki feel more comfortable.

It worked on Riki, who smiled at me. It didn't work on Rotondo, who glared at me. Oh, well. I shut my mouth, poised my pencil, prepared to take more notes, and Rotondo didn't order me from the room, thank God.

"Very well. Tell me what happened. You were fixing up the guestrooms. Do you know where you were when the incident occurred?"

"I'm not sure whose room I was in. I think it was Miss Allcutt's." Another glance at me. "Is yours the room next to the large suite in the west wing, Miss Allcutt?"

"Yes. Next to Chloe and Harvey."

"The one with the pretty dog?"

I smiled at him. "Yes. That's Buttercup, my toy poodle." A glance at Detective Rotondo made me stop talking. Instantly.

"That's the one, then," said Riki, nodding.

"How far away is that room from the staircase from which Mrs. Winkworth fell?"

Riki thought for a moment. "Close. It only took a couple of seconds after I heard the loud argument and the scream to get to the staircase and look down." He shook his head in a convulsive sort of way. "It was awful."

"Did you see her hit the ground?"

"N-no. No, she was already there."

"You say you heard an argument before the woman went over the railing. Did you hear what it was about?"

"No. In fact, I might have heard Mr. Nash and Miss de la Monica arguing." He shook his head hard. "But I don't think that was it. I think the loud argument I heard happened right before the scream." Another, harder, head-shake. "I'm sorry. I was pretty upset at the time, and it's all kind of fuzzy in my mind."

"I understand," said Rotondo, surprising me. I wouldn't have pegged him as possessing an ounce of sympathy in him before then. "And you didn't see anyone else in the upstairs corridor?"

Another hesitation on Riki's part. "To tell you the truth, I'm not sure. I thought I saw something white, but it might have been a curtain or something waving in the breeze. I didn't see a person. At least I didn't recognize anything as a human being. I just remember a fluttering to my left."

"A fluttering, eh? And you have no idea what was fluttering?"

A frustrated head-shake. "No. As I said, I only caught a glimpse, and maybe I didn't see anything at all. If I did, it was probably a curtain. The windows along the upstairs hallway are covered with white lace curtains."

Hmm. The windows were covered with white lace curtains. And Lola de la Monica was covered—to a degree—by a filmy white gown. Something to think about, for sure.

"Can you think of anything else you saw?"

Riki opened his mouth, shut it, and then said, "Well . . . I think I saw a man, but it couldn't have been Mr. Mann or Mr. Nash, because Mr. Nash came up to me a second later, and Mr. Mann was typing. I think. But maybe I'm mistaken. If I did see anyone, I can't honestly say who it was or if it was a figment of my imagination. When I saw what happened, I . . . well, I . . . everything else kind of flew out of my head. If you know what I mean."

I knew what he meant, having come across a body at the foot of a staircase once, but I sensed no one wanted to hear about my history of corpse-finding.

"Where was this man you aren't sure you saw?" asked Rotondo, sounding grim.

"Well . . . Oh, I don't know. I probably didn't see anyone. Or maybe it was a maid. I was really . . . upset at the time."

"What other men are in the house?"

Again Riki hesitated. I got the impression he didn't want to incriminate anyone. At last he said, "Well . . . apart from guests who are here for the evening, there's only Mr. Allcutt, and he was in the drawing room, Mr. Nash, and Mrs. Winkworth's secretary."

Rotondo stared at Riki for another moment or two, and then said, "All right. Don't go anywhere. I'll probably have to talk to you again."

"You mean I can go and finish my work?"

"Yes. But don't leave the house." As an afterthought, he said, "You live here, right?"

"Yes. In the servants' quarters upstairs. All of the serving staff have rooms up there. Well, except for Mrs. Thorne, who has a suite of rooms off the breakfast room downstairs, close to the kitchen. She's the cook-housekeeper."

"And she wasn't upstairs when Mrs. Winkworth died?"

"Oh, no. She and the maids would have been cleaning up after dinner. I honestly don't know if Mrs. Thorne has ever been off the first floor of the house."

"Thank you, Mr. Saito. You may go along now."

So Riki skedaddled out of the room as fast as he could. I liked him, and I could think of no conceivable reason for him to have bumped off the odious Mrs. Winkworth, but I supposed one needed to keep an open mind about these matters.

"Your turn, Mr. Mann," said Detective Rotondo.

And, with a deep and heart-felt sigh, Mr. Delbert Mann straightened in his chair and looked bleakly at the detective.

Chapter Sixteen

Detective Rotondo started off with what I'd come to think of as the standard questions one asks a witness or a possible suspect.

"You were Mrs. Winkworth's secretary?"

"Yes, sir."

"How long have you worked for her?"

"Four months. Well, it would have been four months this coming week."

Rotondo's brow furrowed, making him appear formidable and angry, although I don't actually think he was. Angry, I mean. He was definitely formidable. He said, "She had another secretary when I was forced to watch over the damned movie camera on the set of *The Fire at Sunset.*"

"Yes, sir. That was Miss Gladys Pennywhistle, who left Mrs. Winkworth's employ to marry a gentleman professor at the California Institute of Technology."

"I see. And did you like working for Mrs. Winkworth?"

Mr. Mann hesitated for so long, I feared he aimed to lie, and that's never a good thing to do when there are coppers involved. I'd learned that from bitter experience of my own.

But eventually he said, "No. I didn't enjoy my employment with her. She was a fussy, exacting woman, and quite unpleasant."

"Was she fussy and exacting because you did a lousy job, or was she just miserable in general?"

Straightening in his chair, his cheeks slightly flushed, Mann said, "I am a competent secretary, Detective Rotondo. She had no reason to fuss at me, although she did. Constantly."

To my surprise, Ernie spoke next, "Give us an example."

Rotondo frowned at him but didn't object to the question, which even he would have to admit was a pertinent one.

"She accused me of making mistakes when transcribing notes, but I hadn't made mistakes. I'd typed precisely what she'd said to me. If she disliked the wording after I'd typed what she'd said, it wasn't my fault." He shook his head hard. "That makes me sound petty and foolish, but it's the truth. The woman went out of her way to make life miserable for the people around her. If you don't believe me, ask her daughter and grandson. I swear, if it weren't for Mrs. Hanratty, I'd have quit after my first week."

"You might have been better off if you'd quit anyway," Ernie pointed out, earning another frown from Rotondo.

Mann heaved another large-sized sigh. "You're right. But jobs aren't as plentiful as they once were. I was afraid to quit, because I didn't trust the old woman to give me a good reference. She was like that." He paused for a second and then continued in a ruminative voice, "Although the longer I stayed, the worse she got, so you're probably right. I ought to have resigned after the first week."

"So you didn't like her," Rotondo stated, taking the interrogation back into his own hands. Or mouth.

"No. I didn't like her."

"Miss Allcutt said she heard the two of you arguing during the evening."

After shooting me a huffy glance, Mann said, sounding petulant as he did so, "The woman told me I'd made more mistakes. I usually don't answer her back, but I was angry at her constant carping about things that weren't my fault, so I told her I'd typed precisely what she'd said to me, and if she wanted proof, she could read my notes." He deflated a trifle. "Which was a stupid thing to say, because she can't read shorthand. Even if she could, she'd have told me I'd taken her words down incorrectly. And I hadn't!"

Poor guy. If I'd had a boss like his, I might have been tempted to shove her over a staircase railing. I suppose he could have done the evil deed, although "evil" is perhaps not the correct term for ridding the world of such a pestilential female.

"You were upstairs with her shortly before her death, right?"

"Yes. In the room Mr. Allcutt allowed her to use as an office, which is in the east wing of the house, next to a bedroom. Of course, since she only lives—lived—a block away, she didn't aim to spend the night. If she had done so, I'm sure I'd have been relegated to the servants' quarters." He sounded bitter. "And I certainly have no idea why she needed anyone to write letters for her while she was a guest at a party. Anyhow, I could have stayed home and typed them if they were that important."

"So you had good reason to dislike her."

"But not a good-enough reason to push her over the railing," Mann said defensively. "If people don't like their bosses, they don't go around killing them."

"I could give you statistics," muttered Ernie, which, to my surprise, made Rotondo chuckle rather than glower at him.

"So could I," said the detective.

"Well, I didn't," Mann said irritably. "I just went into that room she used as an office to re-type the letters she said I'd taken down incorrectly. When I heard a scream, it startled me, and I left the office to see what was wrong."

"And did you?"

"See what was wrong?"

"Yeah."

"Not at once. The office is east of the place where she went over. It took a couple of seconds for me to get there. When I did, I saw that Jap houseboy heading down the stairs. Then I leaned over the railing and saw Mrs. Winkworth on the floor."

"Did you see anyone else upstairs?"

"Not immediately. Mr. Nash joined me a second or two later. I think he came from his own room. We both wondered what had happened."

"You talked about it?"

"Yes. Well, only insofar as we asked each other if we knew what had possessed Mrs. Winkworth to climb over the railing and let go."

"You thought she'd committed suicide?"

"Yes. No. Oh, I don't know. She didn't seem the type to kill herself. I could see her killing someone she didn't like, but she was too self-centered to kill herself."

"Right. Let me know if you think of anything else that might be of interest to the case, and keep yourself available for further questioning."

"Thank you," said Mann.

Which brings up a point that may or may not be pertinent to this case. If you're a secretary, you're required to thank people, even if they're interviewing you because they suspect you of committing some vile crime. Secretaries are subservient beings. I was only lucky that Ernie had chosen to hire me and then to put up with my independent attitude. Most secretaries, and Delbert Mann was clearly one of them, were cowed by other people whom they believed wielded more power than they. And they were absolutely right in that assessment. It's a sad situation, but there you go.

"All right, then." Rotondo conferred with Officer Ludlow for a moment or two. They spoke so quietly, I couldn't hear what they said to each other, no matter how much I strained to do so.

"Give it up, kiddo," Ernie told me with a grin. "They're not going to let you into their club."

Frowning at my annoying employer, I said, "Well, I'm involved whether they like it or not. I've been taking notes, too, you know."

"I know."

Turning to us, Detective Rotondo said to Ernie, ignoring me in the process, "We're going to the station now. Do you want to come along to witness Miss de la Monica's interview?"

"Yeah. Thanks. I appreciate your asking me, because I'm at present working for a tyrant." He gave me a saucy grin.

"I'm going, too," I said. "I don't want to be stuck here with my monster of a mother while you're interviewing that other monster, the actress."

Rotondo frowned, and I could almost see a "no" dancing on his lips, but Ernie didn't let him say it. "I need her to take notes, Detective Rotondo. You have your guy, and I have mine." He nudged me, making me scrape my pencil point across the page of my secretarial notebook. Darn him! "And you wouldn't be so cruel as to leave her with her mother, would you?"

"I don't give a damn about Miss Allcutt's mother," growled Rotondo. "I have a case to solve. You're a P.I., which means you're nothing but a pain in the ass to me."

His language offended me, although I suppose that's the way policemen speak to each other when no one of significance is listening. You can imagine how that made me feel, although I didn't voice my displeasure, thereby proving that I can act in my own best interest from time to time.

"Listen, you allowed us to sit in on the other interviews, and I've been hired to help," said Ernie. "I don't aim to get in your way. We'll just sit quietly and listen. Well, and Mercy will take notes. Who knows? We might just be of some kind of help."

"Huh." Rotondo scowled for a moment, then said, "Oh, hell, come along. You can follow us to the station. But no interfering or I'll kick you out, and don't think for a minute I won't."

When it came to policemen, I much preferred Ernie's detective friend, Phil Bigelow, with whom I'd struck up a nice friendly acquaintanceship, to Detective Rotondo. I couldn't understand how Mrs. Majesty could tolerate this gruff man.

"We won't interfere. Promise," said Ernie, still grinning. He was the most annoyingly casual man I'd ever known. But he got his way, which was the important part. "Mercy and I will follow you in my machine."

"Right," said Rotondo. "I'll go speak with the Allcutts, and then we'll head to the station."

Both Officer Ludlow and I closed our notebooks at the same time. We all rose from our chairs, left the dining room and I headed to the drawing room. Mother and Father were still there, although the room had cleared of other people. The two maids, whose names I knew not, were busily picking up cups, saucers, napkins, etc., and scurrying around, trying, unless I missed my guess, to appear invisible to my parents. Made sense to me.

Mother glanced up at us and frowned. No surprise there. "Well?" she demanded. "Who murdered that poor woman?"

Undaunted by her austere question and manner, Detective Rotondo said, "We don't know yet, ma'am. We had to take Miss de la Monica to the station to be questioned, because she kicked up such a dust in the dining room."

My father huffed indignantly.

So did my mother. "Abominable woman. I don't even know why she was here tonight. She certainly wasn't invited."

"We know that, Mother. Evidently she just shows up when and where she pleases."

"I do not approve of that sort of behavior," said Mother, as if we didn't already know that.

"Yeah," said Rotondo. "We don't, either. I'm leaving a uniform here to make sure no one disrupts the various scenes of the crime."

"Scenes of the *crime*?" my mother said, her Boston manner at its chilliest.

"Yes. We'll be back tomorrow, so don't go anywhere. And please don't allow anyone, including the maids, to clean anything upstairs." Rotondo and Ludlow turned around and headed to the door.

"Wait! Wait! You come back here, young man!"

Detective Rotondo? A young man? I squinted after him. Hmm. I guess he was young, even though he behaved like a hardened . . . well, policeman. Which he was, so I suppose that was all right.

Mother's head snapped in my direction. Of course. She had on her best glower when she said, "I don't understand any of this! Why can't we have the mess upstairs cleaned up? And why are we under siege?"

"You're not under siege, Mother," I said, trying to placate the woman, which was more or less akin to taming a raging nor'easter. In other words, it was futile.

"But that man left a uniformed policeman here!"

"That's to make sure no one leaves the house, Mother. And to make sure no one disturbs the crime scene."

With an indignant chuff, Mother snarled, "Crime scene, indeed."

All righty, then. I'd had enough. "Yes, well, we need to get ourselves down to the police station now, so that we may pursue the case you've assigned to Mr. Templeton."

"*You* will remain right here in this house, young woman," said Mother. I noticed she didn't "Mercedes Louise" me this time, perhaps recalling that I could bite when driven beyond endurance.

"I work for Ernie, Mother. I'm his secretary, and I have to take notes during Miss de la Monica's interview. If I don't do it, Ernie has no help at all. You hired him, remember."

She just hated when I spoke up for myself. However, under the present circumstances, she couldn't very well refute my logic. "Very well, but come back here as soon as possible. I don't want my daughter gallivanting all over town alone with a man."

"If I'm with Ernie, I'm not alone," I pointed out, probably to my peril. Before she could leap upon me and batter me senseless, I remembered something important. "By the way, because I've been helping Ernie carry out the duty you assigned him, I haven't been able to get a room ready for him. Perhaps you can have Riki or one of the maids prepare a room for him. On the second floor," I added, lest she go against Ernie's wishes and send him to the third floor with the servants.

I noticed with interest as my mother puffed up like a pigeon with its feathers in a fluff, but it was my father who saved the day. Or the evening. Or maybe the morning. I don't even know what time it was by then.

"That's a good point, Honoria." He lifted his regal head. "Mary Jane."

He didn't lift his regal voice, but I noticed one of the maids in the room jump approximately a foot in the air and twirl around, clutching an errant teacup to her bosom as if she expected to be horsewhipped. Poor thing. Maids were even more put-upon than secretaries. Especially in this house.

"Y-yes, sir?" she whispered as if she feared to speak any louder.

"Will you please prepare a bedroom for Mr. Templeton." It wasn't a question. "Put him . . ." He glanced at Mother, whose lips were as wrinkly as a raisin with displeasure.

After fuming for a moment or two, she waved a hand regally and said, "Oh, give him the last room on the east wing." She switched her glare from poor Mary Jane to Ernie. "You'll have

161

to be satisfied with that, Mr. Templeman—"

"*Templeton*, Mother!" I said, and rather loudly too. "The least you can do is treat the man with the respect he deserves. He didn't *want* to come all the way out here, you know."

"And *you*, Mercedes Louise—"

"Don't you start *Mercedes Louise*-ing me again, either." Maybe I was tired after a long day, or maybe I was just fed up, but I can't recall another single time in my life that I'd stood up to my overbearing mother twice in one day. "That room will be fine." I turned to Ernie. "There's a bathroom right across the hall from it, and I don't think you'll have to share it with anyone but—well, come to think of it, you won't have to share it with anyone now that Mrs. Winkworth's dead."

"Mercy," said my father in a stern tone.

I shrugged, reminding me of Ernie. "It's the truth."

"But don't let anyone into the room Mrs. Winkworth used as an office," said Ernie. "The police still have the place closed off, and I imagine they'll be back tomorrow to dust for prints there."

"Dust for prints?" Father frowned at Ernie. "That room is the one I use for my office. I allowed Mrs. Winkworth to use it this evening."

"They have to take fingerprints," I said. "They've already dusted the stair railing where Mrs. Winkworth was pushed over. I expect you'll have to wait for permission from the police before the maids or Riki will be allowed to clean the fingerprint powder away."

"Fingerprint powder? We have to wait for the *police* to give us leave to clean our own home?" Mother. Indignant. As usual.

"Yes, Mother, just as Detective Rotondo already told you," I said with a sigh. "You've never been involved with a murder investigation before, but any time the police have to investigate something like this, you're not supposed to interfere with the scene of the crime. Or the office used by the murdered person."

I added that last part because I didn't want her to forget it.

"The scene of the crime! I've never heard of such a thing!" There she went, puffing up again. It was an interesting sight, but not one I particularly cared to witness any longer.

"Well, you've heard of it now," said I. "Come on, Ernie. Let's get out of here and down to the police station."

As Ernie and I turned to leave my mother and father, who'd commenced goggling at us, I ignored my mother's angry, "Mercedes Louise!"

"To hell with her," I muttered so that only Ernie could hear.

He laughed, as I might have anticipated, but didn't. So I laughed, too. It felt good.

CHAPTER SEVENTEEN

I'm not sure where, in the overall scheme of things in Pasadena, the Pasadena Police Department headquarters resided, but we were there not long after we'd left Mother and Father's home on San Pasqual.

"You sure know your way around Pasadena," I observed to Ernie, impressed.

"I looked at the map. The station's only west and a little north of your parents' house. If you can call such a palace by so meager a term."

"Don't start in on me being a rich girl again, Ernie," said I, all but snarling.

With a chuckle—curse the man—Ernie said, "Sure thing, kiddo."

"And don't call me *kiddo*, darn it!" I hated when he called me that. Made me feel like his little sister or something, and I wanted to build up my position to that of partner in his firm. At the moment, he didn't need a partner any more than he needed a secretary, but that's neither here nor there. I had faith in our ability to increase the business.

"Very well, your majesty."

"Blast you, Ernie Templeton!"

"Sorry, Mercy. But you have to admit, you're fun to poke fun at."

"Hmph. And you're not supposed to end a sentence with a preposition, either."

This time Ernie laughed out loud. "You're fun at which to poke fun. That better?"

"Not much. Your *which* should be *whom.*"

"Baloney. Who talks like that these days?"

With a sigh, I admitted, "Nobody. Except my parents, I suppose."

"Well then, there you go. You don't want me to act like your folks, do you?"

"No." The mere thought gave me the shivers.

Ernie, unable to stop himself from being gentlemanly no matter how hard he tried, got out of his Studebaker and came around to open my door for me. He even took my arm to help me debark, if that's the term one uses when one leaves an automobile.

"This way, Mercy."

He kept my arm as he led the way from the parking lot to the front door of the police station. Truth to tell, it wasn't exactly a front door. The police station sat behind a large building residing on a corner lot at Fair Oaks Avenue and Union Street. I know that because I looked at the street signs. See? I'm observant. I'd be a good P.I., if ever I could convince Ernie of the fact.

Ernie even held the door for me to enter before him. I could hardly believe how mannerly he was being this evening, but I didn't trust him to continue this behavior.

We both approached a uniformed officer who sat at a desk in the middle of a room. Behind him was a walled-off space with a door leading therefrom. I wondered where Lola had been taken and if she was still cutting up larks. If larks they could be called.

"Detective Rotondo said we can sit in on the interview with Miss Lola de la Monica," Ernie told the copper, who gazed upon us stolidly.

"You Templeton?"

"Yes."

The uniformed fellow hooked a thumb at me. "That your secretary?"

"Yes."

With a grunt, the stolid bloke rose from his chair, which squeaked like Ernie's used to do before I went at it with an oil can. He'd told me once he missed his squeak, but I believe he was only being obstinate at the time.

Opening the door in the wall, the policeman said, "In there. Second door on the right."

"Thanks," said Ernie as we entered through the door and faced a long, bleak hallway.

"Better you than me," said the copper as he shut and locked the door behind us.

Not a promising statement, that. Oh, well. It's not as if we didn't already know what to expect from the demented actress.

"Second door on the right," I repeated, just in case Ernie hadn't heard.

"Yeah. I know."

Very well, I guess he'd heard just fine.

We both stood before the second door on the right and I wasn't sure what to do. Burst in? Knock?

Ernie, who didn't suffer from my scruples, rapped hard once upon the solid metal door, turned the handle . . . and the door didn't budge. Soon enough, Officer Ludlow unlocked the door, beckoned to us, and Ernie walked right on in. So I walked right on in behind him.

Detective Rotondo, who'd been seated at a table, glanced up and grunted when he saw us. "Sit anywhere," he said with a vague wave around the room. Ernie pulled up a couple of chairs and placed them on Rotondo's side of the table. I saw Officer Ludlow mosey off to the side and sit in a chair in the corner as if he didn't want to be noticed. Poor fellow. It was going to take a while for those slash marks and the iodine stains to fade away. I feared he was going to get unmercifully ribbed by his fellow officers in the ensuing days.

Lola, I noticed, sat on the other side of the same table, with a uniformed officer on either side of her. Her expression mulish, she glared at Rotondo as if she wanted to spit in his eye. Rotondo didn't seem to notice; or maybe he just didn't care.

"All right, we're all here," said the detective. To Lola he said, "You had a discussion with Mr. Nash."

I thought for a second she wasn't going to answer the question, but suddenly she seemed to deflate, her stubborn expression softened, and her eyes got misty. What an actress the woman was! Too bad she was such a pain in the rump; I'm sure she'd have had a wildly successful career if only she'd learned to behave.

"I was upset." I noticed her Spanish accent was back and riper than ever. "I ran from the room. I don't know where I went. I don't know the house."

"Did you see Mrs. Winkworth as you ran?"

"I . . . don't know. I don't know. I *don't know!*" She had a darned good screech going for her. If talkies ever became viable to produce, she'd be great. Well, if she'd hadn't been fired, she would have been great.

"You don't know if you saw the woman?" Rotondo said, clearly skeptical.

Lola would have thrown her arms wide if she weren't hampered from doing so by the rock-steady police officers at her sides. "I don't *know!* I don't see anything. I was blinded by tears."

"Yeah? Well, according to our fingerprint folks, your prints were on the stair railing right about where Mrs. Winkworth went over."

Oh, my! I wondered how they managed to get her to sit still

long enough to take her prints. I didn't ask.

With a magnificent shrug, Lola said, "I hold onto the railing. Everybody holds onto the stair railing when climbing stairs."

That might well be true, although the direction of Rotondo's questioning sounded promising. I'd rather see Lola de la Monica convicted of murder than any of the other suspects.

"Huh. You didn't like Mrs. Winkworth, did you?"

"I have no opinion of Mrs. Winkworth." If Lola's tone got any loftier, the police gents would have to pin her down by pressing on her shoulders.

"She sent you threatening letters a couple of years ago."

Another shrug. "I don't care. Stupid woman."

"From everything I've heard about her, Mrs. Winkworth had a wicked tongue. I can envision you racing out of Mr. Nash's room, bumping into Mrs. Winkworth, her saying something nasty to you, you getting mad and tossing her overboard," said Rotondo in a matter-of-fact tone.

"I did nothing!" Lola said. Loudly. "I want an attorney. Get me my attorney." The words were a command, but nobody raced to do her bidding.

"Who's your attorney?" asked Rotondo.

"I don' know his name," she said. Her accent waxed and waned, which was quite interesting. I still thought she was from New York. Maybe New Jersey or Rhode Island. Or, heck, even Massachusetts.

"If you don't know his name, we can't telephone him for you," Rotondo pointed out.

"Call Harvey Nash. He knows. He will use the attorney who works for the studio."

"According to what Mr. Nash told us, you're no longer affiliated with his studio. Your contract wasn't renewed, remember?"

Lola's lips pursed, and I thought for a second or two she aimed to hurl vile vituperations at Detective Rotondo, which sounded like a really bad idea to me. Finally she said, almost pleading, "Telephone Harvey. I'm sure he will help me."

"Whatever you say." Rotondo turned to Ludlow. "Will you please call the Allcutt place and see if you can get Mr. Nash to approve his studio hiring a lawyer for Miss de la Monica?"

With overt reluctance, Ludlow left his corner, headed to the door, unhooked a hoop of keys from his belt, chose one, and unlocked the door. After he left the room, I heard the key twist in the lock again. Boy, I'd never seen such security. In a way, it was comforting. It would have been more comforting if Lola de la Monica weren't in the room with us, but one can't have everything.

Silence reigned as we waited for Ludlow to return. It wasn't long before we heard the door being unlocked, and he re-entered the room, shaking his head. "Sorry. Nash says the studio is through with Miss de la Monica. She's going to have to hire her own attorney."

That speech set Lola off again. She wailed at the top of her lungs, pounded the table with her fists, and thrashed her head back and forth. Her hair, by the way, had dried after I'd drenched it with rose-vase water, and now hung in clumps. For such a gorgeous woman, she didn't make a pretty sight just then.

After a very few seconds of that, Rotondo sighed, rose from his chair, and told the two officers standing beside the termagant, "Take her to a cell and lock her in. Make sure she doesn't have anything she can hurt herself—or anyone one else—with."

"Yes, sir," said the taller of the two officers.

And then the two men each grabbed one of Lola's flailing arms and lifted her bodily from the chair, which she kicked over in her tantrum. Golly. I sure wouldn't want to be a police person, if they had to deal with people like that woman all the time.

After Lola was gone and our ears stopped ringing, Ernie asked Rotondo, "Was that fingerprint nonsense true?"

"Hell, no. I just wanted to see how she'd react."

"You mean you *lied* to her?" I asked, astounded. I didn't realize the police did things like that. Sounded like playing dirty to me.

"Yeah. We lied to her."

"It's a technique used by all good cops. And P.I.s," said Ernie, grinning at me.

"Hmm. Doesn't sound fair to me."

"What would you suggest they do?" asked Ernie. "Treat her like a lady? That broad's no lady, Mercy. I thought you'd learned a thing or two since I hired you."

"I have learned a thing or two, darn it! I just . . . well, I just didn't know the police were permitted to lie to a witness. Or a suspect. Whatever she is."

"Live and learn, kiddo. I mean Mercy."

I gave up and turned to Detective Rotondo, who had picked up a bunch of papers. I guess he'd been making notations on them, although I didn't notice him writing. Interesting. Maybe he was more clever than he at first appeared. My first impression was of a large, solid, solemn man, with no sense of humor and little grace. But if Mrs. Majesty loved him enough to marry him, perhaps he had depths I had yet to plumb. Not that I aimed to do any plumbing in that department. This is just an observation, if you see what I mean.

Ernie held out his hand to Rotondo. "Thanks for letting us sit in on the interview."

"For all the good it did," grumbled Rotondo.

"Well, you never know. My money's still on the secretary, but I'd honestly rather see Lola fry than that meek little guy."

"What about the Jap?"

With a shake of his head, Ernie said, "I can't see him doing anything so drastic. He seems like a nice kid. He also appeared scared to death."

"If that Winkworth witch called him a yellow devil or something equally insulting, don't you think he might have had a brain wave or something and killed her? She really was a bad person."

My goodness! The detective's words shocked me, although I'm not sure why. After all, he'd met her when she was alive, before she'd had to be scraped off my parents' parquet flooring, so he knew her a good deal better than I did. And I hadn't liked her either.

"So I understand. But I expect that lad's been insulted before and lived through it. I doubt he'd have taken his anger out on a little old lady, no matter how vicious she was. Will you be coming back to the Allcutt place tomorrow?"

"Yes," said Rotondo, sounding as if he'd rather do almost anything else. "We still have to take prints from everyone who was in the house at the time of the murder." He turned to me. "That includes you, Miss Allcutt."

"Me?" I pointed at my chest, alarmed. "I didn't push her! I saw her fall, for heaven's sake!"

Rotondo heaved a sigh as big as he was.

Ernie told me, "They take everyone's prints for elimination purposes. They'll know who not to consider as a suspect once everyone's printed." With a grin, he asked Rotondo, "How are you going to get Lola de la Monstress to hold still to have her prints taken?"

"I'll use the biggest men on the force and break her wrists if I have to. That damned woman needs to be locked up as a menace to society."

I didn't envy either Detective Rotondo or the officers who'd have to take Lola's fingerprints. She didn't yield to authority gently. In actual fact, I doubted she ever yielded to anything at all but had to be carried, kicking and screaming, to do anything she didn't want to do.

"Good luck with that," said Ernie.

"Yes," I said. "Good luck. Do you want to take my fingerprints tonight?" After getting over my initial fear that the police might consider me a viable suspect in Mrs. Winkworth's death, the notion of having my fingerprints taken sounded pretty keen. I didn't know anyone else who'd ever had his or her fingerprints taken. I then thought about the police taking my parents' prints, and actually giggled.

"What?" said Rotondo, evidently irked by my merriment.

"I was just thinking about how my parents are going to react to the police taking their fingerprints."

Ernie smiled broadly. "I'd like to see it. You have your work cut out for you with those two, Detective Rotondo."

"Don't I know it." It wasn't a question.

So a very nice young policeman came into the room after having been summoned by Officer Ludlow, and he inked and printed the pads of my fingertips. He gave me a cloth so that I could wipe my hands afterward, but there were still inky smudges on my fingers after I'd cleaned them. Detective Rotondo directed me to a ladies' room, where I thoroughly washed my hands.

Ernie and the detective were standing in the hallway and engaged in a serious discussion when I left the ladies' room. I eased up to them, hoping to hear what they were saying to each other and fearing they'd shut up if they noticed me. That's because they were men, and men don't believe women have brains enough to engage in sensible conversation, the idiots. You'd have thought Ernie, at least, would have learned by this time that I can be relied upon to offer pertinent comments in a murder investigation. Still, I kept mum.

"Good. I'm glad you're staying there," Rotondo was saying as I tippy-toed up to the men. "You can be my eyes and ears, if you're honestly determined to help the investigation and not just get in the way."

Ernie held his hands up, palms out. "Hey, Mrs. Allcutt hired me. I'll help all I can. She's paying me, after all, and she's not a woman to trifle with."

I almost snorted, but held my peace.

"What if Mr. or Mrs. Allcutt turns out to be the murderer?"

Ernie's lopsided grin was a work of art. "That would make Mercy undyingly happy."

Both men turned to me, and I realized my presence had not gone unnoticed.

"Yeah?" said Rotondo.

"Yeah," I said. "I mean, yes, although I doubt either my mother or father would ever bestir herself or himself to do anything at all, much less toss a woman to her death. They have servants to do those sorts of things for them."

Both men burst out laughing, and I decided Detective Sam Rotondo wasn't so bad after all.

Chapter Eighteen

Ernie and I discussed the case all the way back to my parents' house.

"I think it was Lola," I said. "She's just the type."

"Yeah? What's the type? I didn't know there was a type."

"Bother! You know precisely what I mean, Ernie Templeton." I clutched my secretarial pad, which was almost filled from beginning to end with the notes I'd taken that evening. I wished I'd brought my typewriter to Pasadena with me, so I could transcribe the notes into English. "How am I going to transcribe my notes?"

"Your notes?" Ernie peered at me for only a moment. "How the hell should I know? Didn't you bring your typewriter with you?"

"No." I heaved a sigh. "I didn't think my parents would appreciate the noise of me typing, but now I don't know how to get my notes transcribed into a form that can be read by anyone. And I can't use the typewriter in my father's office, because that room is sealed off. Do you know how long the police will keep it off-limits?"

"Don't have any idea."

"Huh. Well, that means I don't have access to a typewriter then."

"Hmm. We'll have to think about this. Maybe somebody has a typewriter you can borrow. Or maybe the police can lend you one."

"Or maybe I can go to the station and transcribe them there." That idea tickled my fancy. I think it would be swell to work in a police station. It might even be more fun than working for a private investigator, although probably not. After all, I was a female and, therefore, not apt to get any truly interesting work to do. On the other hand, I enjoy reading mystery novels. I expect if I got to type reports of real crimes, they might be interesting. They might even spark novelistic notions in my head and allow me to write really good detective books.

"I doubt Rotondo would appreciate that. He wants us on the spot, as it were."

"I suppose so. Well, maybe Harvey can have someone bring my typewriter to me."

"How about Lulu?" asked Ernie. "She'll have the rest of the week off, won't she? Maybe she can take one of those red cars to Pasadena and bring your typewriter with her."

The red cars, by the way, were red trolley cars that ran on tracks from Los Angeles to Pasadena and, I suppose, other places as well.

"Ernie! That's a brilliant idea! I'll telephone Lulu tomorrow and see if she can do that. I'm sure she'd like to be in on an investigation, too."

"Wait a minute, Mercy. I don't know about that last part."

"Lulu's helped me before in investigating stuff," I said stiffly.

"She was also with you when the two of you were picked up as prostitutes."

I felt my cheeks heat. "Darn you, Ernie Templeton! You know good and well we were on the trail of a thief at the time. The whole thing was a misunderstanding."

"Yeah, yeah. I know." I could tell he was trying not to laugh, the rat.

By that time we were on San Pasqual Street. I'd expected to arrive to a house dark as night. I certainly didn't anticipate my parents being kind enough to leave any lamps turned on for Ernie and me. To my surprise, the house was fairly aglow with light.

"Good heavens, why are all the lights on?" I muttered.

"Damned if I know," said Ernie as he pulled into the drive and pushed the button to alert anyone handy to open the gate for us.

"Who is it?" came a voice from the speaker attached to a gatepost. I think, although I'm not sure, that the voice belonged to Riki Saito.

"Miss Allcutt and Mr. Templeton," said Ernie, all formality. I gaped at him, although it was probably too dark in the Studebaker for him to notice.

The massive gate began to open, and Ernie drove his ratty machine up to the front door. "Better get out here, kiddo. I'll hide my disgraceful car so it won't sully your parents' view."

So I did. And without even chiding him for calling me *kiddo* again. In truth, all of my internal alarm bells had gone off when I'd seen all those lights emanating from the house. I ran to the front door, which stood open, thanks to Riki, who held it for me.

"What's going on, Riki?" I asked. "Why are all the lights turned on?"

"Mr. Mann seems to have gone missing," said Riki. "The servants are all searching for him." He lowered his voice. "Your parents are livid, and the policeman who was supposed to be watching everyone is embarrassed."

I sagged a bit. "Oh, dear. I'm sure they are. I'm sorry, Riki."

"Naturally, your folks think that because Mr. Mann took off, he's the one who killed Mrs. Winkworth."

"Naturally. I guess his desertion is kind of like a confession."

"I guess."

Riki didn't sound convinced, but Ernie had arrived at the

front door by that time, so I didn't question Riki. Rather, I told Ernie, "Mr. Mann has evidently flown the coop."

Ernie's eyebrows soared like larks ascending. Or perhaps caterpillars, although his eyebrows were nowhere near as bushy as Detective Rotondo's.

"He took off, did he? Silly thing to do. Where was the officer assigned to stay here when Mann took off?"

"I don't know, sir. But the poor guy couldn't watch over everyone at the same time. People were all over the house," said Riki, making a valid point, although I doubted my parents or Detective Rotondo would agree.

"True, true," said Ernie. "We'd better call Rotondo."

"Oh, dear. He won't be happy about this," I muttered.

"Of course he won't. Can't say as I blame him."

"No," I said. "I don't blame him either. But what a stupid thing for Mr. Mann to do! It's almost as if he's confessing to the crime."

"Looks that way," said Ernie.

"I still prefer Lola," I said with faint stubbornness. Very well, so it *did* look as though Mr. Mann had made a daring escape before he could be arrested for murder. It still seemed to me like a stupid thing to do. He could at least have waited until someone actually accused him of doing the deed before announcing to the world he'd done it, which is precisely what he'd done by running away.

Because I couldn't help myself, I asked, "Why is everyone sure he took off voluntarily? Could he have been forced into . . . running away? Or been kidnapped? Or something like that?"

Both Riki and Ernie gazed at me, Riki with surprise, Ernie with resignation.

"You don't like anything to be easy, do you, Mercy?"

"It's not that," I said, my brain cells scrambling to find words to put to my suspicions. "It's . . . oh, I don't know. All right.

He's probably guilty as sin and is trying to escape justice."

"Precisely. Let me telephone Rotondo." He pulled a card from his suit pocket and peered at it as I led him to the telephone room.

Even I could hear Detective Rotondo roar when Ernie gave him the news. Ernie winced and pulled the receiver away from his ear.

"Where the hell is Gunning?"

"I don't know who Gunning is," said Ernie softly. I guess he was attempting, by example, to soften Rotondo's rage.

It didn't work. "Dammit, Gunny's the uniform I stationed there! Get him right now!"

Riki had come with us, and I turned to him. "Do you know where Officer Gunning is, Riki?"

"I think he's in the kitchen," said Riki. "I'll go fetch him."

"Thank you."

"Riki is going to find him and bring him here," Ernie said over the wire.

"Damn it!" Rotondo's voice was a trifle softer, but not very.

A couple of minutes later, a downcast uniformed police officer made his way into the telephone room. Ernie and I both looked upon him with sympathy writ large on our features. Well, I presume I appeared as sympathetic as Ernie did. I couldn't see myself.

"Detective Rotondo wants to speak to you," said Ernie, handing poor Officer Gunning the telephone receiver.

I heard Gunning sigh deeply as he accepted the receiver. Ernie moved aside, and the policeman took Ernie's place in front of the wall phone. "Gunning here, sir," said he.

Ernie and I exchanged speaking glances as Detective Rotondo's roar sounded again in our ears. As Ernie had done before him, Gunning removed the receiver from his ear, waited until Rotondo had quit shouting and then said, "I'm sorry, sir. I'm not sure when he left. I was walking around the place, trying to keep tabs on everyone, and he slipped out sometime between twelve-thirty and one-thirty."

Good heavens, was it that late already? I decided then and there to buy myself one of those newfangled wristwatches, so that I could check the time any old time I wanted. That sounds odd, but I'm sure you know what I mean.

Rotondo's voice had quieted, and Gunning again held the receiver to his ear. "Yes, sir." Pause. "Yes, sir." Pause. "Yes, sir." Pause. Gunning cleared his throat. "It occurred to me, sir, that Mr. Mann might have returned to the Winkworth estate."

I presume Rotondo asked why Mann would do such a thing, because Gunning then said, "Perhaps to pack his belongings and head to the train station. Or something like that."

Ernie gestured for Gunning to hand him the receiver. Gunning listened for another few moments, then did as Ernie had bade him do.

"Detective Rotondo?" said Ernie. "Yeah, it's Templeton. You want me to go to the Winkworth place and look around?"

A roared "No!" assaulted my ears. Once again, Ernie yanked the receiver away from his ear.

"This is a huge place, Detective. One man can't cover it all, unless you stick all the inhabitants in one room, and you didn't do that."

Tsk. I didn't think it was wise to virtually accuse the detective, who seemed to take his job *extremely* seriously, of mishandling a criminal investigation.

Ernie nodded as he listened. "Yeah, I know. Budget cuts. We had 'em in L.A., too. Your guys probably aren't on the take like the L.A. coppers are, or I'd think maybe Mann slipped Gunning a little cabbage."

Although I had no idea what Ernie was talking about, evidently Gunning did, because he stiffened up like Lot's wife turning into a pillar salt. His face turned red, and he gave Ernie a furious scowl. Ernie grinned at him. He would.

"Yeah, yeah," said he. "I know. Your guy's as pure as the driven white stuff." Pause. "All right. Mercy and I will stay here, although I could go with Gunning and check out the Winkworth place before you can get there." Another pause, this one longer. "Right. Official police business. That's jake."

I think "jake" means "all right." I still needed to learn what "cabbage" was.

"Right," said Ernie, and he handed the receiver back to Gunning.

"What does 'cabbage' mean?" I asked Ernie as soon as his ear was free.

"Long green. Lettuce. Kale."

"Darn you, Ernie Templeton, I know good and well you weren't talking about vegetables!"

With one of his more irritating grins, Ernie said, "I told Rotondo I was pretty sure Gunning wasn't on the take or I'd have suspected Mann of having bribed him with dough to let him escape."

"Dough? What—" And then I understood. "Oh. You mean money."

"Got it in one, kiddo."

"Stop calling me *kiddo*! You're as bad as my mother with her *Mercedes Louise*s."

Ernie slapped a palm over the part of his body that might have contained a heart if he'd had one, which at that moment I doubted. "You wound me, Mercy. I'm nowhere near as bad as your mother."

"Well . . . that's true. But I still don't like it when you call me kiddo."

"All right. I'll try to remember not to do that. But we'd better talk to your folks, whether we want to or not, and try to figure out who was where when Mann cut and ran. Let's get a wiggle on."

All of Ernie's slang was giving me a headache. Or maybe the late hour and my increasing feeling of exhaustion were making my head spin. "I don't want to."

"I don't either, but you know we have to."

"Very well. Let's get it over with."

Mother and Father were, as I'd suspected they'd be, in the drawing room, only they'd manage to unbend enough to sit, Mother on a sofa, Father in a chair. I don't think I'd ever seen them sit on a sofa together, which made me wonder how they'd managed to produce three children. Not that sofas and babies have anything to do with each other as a rule, but my parents didn't seem . . . "close," I guess is the word I want. People had to get really close to each other in order to produce offspring, after all, and as nearly as I could judge the matter, Mother and Father barely spoke to each other. Oh, well. What did I know? Clearly not much.

Father spoke first when he saw us enter the throne room. I mean the drawing room. "Well? What did that actress have to say for herself?"

"Not a whole lot," said Ernie. "She'd been upstairs with Mr. Nash, who gave her the bad news that her contract wasn't going to be renewed. She threw a couple of tantrums, and they're keeping her overnight at the jail because she attacked a policeman."

"Well, *really*!" My mother's brow furrowed so much, you could have planted some of Ernie's cabbages in the ruts.

"She might have done the deed, although nobody knows yet," said Ernie.

"That Mann fellow is obviously the culprit," said Father, frowning. Not that he was any angrier than usual; he just always frowned.

"We don't know that either, although running off was a stupid thing for him to do," said Ernie.

"I should think his actions are as good as a confession," said Mother.

"Maybe," said Ernie.

Suddenly I had a thought. I know, how surprising, huh? But really . . . "Say, Mother and Father, don't you have a chauffeur tucked away somewhere on the property?"

Mother, Father, and Ernie all turned their heads and stared at me.

CHAPTER NINETEEN

Feeling a little foolish under their scrutiny, I shrugged. "Well, nobody's even thought about him. It just occurred to me that someone ought to check up on him. I mean, he probably wasn't even in the house at the time of Mrs. Winkworth's death, but . . ." I couldn't think of anything else to say.

"Nonsense," said Father. "Roberts is a perfectly respectable young man. He sleeps in an apartment above the garage, and he seldom even enters the house."

I didn't blame Roberts for not wanting to enter the house, but thought I'd better ask, "Was he there all evening?"

"How should I know?" demanded Father. "I don't keep track of him. However, I do know that he takes excellent care of the machine, and it's always filled with gasoline and shined to a high gloss every time I put it to use."

Huh. *He* put it to use, did he? He put *Roberts* to work, was more like it. And just because Father said the man was a solid citizen didn't mean he was one. Father seldom paid attention to anyone he considered beneath him, which was the entire rest of the human population of the world.

"That's a good idea, Mercy," said Ernie, surprising me. "We'd probably better talk to this guy"—he returned his attention to Father—"Roberts, did you say his name was?"

Still frowning, Father said, "Yes."

"And be sure to talk to the maids, as well," said Mother. "You never know about servants."

Huh, as Ernie—or Detective Rotondo, for that matter—might have said. Mother and her buddies in Boston were always complaining about "the servant problem." According to them, nobody wanted to work for a living any longer. And then they had a collective fit when one of their daughters decided to get a job. You figure them out; they're beyond me.

"What time is it?" asked Ernie.

Father took out his pocket watch and peered at it. "It's almost three o'clock. Do you intend to question Roberts and the maids now? At this hour?"

Ernie stood there, presumably undecided, for a moment, then said, "No. I imagine they all need their sleep after an eventful day. They have to get up early, no matter what time they get to bed, right?"

There wasn't a hint of sarcasm in his voice, and I gave him credit for it. I'd have been sarcastic as heck if I'd asked the question. Then again, I suppose Ernie had learned how to talk to all varieties of people during his career both as a police officer and a private investigator.

Mother sniffed. "The servants get up at six o'clock in order to prepare the house for us. Mrs. Thorne cooks breakfast, and the maids and Riki clean and dust before we get up. None of us require the maids to bring us breakfast in our rooms. We always go down to the breakfast room, unless one of the family is ill, of course."

"Of course," said Ernie, still not sarcastic.

"What time did the servants finally get to bed?" I couldn't help myself; I had to ask.

With one of her better regal glares, Mother said, "I have no idea, Mercedes." I saw that cursed *Louise* dancing on her lips, but she spake it not. Good thing, too.

"Don't you think they deserve to sleep in, too?" I asked.

Father, who was already rigid as a pike, stiffened even more.

"We pay our servants a good wage, Mercedes. They understand their duties, and they perform them, or they look for work elsewhere."

"Right," I said. Turning to Ernie, I said, "We'd probably better just go to bed. We can get up at six if the servants can." I didn't look at my parents.

"I suppose so. I especially want to interview Roberts. You'll have to take notes again."

Which reminded me of something important. Bracing myself for an explosion, I turned again to my mother. "I'm going to ask Lulu to bring me my typewriter so I can transcribe all the notes I've been taking for Ernie and the police."

"*Lulu?* That *hussy?* I won't have that female in my house!"

"Nuts. Lulu's my friend, and she's going to be doing me a favor." I hoped. "And she's no more a hussy than I am, and I'm not. A hussy, I mean."

"Mercy's right," said Ernie, bless his loyal heart.

"Why can't you use the typewriter in my upstairs office?" Father asked. His question wouldn't have been unreasonable under other circumstances.

"Because that room is off-limits until the police tell us otherwise," I told him. "It's the last place anyone confesses to having seen Mrs. Winkworth before she went over the stair railing."

Mother puffed up like one of those African adders I've read about in *National Geographic*. "This is ridiculous," she said. "I don't believe the police have the right to invade our home and tell us which rooms we can and cannot occupy."

"You're wrong there, Mother," I told her, and boldly, too. "The police have every right to cordon off a crime scene."

"I thought the staircase was the crime scene."

I sighed. "Please, Mother. Just follow the directions the police give you, and everything will be back to normal in a jiffy."

Mother's eyes widened, and she puffed up some more. I expected an explosion, but suddenly her breath left her in a huff. "Oh, very well," she said, sounding like a pouty schoolgirl. "Go to bed, both of you. I'll be sleeping late in the morning."

"So shall I," said Father.

And they rose as one and marched out of the drawing room together.

I watched them go and whispered to Ernie, "Wow, that's the first time I've seen them do anything together in a long time."

With a chuckle, Ernie said, "You're becoming downright evil, you know that, Mercy?"

"It's the company I keep," I said, my voice as dry as the Sahara.

"Probably," said Ernie. "But now that you brought him up, I have a real hankering to check up on this Roberts character who drives your father's car."

"Now?" I asked with dismay.

"Yeah. I won't keep him long. I just want to make sure he's where he's supposed to be and ask him if he noticed anything unusual at the time of the crime or thereabouts."

"From his room over the stable? What could he see?"

"Damned if I know. But I'm going to ask."

Wearily, I said, "Very well. I'll come with you."

"You don't need to," said Ernie, giving my shoulder a pat. "You look bushed."

"Thanks ever so much. However, if you're going to see Roberts, *I'm* going to see Roberts. You needn't think you can leave me behind in your investigations, Ernie Templeton. I'm your assistant, remember?"

"You're my secretary."

Botheration. He would mention that silly little point, wouldn't he? I remained undaunted. "Nevertheless, I shall accompany you. I feel responsible for you being here, after all."

"Nuts. Your mother made you telephone me."

"Yes. And I'll be darned if I'll give her an excuse to carp at me."

With a chuckle, Ernie surrendered the point. "All right. Anyhow, you've got to show me where this Roberts character lives."

"I'll take you. We can go out the service porch off the kitchen."

So we did. And we walked to what used to be the stables. Once we got there, we had to climb the staircase to the apartment over the stables. I'm sure, in the olden days, two or three stable boys probably occupied those rooms, but Father only needed one chauffeur. I was out of breath and absolutely *longing* for my bed by the time we reached the top of that stupid staircase.

Ernie knocked on the door.

Nothing happened. So Ernie knocked on the door a little harder.

Still nothing happened.

Finally, Ernie called sharply, "Roberts! You in there?"

Silence.

Ernie and I exchanged a befuddled glance. Well, my glance was befuddled, mainly because my brain was about to shut down from weariness. I'm not sure what Ernie's glance revealed, but he said, "Huh. I guess Roberts isn't as predictable as your father thought he was."

"I guess not. What now? We can't drive all over Pasadena looking for my father's chauffeur."

"I doubt old Roberts is very far away."

"He's not old. He's a fairly young man. Good looking, if you like the thin, rangy type. Has light blond hair. Doesn't smile much." Of course, I'd only seen him a couple of times, so perhaps I was wrong about that last part.

"In that case, I suspect he's definitely not very far away."

187

"What do you mean?"

"Toddle along with me, kidd—I mean Mercy, and learn a thing or two about human nature."

"There's not much else I can do under the circumstances," I said unhappily. I didn't feel like toddling any longer, darn it. I wanted to go to sleep.

"This won't take long," Ernie promised.

He led the way back to the service porch and stopped walking so suddenly, I very nearly bumped into his back, which irked me. Anything would have irked me at that point. I was beyond exhausted.

"Is there a back staircase that leads to the servants' quarters?"

"Sure. It's right there." I pointed to a door in the wall of the service porch. "The servants' quarters are three floors up." I opened the door, revealing a dark, narrow staircase.

Ernie, being taller than I, spotted the dangling cord to the overhead light before I did, and he pulled it. And then there was light. What's more, it hurt my eyes, which had become accustomed to darkness. I shaded them and said testily, "Are you going to wake up all the servants now?"

"I just have a hunch," said Ernie mysteriously.

I wasn't in the mood for mystery. "Well, get at it then."

"Tut tut. Don't be crabby. This'll only take a couple of minutes." And he started up the stairs.

After heaving a heartfelt sigh, I followed him. Unwillingly.

Once we reached the top of the staircase, we saw a row of doors. All were shut.

"What's the layout here?" asked Ernie.

"This is where the maids and Riki sleep. I don't know whose door is which. Or which is whose." I actually thought about which phrasing was more appropriate until I decided my tired brain was just playing a game with me and gave it up.

"Well, then, I guess we'll begin with the nearest one." And he stepped up to a door and knocked.

A grunt sounded from inside the room. Then footsteps. Then the door opened a crack, and an extremely sleepy-looking Riki Saito peered out. "Huh?" said he. "I mean, may I help you?"

Boy, if that didn't show intrepidity, I don't know what did. Here was Riki, after a very stressful day during which he'd probably had to work overtime, being polite to a person who'd just knocked on his door in the middle of the night. Training. Training and fear, I imagine. He didn't want to lose his job, not that Ernie or I had any say in his hiring or firing—or would suggest either if asked by my awful parents.

"Sorry to disturb you, Riki," said Ernie with one of his kinder smiles—the kind he never uses on me. "Just checking to see if Roberts is up here somewhere."

Riki squinted at Ernie. "Roberts? Who's—oh, the chauffeur. He should be in his rooms over the garage. If he's not there, I don't know where he is."

"Thanks, Riki. Sorry to have disturbed you. Hope you can get back to sleep."

"Yeah. Thanks."

"I'm so sorry, Riki," I said, unable to stop myself because I felt so awful about having made him come to the door on account of one of Ernie's whims.

"It's all right, Miss Allcutt. 'Night."

"Good night. Please get as much sleep as you can."

"Uh." Riki shut the door in our faces.

"You're a beast, Ernie Templeton! That poor boy—"

"Yeah, yeah. I know. But I want to find Roberts."

"You're impossible."

"You're the one who wanted to come with me."

"I didn't *want* to. What I *want* is to go to sleep."

"Quit carping. Let's see what's up here." And darned if he didn't knock at the next door down the hall.

We heard a squeak, then a rustle of fabric—probably bedclothes—a few tentative, light footsteps, and then a tiny voice at the keyhole of the door. "Who is it?" a female whispered.

"Detective Templeton," said Ernie. I guess he spoke the truth, but he made the words sound as though he belonged to the police department, and he didn't, which meant he was fibbing. I didn't approve, although I didn't say so.

"Um, what do you want?"

"I want to know where Roberts is," said Ernie in a stern voice.

Whacking him on the shoulder, I whispered, "Ernie! What are you doing? That girl can't—"

The door opened, cutting off my protest. The maid who wasn't Mary Jane stood before us, her nightgown rumpled, and her head hanging in what looked like shame to me.

My mouth fell open when I heard Roberts's voice behind the girl. "What's up, Celia?"

"This detective is looking for you," said Celia morosely.

"You mean Roberts is *here*?" I cried out a trifle too loudly.

Celia winced. Ernie said, "Shut up, Mercy. You don't want to wake the whole house."

Roberts loomed up behind poor Celia. "It's not what it looks like," he said, which was a flat lie, if I knew anything at all.

He went on to elaborate. "Celia and I are engaged and are going to be married next month. We weren't doing anything wrong. She was scared because of the murder and all, so I told her I'd stay in her room tonight."

"Ah," said Ernie without a hint of irony. "A valiant knight guarding his lady-love."

Roberts gently shoved past Celia. He still wore his livery, so maybe he'd told the truth after all. I mentally erased the evil thoughts I'd been thinking.

"Yes, darn it," said Roberts. "I know this looks bad, but we weren't doing anything wrong. For Pete's sake, somebody got *murdered* in this house tonight. Last night. Whenever it was. Celia was scared, and I've been sleeping in the chair next to her bed." He shot me a worried frown. "But please don't tell your parents, Miss Allcutt. They wouldn't understand."

"Hell," said Ernie. "*I* don't understand. Why didn't Celia just spend the night with the other maid? Why'd she have to call you in to stay with you?"

"She didn't *call me in.* I volunteered." Roberts straightened. I guess he was trying to appear noble.

"All right, all right," said Ernie. "What I want to know is where you were at the time of the murder, Roberts."

Roberts shrugged. "Since I don't know when the murder happened, I can't tell you where I was."

Ernie gave me a quizzical glance, and I said, "It was about eight or eight-thirty. Somewhere around that time."

"In that case, I was in my room reading the newspaper," said Roberts, tugging on his jacket and trying to press the wrinkles out with his hands.

"How'd you and Celia meet up tonight?" asked Ernie.

Celia and Roberts looked at each other. Then Celia whispered, "I went out to his room after we were through cleaning up. I was frightened. I've never been in a house where anyone's been murdered before."

"Huh. Very well," said Ernie. "You'd better get back to the stable now, Roberts. Celia will be just fine for the rest of the night without you guarding her. The place is full of policemen."

Celia and Roberts exchanged a somewhat frantic glance, and then Celia drooped a bit. "It's all right, Brandon. I'll be all right now. At least I feel safer knowing the police are in the house. But what about you? You're all alone out there in that—"

"I'll be fine," said Roberts. I could tell he was embarrassed.

191

After all, *he* was a *man*, and *men* weren't afraid of any old murderers.

I'm sorry. I become astringent when I'm extremely tired.

"Let me get my cap," said Roberts, and he hurried to where he'd left the said object, gave Celia a quick peck on her still-burning cheek, scooted out the door, past Ernie and me, and lammed it down the stairs and out to the stable.

Because I thought I should, even though her behavior had shocked and disturbed me, I said, "You'll be all right, Celia. Go back to sleep now." And then, because I couldn't help myself, I added, "You'd probably better not ask Roberts up to your room anymore. If my mother or father hears about this, you and Roberts will both be history."

"But we weren't—"

"Doing anything." I sighed. "That won't matter to Mother or Father, believe me."

"Yes, ma'am."

I didn't appreciate being called ma'am, but I didn't tell her so.

Ernie and I trudged down one flight of stairs, and I opened the door to the second floor of the family's winter mansion. "I'll see you to your room, Ernie."

"Thanks."

"How'd you know Roberts would be in one of the maids' room?" I asked because I couldn't stop myself. The subject of Roberts and Celia was an embarrassing one, but I was more interested in garnering unto myself information about the detective business than worried about being embarrassed.

"I didn't. I just thought it was a possibility. Hell, I could just as easily have been wrong."

"And you'd have awakened all the servants for nothing."

"Yeah."

I thought for a moment. "Hmm. I don't think you'd ever do

anything for no reason. I think you have well-honed investigative skills."

"Is that a compliment?" Ernie asked, feigning incredulity.

"Oh, stop it! I'd never in a million years have thought about looking for Roberts in the maids' quarters."

"You haven't been doing this job as long as I have."

"I guess not."

I also guessed it would take more than mere years to educate me to the baser elements of human behavior. Not that, if one were to believe them, Roberts and Celia had been doing anything naughty. But I'd told Ernie the truth. I'd never even have *thought* about looking for a man in a maid's room. Never. Ever.

Boy, I had so much learning to do about the detective business, it was downright depressing.

CHAPTER TWENTY

But I didn't want to think about my shortcomings anymore that day. Or maybe it was the next day. Whenever it was by that time. I led Ernie to his room, pointed out the bathroom across the hall, and then I all but dragged my worn-out carcass to my own room, where a delighted Buttercup greeted me. I was so tired, I almost snapped at her, and was ashamed of myself.

I didn't even bother to undress completely. I just shoved off my shoes, took off my dress and threw it over a chair, yanked off my girdle and bust-flattener, and plopped down on my bed in my slip. Buttercup leaped up and snuggled against me. We were both asleep within seconds. Someone knocked lightly upon my door far too early on the morning following the excitement. I groaned aloud.

Buttercup, perhaps more desperate than I, jumped off the bed and ran to the door, wagging like mad. I felt guilty for having left her alone so long the day before—and for not taking her outside to do her business before I went to bed.

Because I knew I had a lot to make up for with my dog, I dragged myself out of bed, fumbled for the robe some kind-hearted—or, more likely, obedient—maid had laid out across its foot, and stumbled to the door. I scooped up Buttercup before I opened it.

"Time for breakfast, sleepyhead," chirped Chloe, as if I'd been sleeping since the day before yesterday.

"Augh," I said.

"You look like you've been rode hard and put up wet," said my sophisticated sister.

I squinted at her through half-closed eyelids. "Huh?"

"That's a line from one of Harvey's pictures. I thought it was cunning."

"Huh."

"Good Lord, Mercy, what's the matter with you?"

"Didn't get any sleep last night. Ernie and I were detecting until about three this morning."

Chloe's lovely eyes opened wide. I envied her those clear eyes. Mine felt as though somebody had thrown sand in them. "I've gotta take Buttercup out to pee," I mumbled, still half-asleep.

"For heaven's sake, Mercy. Go back to bed. I'll take Buttercup outside."

I handed her my dog. "Can't," I said, turning to go to my dressing room.

"You can't what? Go back to bed? Why not?"

"Gotta help Ernie detect some more. The police will be back here this morning, and I have to be ready for them."

"Why?"

"Because it's my job."

"For God's sake." While my sister had never been as anti-job as my parents were, she'd never understood my need to become one of the worker proletariat. I wasn't up to educating her that morning.

"Thanks for taking Buttercup outdoors. I'll get dressed and go downstairs as soon as possible."

"Ernie's already up and doing," said Chloe.

I turned and stared at her. "He is?"

"He is. In fact, he's the one who sent me up here to wake you up."

Bother! Ernie was making me look like a malingerer. "I'll hurry."

"Golly, Mercy, I think you need more sleep."

Annoyed, I snapped, "I do, but I'll have to get it later. Take Buttercup outside, will you?"

"Don't you be cranky with me, Mercy Allcutt! It's not my fault somebody killed that horrible old woman."

I darned near broke down and cried, I felt so pathetic. Remorseful, I turned and said, "I'm sorry, Chloe. I'm just so tired. Thank you very much for taking care of Buttercup. I'll be downstairs as soon as I can be."

Chloe sniffed, but, with Buttercup in her arms, she exited the room, saying as she did so, "That blockish policeman will be here any minute. Ernie asked me to tell you that."

That blockish policeman? Who the heck . . . ? Oh. Sam Rotondo. Daisy Majesty's Sam. "Good grief, what time is it, anyway?"

"Eight o'clock."

Shocked out of my lethargy, I said, "Oh, my. I meant to be up at six."

"*Six?* For God's sake, Mercy, you're not a detective. You're a secretary! You don't have to sacrifice yourself this way."

"It's not a sacrifice," I told my sister. "I'm learning a whole lot about the real world and how real people live in it."

With a sniff, Chloe said, "Well, I certainly hope not many of your *real* people go around killing each other all the time." And with that, she turned and walked off with Buttercup.

Feeling slightly abandoned, I went to the bathroom adjoining my room. Although I didn't have time to take a bath, I washed my face and other extraneous portions of my anatomy, using a washcloth and standing on a bath mat so as not to make puddles on the bathroom floor. I didn't want to risk my mother's wrath. Even though she'd never do any housework herself, if she learned somehow that I'd made a mess, she'd never let me live it down.

I'd almost returned to the human race after I'd donned a sensible day dress, pulled on some cotton stockings, and shoved my feet into my old house shoes. I should have done all that right after last night's séance, but I didn't think about changing into comfortable clothing before Ernie and I went to the police station. Not having to wear a corset gave me a feeling of freedom, even though I still needed about twelve hours of sleep.

Breakfast was over by the time I got downstairs. Fortunately for me, Mother and Father had made good on their promise to sleep late, and they weren't around to scold me when I entered the kitchen. There I found Ernie, eating a plate of scrambled eggs and toast and chatting up a storm with Mrs. Thorne.

The cook saw me and gave me a huge smile, something I seldom received from members of my parents' household. I liked her for it. A lot.

"Good morning, Miss Allcutt!" said she. "Mr. Templeton here has been telling me all about the adventures you two had last night. You must be exhausted, dear. Let me fix you a plate."

Oh, my, *no one* associated with my parents had ever been this nice to me. "Thank you very much, Mrs. Thorne. I don't want to be a bother."

"Nonsense. You just sit yourself down right there and have a bracing cup of coffee. There's nothing like coffee to perk a person up if she's not had enough sleep."

"Thank you." I wasn't a particular fan of coffee because I thought it tasted bitter, but I had noticed that it did indeed perk a body up. "You're very kind."

I noticed Ernie grinning at me, and I sat with a *whump* in the chair across from his. "What are you grinning for?"

"Nothing. It's just . . . you look like heck, kiddo. I mean Mercy."

"Thanks a lot, Ernie." How depressing. My boss had actually told me I looked like heck.

"It's all right, Mercy. You didn't get any sleep. You don't really look bad. You just look tired."

"Right. I don't believe you."

He patted my hand, which I'd carelessly left on the table. Honestly, parts of my body didn't seem to belong to me that morning. I'd probably lose my head next.

"Buck up, Mercy. Detective Rotondo will be here soon, and you can help me start detecting again."

It's probably a good thing Mrs. Thorne planted a plate before me just then, or I might have smacked Ernie's hand. Or maybe his face. He seemed entirely too frisky. I was barely alive, and he sat there cracking jokes. It wasn't fair. Without another word for Ernie, I dug into my breakfast. It tasted *so* good.

After breakfast and three cups of coffee, I felt almost ready to face the day, although my brain was still a bit fuzzy. I hoped the coffee would cut through the fuzz. It sure cut through the rest of me.

The doorbell rang, and Ernie rose from the table with a sigh. He hadn't said anything to me as I ate and drank. He spoke now. "That's probably Rotondo. You ready for another day, Mercy?"

"Almost. I need to . . . go to the cloak room for a minute."

How embarrassing. Nevertheless, I knew I wouldn't be able to hold it in for another half hour, much less the hours and hours Detective Rotondo would probably be here. So, as Ernie chuckled annoyingly, I ran to the downstairs bathroom.

When I exited same, I found Ernie and the detective and one of his minions standing in the huge hallway. I joined them.

Rotondo frowned when he saw me. "Have you transcribed the notes you took yesterday, Miss Allcutt?"

"Have I *what?*"

"He thinks you should have stayed up all night typing your notes, Mercy. That's what a real policeman would do, after all," said Ernie with one of his more irksome grins.

"Oh, does he now?" I said, stiffening up like cement setting.

Rotondo stopped what would surely have become a squabble. "No, no, no. I'm sure you didn't have time to type your notes yet. But you might want to do that today sometime when you have the chance. They might come in handy."

I didn't believe him, mainly because I sensed he was humoring me. I said, "I shall transcribe my notes as soon as I possibly can, but I don't have a typewriter with me, and I haven't had a chance to call Miss LaBelle, who might be able to bring my typewriter to Pasadena."

"You want to bring a typewriter here? From where? Where do you live?" demanded Rotondo.

"Bunker Hill in Los Angeles."

"Bunker *Hill?* In Los *Angeles?*" The detective's face darkened and I swear he grew larger.

Ernie spoke up, probably because he thought either Rotondo or I were about to erupt like Mount Vesuvius. "It would take a long time for Lulu to get the typewriter here. Why don't you type your notes up in your father's office, Mercy? There's a typewriter in there, isn't there?"

Huh. Good point, although it was, perhaps, an equivocal one. It was also one we'd discussed the preceding night. Morning. Whenever we'd talked about it. "Are the police through in there? If they've finished with Father's office, I guess I can use his machine."

"They're not quite done, but you should be able to use the typewriter in a half hour or so. I'll leave orders to admit you," said Rotondo.

"And while you're transcribing your notes," said Ernie, "Detective Rotondo, Officer Ludlow, and I are going to the

Mountjoy place to see what we can see."

"I want to go with you," I said, sounding slightly whiny.

"Nuts. You can see the place another time. We just need to find out if Mann is there."

"I thought your detectives went there last night," I said, frowning upon Detective Rotondo.

"We did. He wasn't there."

"Oh." Well, *that* took the wind from my sails. "You don't need me to take notes?" I asked Ernie, staring at him hard to let him know I'd catch him if he lied.

"Nope. Your notes from yesterday will be more useful than your presence in this instance, Mercy. Honest." He had the effrontery to cross his heart!

"Very well." Indignant didn't half cover my feelings when I left those awful men and trudged up the twisty staircase to my room.

I noticed uniformed officers prowling the upstairs hallway, a couple of them on their hands and knees. I guess they were looking for scuff marks or something like that, although I didn't know it for a fact. I also wondered if I'd be allowed into my father's office, since it hadn't been a half hour since I'd talked to Detective Rotondo.

Therefore, because I wanted to give them enough time to do whatever they needed to do in that room, I gathered up Buttercup, whom Chloe has thoughtfully returned to my bedroom after she'd brought her back indoors, and let her follow me downstairs again and out the back, where she romped a bit, watered several plants, and deposited a very small pile next to the rose garden. Dutiful dog-owner that I am, I'd thought to bring an old newspaper outside with me, so I picked up Buttercup's delicate pile and deposited it in a trash can next to the stables.

As I stood next to the stables, I glanced upward toward where

Roberts slept, and Ernie's and my conversation with him the night before or this morning—I'd totally lost track of time by then—played through my mind. Then I remembered Riki Saito saying he thought he might have seen a man in the upstairs hallway about the time Mrs. Winkworth fell to her death. Hmm. Could Riki have seen *Roberts*? Could it have been *Roberts* who'd shoved Mrs. Winkworth over the balcony railing?

Of course, there was no reason I knew of why Roberts might want to kill Mrs. Winkworth. Then again, if Mrs. Winkworth had caught him upstairs with Celia, she'd probably have told on him. On the other hand, Celia had been busy downstairs at the time of the murder. Hadn't she? I shook my head, trying to make my brain start functioning properly. Didn't work.

Therefore, after Buttercup had romped enough, I called her to me. She didn't seem awfully happy to have her play time interrupted, and I begged her pardon. But I had work to do, blast it. "I'm sorry, Buttercup. After we find the mean old murderer of that mean old woman, I'll take you outside, and we can walk for miles and miles and miles."

And that, by gum, was a promise I aimed to keep.

CHAPTER TWENTY-ONE

Although I'd rather have kept her with me, I left Buttercup in my bedroom after I'd gathered my secretarial pad and headed toward my father's office, hoping it would have been cleared of coppers.

It hadn't been. Bother. I tapped a uniformed man on the shoulder, and he turned around and frowned down upon me. He was quite tall.

Nevertheless, I had a job to do. "My name is Mercy Allcutt, and I've been assisting Detective Rotondo and Mr. Templeton. I have a ton of notes to transcribe from all the interviews conducted yesterday after Mrs. Winkworth's demise. Detective Rotondo wants me to have them transcribed by the time he and Mr. Templeton return to the house."

The officer stared at me, his eyes narrowed, for what seemed like eternity. Then, without speaking to me, he called into the room, "You about done in there, Joe? There's a lady needs to type something for Rotondo. He told me to admit her when you're through."

Another officer, who looked approximately as stern as his companion, appeared from the innards of the office. "Yeah. I don't think there's anything in there. We've printed everything." Joe glanced at me. "You got a rag, ma'am? There's fingerprint dust all over those typewriter keys."

"You mean you don't clean up after yourselves?" I didn't mean to sound snobbish. The words just popped out.

"No, ma'am. Our duty's to solve the crime. We aren't a maid service."

Blast. "Very well." I turned on my heel and aimed for the staircase again. I swear, if this week ever ended and I got to go home again, my legs would never be the same. I hadn't walked up and down so many stairs in my life. And that includes the stairs in my own lovely home on Bunker Hill. Heck, I only had to walk up and down them a couple of times a day, and they weren't nearly as steep and twisty as those in my parents' house.

Once downstairs, I aimed myself at the kitchen again, hoping Mrs. Thorne would direct me to a maid. Or at least a dust cloth. As I approached the butler's pantry, however, I heard voices. Surreptitious voices. Or maybe they weren't.

Naw. They were. Two people were whispering together, and they didn't sound happy. I tiptoed to the pantry door and stuck my left ear against it.

"Damn it, Celia, don't tell anyone!"

Roberts! I'd know that whisper anywhere.

"But, I'll lose my job!" Celia sounded as though she were crying.

"Don't cry, Celia," said Brandon Roberts, verifying my suspicion. "Everything will work out all right."

"How can it work out all right?" asked Celia as fiercely as a person who's both crying and whispering can sound. "You *have* to tell the police what you know about that woman."

"If I do that, they'll arrest me, damn it. Do you want a jailbird for a husband?"

My goodness! I suppose it wasn't nice to listen in on other people's conversations, but this one was mighty interesting.

"They won't arrest you, because you didn't do anything," said Celia, sobbing some more.

"Nuts to that. They'll arrest me because I'm easy to blame,

and because I have a history with the old bat."

Roberts had a history with *Mrs. Winkworth*? She was the only old bat I could think of. Well, except for my mother, but she was still alive and healthy, as far as I knew.

"But you didn't do it," said Celia, sniffling now.

"Stop crying, Celia. It'll be all right, baby. I didn't do anything, and they can't prove I did, but they might try if I tell them the truth. Then they'll pin it on me sure as the devil."

"Oh, but Brandon, I hate keeping secrets!"

"Please, sweetheart. Keep this little one. It might save my life."

Hmph. What about Mrs. Winkworth's life? Rather than asking that pertinent question, I backed up a ways and then stomped heavily toward the butler's pantry. I heard frantic scuffling on the other side of the door. When I pushed the door open, the pantry was empty of people, Celia and Roberts having fled into the kitchen, since that was the only other room they could get to from the pantry.

Mrs. Thorne was kneading bread when I entered the kitchen for the second time that morning. She glanced up and smiled at me. "Good morning again, Miss Allcutt."

"Good morning again, Mrs. Thorne." I smiled back at her. "Say, did you just see Celia come through here?"

Mrs. Thorne's smile vanished. "I certainly did. Along with that Roberts of hers." She shook her head. "I swear, young people these days. In my day, you wouldn't find a chauffeur and a housemaid spooning in the master's house."

"Oh, are they sweethearts?" I asked, doing my best to sound innocent.

A sniff preceded Mrs. Thorne's, "Sweethearts? I suppose you might as well call them sweethearts. If they're doing anything else together, I don't want to know about it. But he's got poor Celia in a state this morning, is all I have to say about it."

"Oh, dear. That's too bad." After contemplating questioning Mrs. Thorne some more, I decided against doing so and asked, "Do you have a dust rag I can borrow? I have to type some notes, and the policeman upstairs says there's fingerprint dust all over the typewriter keys."

Another sniff, this one louder. "Those policemen! Coming into a decent household and making a mess of it. I don't hold with things like that, I don't."

I didn't either, although I didn't say so.

"Celia?" Mrs. Thorne bellowed, nearly deafening me. "Celia, get your dust rag and go upstairs and tidy up the mister's office. Miss Allcutt has to type up some notes."

And Celia appeared from the breakfast room, her eyes puffy and her nose red. She kept her head down, gave me a brief curtsey, and said, "I'll do that right now, Miss Allcutt."

"Thank you, Celia."

She toddled off to get a dust cloth, and I waited for her, contemplating a plan of attack. I aimed to ask her what she and Roberts had been whispering about, even if doing so did peg me as a snoop. Darn it, a woman had been killed, and if Roberts had a prior history with Mrs. Winkworth, Ernie, if not the police, needed to know about it.

Therefore, when Celia and I were alone in the upstairs hallway heading to my father's office, I said, "I heard you and Roberts talking to each other this morning, Celia. Exactly how did Roberts know Mrs. Winkworth."

Goodness, but the girl could move fast when she was provoked. She whirled around so quickly, her apron ballooned out around her. Her eyes got huge, her face got red, and she looked as if she might faint. I hurried to her and put a comforting hand on her arm. She shook off my hand as if it were a rattlesnake that had just bitten her.

"You *heard?* You were *spying* on us?"

"No, I wasn't spying on you!" Curse it, this morning was already awful, and I feared the rest of the day wasn't going to get much better. "But I heard you when I went to get something with which to clean off the typewriter keys in Father's office. You need to tell me about it. Or you can tell the police. If it were I, I'd talk to me before I'd talk to the police. I can then tell my boss, Mr. Templeton, and it's possible the police won't even have to know about Roberts's involvement with Mrs. Winkworth."

"He wasn't involved with her!" Celia said adamantly. "He wasn't!"

"He said he was," I reminded her.

And then poor Celia buried her face in the dust rag (ew) and sobbed as if her heart were about to break into shards. Horrified, mainly because I didn't think the face-in-the-rag thing was a good idea, I grabbed the cloth and tugged it away from her.

"Don't do that! For heaven's sake, calm down."

She didn't calm down. She even wailed. Lord. I grabbed her wrist and tugged her a few paces to my room, opened the door, and shoved her in, following her and shutting the door quickly behind me before anyone saw or heard us. I tossed the dust cloth on the table beside a chair. Buttercup, unaware that some sort of tragedy was taking place in front of her very eyes, was overjoyed that I'd brought another human to meet her and leaped upon Celia's apron.

"Down, Buttercup," I said sternly.

My darling doggie looked crushed, but she did as I'd commanded. I picked her up.

"Good girl." She licked my cheek. I turned to Celia, who was now choking on her sobs. I gestured her to a chair in the corner next to the table, and she walked over and collapsed into it.

"Calm down now, Celia. There's no need for you to be carrying on like this."

All I got for my trouble that time was another wail. I'd heard that the best way to stop a woman from being hysterical was to slap her face, but I didn't think I'd better do that. Someone was sure to ask her why her cheek bore a red handprint. Maybe I should throw a glass of water over her? No, that wouldn't work either, because someone would comment on her state of water-loggedness. Bother. Then I had a brilliant idea—or maybe it wasn't, but it worked. I walked over to her and put Buttercup in her lap.

Celia hugged my dog so hard, I feared for Buttercup's ribs, but at least she stopped weeping and stared up at me, her cheeks streaming tears. She hiccupped a couple of times and then said, "If you tell the police, they'll arrest Brandon."

"They won't arrest him if he didn't commit the crime."

She shook her head so hard, her neat little bun came undone. Ever since I'd taken the tremendous (for me) step of having my hair bobbed, I didn't understand why any American girl would want long hair, but I didn't mention that to her. Rather, I said, "Just tell me the story, and I'll discuss it with Ernie when he gets back."

"I shouldn't."

"If you don't, I'll have to tell the police what I heard the two of you saying to each other." I know that might sound cruel, but I couldn't very well withhold information, however inconsequential it might seem on the surface, from someone with official authority, and I'd sure as heck rather tell Ernie than Detective Rotondo. Ernie might be a shade too insouciant, but he wasn't big and looming and grumpy-looking like Rotondo was. I still didn't understand the attraction between him and Mrs. Majesty. But love, as the poets say, is blind. Or maybe it wasn't the poets. Whoever said it, the old saw seemed to be true.

"Celia. You know you can't keep any information regarding Mrs. Winkworth and Brandon Roberts a secret. The woman

207

was murdered. The authorities need to know everything if they're going to get to the truth."

Burying her head in my dog's soft fur, Celia said something I didn't hear.

Annoyed and impatient—I had notes to type up, darn it—I said, and sternly, too, "Celia, tell me now. I have other things to do and can't waste all morning trying to get you to stop crying and making my dog all wet."

It might have been playing dirty to mention Buttercup, but Celia's head jerked up, she grabbed the stupid dust cloth from the table next to her chair and began drying the poodle's wet fur. I snatched it out of her hand, put my hands on my hips, and growled, "Spill it. Now."

Sniffling piteously—I went to my dresser drawer, withdrew a clean hankie, and handed it to her—Celia whispered, "He's her grandson."

I'm pretty sure my mouth fell open. I'm entirely sure my eyes widened. As soon as I managed to get my mouth shut, I opened it again to say, "Brandon Roberts is Mrs. Lurlene Winkworth's *grandson*?"

Celia nodded, looking miserable. "I shouldn't have told you."

"Yes, you should." Tapping my cheek with my finger until I remembered the dust rag and threw it onto my bed, I thought about this latest wrinkle, and . . . absolutely nothing occurred to me. Then I decided I should probably do exactly as I'd told Celia I'd do and tell Ernie this interesting tidbit of information. He'd know what to do.

And then Celia's reluctance withered like a flower in the hot sun, and she began blurting out the whole story. "But they never knew each other. Brandon was born to Mrs. Winkworth's daughter. Not Mrs. Hanratty, but the daughter named Violet. Mrs. Winkworth didn't approve of the man Violet married, and she never spoke to her again. Brandon didn't even know Mrs.

Winkworth lived in Pasadena when he moved out here. He's a trained automobile mechanic, you see, and he worked his way from the South to California, and he got a job at the Hull Motor Works here in town. That's where Mr. Allcutt found him, and he hired him. Brandon makes more money working for your father than he did at the Motor Works, although he liked the job at the Motor Works better."

"I can understand that," I said.

A spate of silence ensued. Celia appeared uncomfortable, a condition that made a good deal of sense to me.

"So Brandon knew Mrs. Winkworth was his grandmother, even though he'd never had anything to do with her as a child?"

"Oh, yes. His mother told him all about her mother, whom she . . . didn't care for, according to Brandon."

"Yes, well, who could?" said I, my state of abstraction rendering me a trace too honest. "But never mind that now. Let me think about this. I won't tell the police. I'm going to tell my boss, and he'll know precisely what to do." Then I thought about something else. "But if he was in his own little apartment above the stables, he couldn't have had anything to do with the woman's murder."

If Celia's head hung any lower, it would be in her lap, Buttercup having jumped off after I snatched the rag away. "He . . . he was in the house. Upstairs. He . . . wanted to get to know his grandmother. He didn't believe she could be as awful as his mother said. But . . . well, their meeting didn't go well."

I was stunned for a second or two, but then told myself to buck up. "I can imagine. So this is simply wonderful. We have Riki Saito, your gentleman friend, Miss de la Monica, my brother-in-law, and Mr. Mann all upstairs when the old cow bit the dust. Golly, Ernie's going to love this."

Pleading eloquently with her pretty blue eyes, Celia pleaded inelegantly with her tongue. "Do you *have* to tell him?"

"Yes," I snapped. Then I said, "But get up now, stop worrying about your beloved, and clean my father's office. I have work to do in there."

She heaved one of the more enormous sighs I've ever heard and got out of the chair. Silently she went to the door, me following, opened it, and walked to my father's office. Once there, she cleaned fingerprint dust off the typewriter first as I organized my notes and squinted at them to make sure I could interpret what I'd written down.

When she was through with the typewriter and desk, I placed my notebook on the desk beside the typewriter, and sat in the chair. Then I got up again, found a thick book on a bookshelf, and put it on the chair seat. My legs were shorter that those of whoever had used the typewriter last, who was probably Mr. Mann, unless someone had sneaked in here to type something in secret, which I doubted, typewriters being rather noisy instruments.

As I typed, Celia cleaned the rest of the office to the rhythm of my tap-tap-tapping. I don't have a clue where she went after she'd finished with the office and left the room. I probably should have given the matter some thought. Oh, well.

By the time Ernie and the policemen got back from the Winkworth estate, bearing with them Mr. Delbert Mann, I'd just finished typing the last of my notes and was hoping I'd be allowed to go to the Pasadena Police Station with the guys when they next questioned Lola de la Monica. My money was still on her, mainly because she seemed such a difficult creature.

First though, I needed to tell Ernie the latest.

CHAPTER TWENTY-TWO

"And don't leave again," I heard Detective Rotondo saying to
Mr. Mann when I reached the curving staircase.

"I won't. It was a mistake. I thought you meant I shouldn't
leave town. I didn't know you meant me to stay *here*, in this
house."

"Right. Even though that's what we told you to do."

"But I didn't understand your words to mean that." Mann
had begun to whine.

The men had gathered at the bottom of the staircase. Extra
policemen were brushing fingerprint dust on the staircase railing as I passed them. They were dusting the entire railing and
not just the spot where Mrs. Winkworth went over. Interesting.
I clattered down the stairs and darned near ran poor Mr. Mann
down, my momentum was so great. However, I managed to
stop before I disgraced myself, and then thrust a thickish pile of
papers at Detective Rotondo, interrupting Mr. Mann's excuses,
which sounded lame to me.

"Here," I said, out of breath from dashing down the hall and
the staircase. "My notes."

Rotondo was slow to take them from me, but he did eventually. His reluctance annoyed me, and I kind of wanted to take
the notes back and smack him in the face with them, but I
recognized the urge to be not merely improper and stupid, but
born of my state of anxiety and exhaustion. Therefore, I ignored
him and turned to Ernie.

"I need to speak to you. Privately. Now."

"Have you learned something we need to know that regards the case, Miss Allcutt?"

Rotondo. Of course. What a spoilsport the man was!

So I turned to him and said, "I don't know. But Ernie will."

The detective didn't look pleased when I grabbed Ernie's arm and dragged him off toward the sun porch.

"If you want to be in on Mann's interview and go to the station with us, be back here in ten minutes. I'm going to read these notes," Rotondo called after us.

Ha. At least he aimed to read all my hard work.

"What's so all-fired urgent, Mercy?" Ernie said when we got to the sun porch and I closed the doors, not fancying anyone interrupting us.

So I told him Celia's story. Well, properly speaking it was Brandon's story, but . . . oh, never mind.

I do believe Ernie's mind boggled almost as much as mine had when I reached the end of my narrative.

He said, "Shit," after a second or two of stunned silence.

"I wouldn't put it that way, but yes, we have another viable suspect."

"Where's Roberts now?"

"How should I know?"

"Where's the maid?"

I huffed an impatient breath. "I have no idea! I was trying to type those wretched notes for that ghastly detective. I wasn't spying on my parents' servants."

With a shake of his head, Ernie said, "You probably should have spied on those two. For all we know, they've both run off."

"Oh." See? I told you I ought to have spared a thought to what Celia did after she'd finished cleaning my father's office.

"We'd better check on the chauffeur before we tell Rotondo this. He's not such a bad guy, by the way. He just acts impassive on the job. He's all right when he's not working."

"If you say so. Oh, Ernie, I didn't even think about keeping an eye on those two. If they've taken it on the lam, it'll be all my fault." I felt about two inches tall.

" 'Taken it on the lam'? You've been hanging out with Lulu too much, Mercy."

"Fiddlesticks. If I'd been hanging out with Lulu this week, I could have avoided this whole mess."

We didn't stand still as we talked to each other. Rather, Ernie had opened the door from the sun porch to the outside, and we were hurrying to the stable area. When we got there, sure enough, we heard voices emanating from the upstairs apartment where Brandon Roberts resided. One of the voices belonged to Celia.

"Don't do it, Brandon!"

"Dammit, Celia, if I stick around here, they'll arrest me!"

"No!" Celia, I noted, was crying again. The woman could double as a garden hose.

"Get out of my way. I'll catch a bus in front of Cal Tech."

The California Institute of Technology, near my parents' house in Pasadena, was colloquially called Cal Tech, in case you needed someone to decode that term.

"No! Don't go, Brandon! I love you!"

"I love you, too, but I'd rather love you as a free man than a jailbird."

Ernie heaved a sigh and hollered up the staircase leading to Brandon's apartment, "Come down here, both of you! Nobody's going anywhere."

Silence ensued. In between the various dramatic scenes, silence seemed to ensue a whole lot that day.

"M-Miss Allcutt?" Celia's trembling voice asked.

"Yes. I'm here with Mr. Templeton. You both need to come down here now. The police are in the house, and they need to talk to Brandon."

I heard Brandon's grumbled, "Dammit," before the couple emerged, Celia first, from the apartment. They dragged themselves down the staircase as if someone were holding a gun at their backs.

"All right now," said Ernie, using his official voice. I hadn't heard it often since I'd gone to work for him. "Come on along with us. And don't worry. Nobody's going to lock you up if you didn't do the deed."

"Huh," said Brandon Roberts.

Celia only sobbed. I despaired of the poor girl.

Detective Rotondo, glowering, met us at the door of the sun porch when we approached the house. "Where the devil did you get off to? I thought you wanted to come to the station to talk to that idiot actress."

"We just discovered another problem, Detective," said Ernie.

Celia wailed. Again I felt an urge to smack her, but I restrained myself.

"Christ," muttered the detective. "Now what?"

"Turns out Brandon Roberts here is Mrs. Winkworth's heretofore unknown grandson."

"He's *what?*" Rotondo roared, staring at the four of us as if he'd as soon stomp on us like several pesky insects.

I offered as simple an explanation of the mess as I could. "Mrs. Winkworth's other daughter, Violet, was cast off by Mrs. Winkworth when she married a man Mrs. Winkworth didn't like. Brandon is Violet's son. When he learned Mrs. Winkworth was here, in this house, he decided to meet her. He didn't believe she could be as awful as his mother said she was."

"Yeah?" said Rotondo.

" 'Cast off'?" said Ernie, grinning at me like the fiend he was.

I cast *him* a baleful look and spoke to the detective. "Yes. But he was wrong. She was precisely as awful as his mother said she was. But, according to him—and Celia, who's his young woman—he didn't kill her."

"Cripes," said Rotondo.

"So now we have another suspect to question," added Ernie.

"Yeah, yeah." Detective Rotondo glared at Roberts for a moment. "Well, hell, I guess I'd better talk to you before we go to the station." He turned to me. "Where can we interrogate this guy?"

"Uh . . . I don't know. Oh. I guess you can use my father's office. I'm finished in there, and I don't believe Father will be using it." I glanced around, although I didn't see anything interesting. "Does anyone know if my parents are up and about yet?"

"Not a clue," said Ernie.

"Well, I don't suppose it matters. If they're up, maybe we'll be lucky and miss them."

After an eye-roll I did *not* appreciate, Detective Rotondo said, "Will you lead us to the office, please, Miss Allcutt?"

I sniffed and said, "Yes. Come this way, please."

So I led the way to my father's office, dodging police officers flicking fingerprint powder all over the place. To the detective's growling disapproval, I popped into my room to fetch another notebook along the way. There were pencils aplenty in the office. And to heck with Rotondo.

I didn't learn much from Rotondo's interrogation of Brandon Roberts. Celia wept through the whole thing, using up another one of my hankies, and Roberts told the police the same story Celia had told me, only adding one significant detail.

"Where did this encounter with your grandmother take place?" asked Rotondo.

It was a good question, and one I hadn't thought to ask. Perhaps when this ghastly week was over, I'd write down a little instruction sheet for myself. I could refer to it when refining my detectival skills.

"At the head of the staircase," said Roberts.

The chauffeur looked to be in a foul mood and was surly and snarly. Not that I blamed him much for that, but I do believe he'd have made a better case for himself if he'd sat in an upright posture and spoken with firm confidence. But he didn't ask me how to behave, and I didn't tell him. I certainly did wish Celia would quit crying, though.

"Ah. The good old head of the staircase," growled Rotondo. "That's where everyone met up with the woman."

I raised my hand. Before he could tell me to keep my yap shut, I said, "Riki Saito claims not to have seen her at all until after she was dead, and my brother-in-law was chatting with Miss de la Monica in his and Chloe's suite. I don't believe he saw her either. And Mr. Mann saw her in my father's office."

"Well, somebody pushed her over that railing," said Rotondo, still growling. "So that pretty much leaves you, Mr. Roberts."

"No!" Roberts jumped up from his chair and stood there, quivering, fists clenched at his sides. "I didn't push her! I didn't do anything to the blasted woman except introduce myself! When she told me to go to hell, I left her alone at the top of the stairs."

"Oh?" One of Rotondo's eyebrows lifted. "Where'd you go after you left her? Nobody seems to have seen you afterwards."

"Of course no one saw me. I was upset. I went down the servants' staircase. The nobs probably don't even know the servants' staircase exists, but they'd have a fit if a servant sullied their own glorious staircase." His sneer was a work of art.

He was also telling the truth—about my parents being horrified if a servant dared to use the main staircase—although I decided I'd better not say so.

"Didn't Saito use the main staircase?" asked Ernie, looking at me.

"Yes, but he was in a state of shock over what had just happened. You know, Mrs. Winkworth landing on the parquet flooring." I shuddered as I remembered the scene.

"Huh," said Ernie.

"Well, hell," said Rotondo. "Then who the hell pushed her over?"

"*I* don't know," said Roberts, subsiding into his chair again and sounding defeated. "But it wasn't me. I sure understand why my mother told me her mother was a cold-hearted bitch though."

His language offended me, although I should have been accustomed to bad language by that time, what with Ernie and Detective Rotondo swearing all the time.

I did say, because no one else had mentioned it, and I believed it to be of some importance, "Miss de la Monica claimed to meet her at the staircase railing." I figured a reminder wouldn't go amiss at this point.

Detective Rotondo heaved a sigh. "Yeah. We have to talk to that bi—uh, woman again, don't we?"

"Yes," I said firmly, not intending to be left out of the interrogation committee.

"But first we need to talk to Mann."

Oh, goody. More notes. I really liked being on the inside of an investigation for once. Generally I had to pry information out of Ernie.

"Roberts, you stay here. Don't go anywhere. Don't leave the house."

"Yeah, yeah," said Roberts. "But if the Allcutts see me indoors, they'll fire me." He shot me a nasty look, which I didn't deserve, but oh, well.

"Stay in the kitchen then. They never go in there, do they?" said Ernie.

"Good idea," said I.

"The kitchen? I'm a chauffeur, not a cook!"

Detective Rotondo showed not a jot of sympathy, which was pretty much what I'd expected of him. "Go to the kitchen or go to jail. The choice is yours, Roberts. And don't leave the house."

"Oh, all right," said Roberts, getting out of the chair and slouching off to the servants' staircase.

"Do you think I ought to follow him to make sure he does what you told him to do?" I asked the detective.

"Couldn't hurt," said Rotondo. "When you've got him peeling potatoes or whatever needs done, we'll be interviewing Mann here in the office."

"Excellent," I said, and scooted off after Roberts.

He heard me following him and turned to look, but I guess he didn't dare frown at a daughter of the house, because he just turned back again and continued down to the service porch. I got there about three seconds after he did, and noticed that he was as good as his word—or as good as Detective Rotondo's command—and went into the kitchen.

Mrs. Thorne greeted him with surprise. "Roberts! What are you doing here?"

"Police orders," he said sullenly.

"He's here to give you a hand, Mrs. Thorne," I added brightly. "Do you have anything he can do to help you? The detective doesn't want him to leave the house."

"Is that so?" After giving me a surprised glance, Mrs. Thorne turned to Roberts and fingered her plump cheek.

I got the feeling Roberts was going to be put to good use when a smile appeared on Mrs. Thorne's face, and she reached into a cupboard.

"Get a rag, young man. You're going to polish the silver."

Roberts heaved a sigh, and I ran back up the servants' stairs. I didn't feel like running, but I also didn't trust Rotondo to wait until I got to the office before he commenced questioning Delbert Mann.

But I wronged the fellow. One of the uniforms was just escorting Mann to the office when I got there. I hurried inside and took a chair where I could hear but not be too noticeable. I was operating on the principle that a suspect might be more forthcoming if he didn't see someone taking down his every word. I hadn't thought about this aspect of note-taking the prior day, and none of the men had told me to hide in a corner, but what the heck.

"Sit there," Detective Rotondo told Mann, pointing to a chair in front of Father's desk. Naturally, the detective took the seat of most importance, behind the desk. Made sense. The person running the show should sit there.

Mann sat, his posture defeated, his unhappiness clear to read upon his countenance, which wasn't prepossessing at the best of times. Come to think of it, I didn't know that for a fact, since I'd never seen him in the best of times. But I had a feeling. Other uniformed officers and Ernie scattered themselves around the room, the police people standing, Ernic slouching into a nice leather chair, which was just like him.

"All right," continued Rotondo, "why'd you run for it?"

Mann's lips pinched together for a second before he said, "I already told you why. I understood you to say I shouldn't leave the area, not that I shouldn't leave this house. I live a block away, for God's sake. It's not as if I took off for Alaska."

"Nuts. You knew very well I meant for you to stay here." The detective tapped the desk with a thickish forefinger. "Now why'd you run?"

"I didn't run!" Mann insisted. "I just thought I might as well go home."

"You taking off like that is about the closest thing to a confession I've ever seen," said Rotondo in a conversational tone of voice.

That caught Mann's attention, and he jumped out of his chair, his face turning red as I watched. "It wasn't a confession! It was a mistake!"

"The rest of the folks around here are pretty much convinced you ran because you did in the old woman."

"I didn't!" cried Mann, his fists clenching at his sides, his face flaming an almost fuchsia color. Interesting effect.

"And," said Rotondo as if he didn't have a quivering human male all but incinerating in front of him, "I agree. When you ran, you all but told us you killed your employer."

"That's not true!" yelped Mann.

"Yes, it is," I said, God knows why. Sometimes I can't keep my trap shut for love or money. "My parents even told the detective they were sure you were the murderer because you took off."

Rotondo shot me a glare that told me to shut my trap or leave the room, so I shut my trap.

"But I *didn't* kill her!"

"You hated her," Ernie said from his easy chair.

Mann turned abruptly to face Ernie. He reminded me of some wild animal caught in a snare, although if you'd asked me the day before if the mild-looking Delbert Mann could look like anything more wild than a field mouse, I'd have said no.

"Yes, I hated her! She was a vicious, miserable old woman. But I didn't kill her!"

"If you hated her so much, why'd you stay in her employ?" asked Rotondo, his voice still conversational.

Mann sank back into his chair, defeated again. "I already told you. Jobs aren't easy to find anymore."

"Nuts," said Ernie. "I advertised for a secretary for two

months before Miss Allcutt showed up and made me hire her."

I opened my mouth to protest this blatant lie, but shut it again before I spoke. It had suddenly occurred to me that perhaps Ernie and Detective Rotondo were weaving a subtle web around Delbert Mann. Ergo, I kept taking notes, watching when I could, and decided to write this web-weaving ploy into my detective's manual when I had a chance.

"Well, *I* couldn't find a job for a long time," said Mann, whining now. "And I didn't want to quit because I was afraid I wouldn't be able to find another one."

"That won't wash," said Rotondo, slapping a newspaper on the desk in front of Mann. "That's yesterday's *Pasadena Star News*. There are eleven secretarial positions open in and around town. That's a lot of jobs."

"If I'd quit, she'd have given me a bad reference," said Mann, sounding desperate.

"Applesauce," said Ernie. "You could have left her out of your list of employers."

"Just confess now and save us all this time and nonsense," said Rotondo in an even, almost friendly voice. Almost.

"Oh, God!" Mann sort of folded over and covered his face with his hands.

"God's not here at the moment," Rotondo said dryly. "It's only us chickens. So tell us. Why'd you stay with a woman who treated you like dirt and whom you hated?"

I was pleased he'd said "whom," not that it matters.

"You'll think I did it if I tell you," Mann said. I think he was trying not to cry.

"A whole lot of people already think you did it," said Ernie. "Including most of us in this room."

Believe it or not, a spate of silence ensued.

Mann broke it when he lifted his head, removed his hands,

and said, "All right. I'll tell you. She . . . she had something on me."

I squinted at him, not understanding his words, although I'd written them down in my secretarial pad precisely as he'd spoken them.

"Yeah? What did she have on you?" asked Rotondo, who evidently didn't suffer from my own lack of understanding.

"She . . . she found out I'd stolen something from a person I'd worked for. I don't know how she found out. For the good Lord's sake, that was back in Missouri!"

"Yeah? You get caught for it?" Rotondo again.

"Yes." Mann had begun to turn sullen. "It wasn't grand theft or anything like that. I just stole a gold coin that was worth some money. I'd aimed to pawn it, but I'd never done anything like that before, and I didn't know how to find a pawn shop or anything. I took it to a coin dealer, who seemed suspicious, and I guess the dealer notified the police. He didn't even offer a price for the coin, and his attitude scared me. I'd planned to return the coin the next day, but the police found the coin on me when they came to the boarding house where I lived the same day I visited the coin dealer."

"You go to jail?"

"Yes. I served three months and had to pay restitution. Even though the bastard got his stupid coin back!"

"People don't like it when other people take their things," muttered Ernie. "And it's really not a nice habit to develop."

"I know that," said Mann, hanging his head again. "It was the first and last time I ever even thought about doing anything criminal. But the old bitch found out."

"Which old bitch?" asked Rotondo rather poetically.

"Mrs. Winkworth. She was good at that. She dug and dug and dug, and wrote letters and asked questions, and she finally got her wrinkled old hands on a newspaper account of my

criminal career." He snorted. "A gold coin. Three months in jail
and restitution. Some career. And all for the sake of a stupid
coin I didn't know what to do with after I stole it anyway."

"And she threatened to tell people about this . . . mistake of
yours if you quit her employ?"

"Oh, yes. She said I'd never get another job in Pasadena or
vicinity if I left before she'd had her fill of me." He looked up at
Rotondo, his eyes pleading. "She did that, you know. She dug
up dirt on people. I'm not the only one. Did you know she sent
her own grandson poison-pen letters once? Well, she did."

"Yeah. I know about that."

"She was a filthy blackmailer," said Mann.

"You still made a bad mistake by running."

"I guess so. But I was hoping to go through her office and
destroy the evidence of my Missouri crime before anyone else
found it. That's why I left here last night."

For some strange reason, I believed him.

Another spate of silence filled the room. I'm being candid
here. At last Rotondo rose from my father's chair and pinned
Mann with a stare that would have had me cowering. Actually,
it had Mann cowering, too.

"All right. You can go now. But *do not* leave this house. Do
you understand me today? Did I speak clearly enough for you
this time? Don't leave this house."

"I understand," mumbled Mann.

"Good. Because if you run again, I *will* take your actions as a
confession."

"I won't run," Mann mumbled.

A uniform escorted Mann out of the room. I wondered for a
moment where he aimed to store Mann, but I didn't wonder
long because Rotondo said, "Is there lunch to be had in this
place, or do we have to get sandwiches somewhere else?"

"I'm sure Mrs. Thorne will be happy to feed you, Detective,"

I said, knowing Mrs. Thorne to be a nice woman and hoping my mother wasn't anywhere close by.

"Can you arrange that for us? We can eat in the kitchen or something," said Rotondo.

"Will do," said I, and I did.

CHAPTER TWENTY-THREE

I met Chloe as I tramped toward the spiral staircase in the upper hall. "Hey, Chloe. Do you know where the parents are? I don't want to see them if I don't have to."

"You're in luck then, because Mother said she and Father were going to remain in their own quarters until the police have finished their investigation and gone away."

"Thank God. I have to arrange lunch for the coppers, Ernie, and me, and then we're going to the station to talk to Miss de la Monica again."

Chloe shuddered delicately. Chloe did everything delicately. I'd always wanted to be more like her in that regard. "Good luck."

"Thanks."

And I resumed my march to the kitchen, where the kind Mrs. Thorne pooh-poohed the notion of anyone having to dine in her domain, and made Mary Jane set the table in the breakfast room. Then she proceeded to fix a smashing lunch with a whole lot of delicious sandwiches, potato salad that must have been lurking in the Frigidaire already, and carrot, celery and cucumber slices. She served us cookies and ice cream for dessert. The woman was almost as good a cook as my own Mrs. Buck at home. Which I missed like fire.

Although it was rude of me, I hurried through my own luncheon because I wanted to take Buttercup outside to romp for a minute or two before we left for the police station.

225

I rose from the table before anyone else had finished and said, "Don't go anywhere without me. I have to take care of my dog."

"Huh," said Rotondo.

"Give her a pat for me," said Ernie.

"I will." I went to the kitchen before I climbed those blasted stairs again, because I wanted to thank Mrs. Thorne sincerely for the lovely lunch she'd given us.

"Oh, pshaw," said she. "It's my job. And I love feeding people."

Lucky for us.

Buttercup was ecstatic when I carried her downstairs and into the backyard.

Naturally, she didn't get to remain ecstatic long. I suppose it was ten minutes later when Ernie joined us in the backyard. Buttercup was overjoyed to see him, so he knelt and gave her a good pet.

"Time to go, Mercy. Rotondo's kind of like a freight train. Once he starts, nobody can stop him."

"Good description. Poor Buttercup." I apologized to her all the way back to my bedroom, where I left her, looking droop-eared and depressed, and hightailed it downstairs.

It didn't take me long to find the men, as they'd gathered in the huge hallway from which the staircase ascended. I joined them seamlessly, clutching my secretarial notebook and three pencils, and wishing I'd taken the time to go to the bathroom. But there was a ladies' room at the police station; I didn't think anyone would mind if I used it one more time.

"I'm ready for Lola de la Monica," I said unnecessarily.

"Very well," Rotondo said, eyeing my pencils. But I wasn't taking any chances of having to leave the interview room in order to sharpen one. "Let's go. I hope to God she's calmed down after spending a night in the clink."

I'm sure we all hoped the same thing.

Because my automobile was so much nicer than Ernie's, we took it to the Pasadena Police Department. Ernie drove. I loved my pretty 1924 Moon Roadster. It was a lovely light blue color.

We arrived at the station at about the same time as did the police contingent. Did I mention Detective Rotondo had left, besides the police people fingerprinting the place, two uniformed officers to keep tabs on the denizens of my parents' house? Well, he did. With firm instructions to allow *no one* out of the house, and that included Roberts and Mann.

This order meant that, if my father decided he wanted to go anywhere that day, he'd be out of luck, and would probably fire Roberts out of spite. My father didn't approve of inconvenience to his own personal self. I decided I'd feel sorry for Roberts later. For all I knew at the time, he was a hot-headed murderer. I did excuse him from being cold-hearted, which I believe speaks of a good deal of restraint on my part.

But never mind that. Ernie, Rotondo, his minions, and I entered the Pasadena Police Department at approximately the same time, and Rotondo led us through the same doorway and into the same hall we'd seen the night before. He opened a door on the right, and we all filed in. Then he turned to one of his underlings—I don't know where Officer Ludlow was that morning, but I hoped he was taking care of his scratches—and said, "Bring Miss de la Monica in here. And don't forget to bring a couple pairs of handcuffs with you. She's a hellcat."

"Yes, sir." And the uniformed man departed.

"Do you think he can handle her by himself?" I asked, not meaning to cast aspersions on his deputy (or whatever he was) but remembering the preceding night perhaps too well.

"Good point," said Rotondo, surprising me. He turned to another uniform. "Matthews, go with him. If she gets out of hand, cuff her and carry her."

"Yes, sir." And off went Matthews after the other police person.

We commenced sitting in the silence that ensued after Matthews's departure. I don't know about the rest of them, but I was busy mentally bracing myself for the interview to come and knowing I was in no condition to survive another abrasive encounter with Lola de la Monica.

But evidently a night in the hoosegow had daunted even so demented a specimen of human hellionhood as Lola de la Monica. Her head drooped as Matthews and the other uniform led her, handcuffed but not screaming or kicking, into the interrogation room. When she lifted her head to see who was there to confront her, she appeared about as bedraggled as a woman could appear. Served her right.

"What you want with me?" she said, lifting her head in an effort at defiance.

"We still need to question you about your encounter with Mrs. Winkworth yesterday evening," said Rotondo. "You pitched a fit last night, assaulted a police officer, and had to be locked up. Will you behave today, or do you need more cell time?"

Her back stiffened a bit. "I will answer your questions."

"Good. Have a seat."

The two uniforms deposited her in a chair, although they didn't remove the handcuffs. Rotondo nodded at them and glanced at Lola's feet as if to warn them to be on the alert for flying legs.

"Before we begin the interview, we'll have to take your fingerprints. Will you behave, or do we have to break your wrists?" asked Rotondo, sounding as if he weren't joking.

The actress bridled. "My fingerprints? You said you already had my fingerprints. Why you lie to me?" I noticed her fingers, cuffed behind her back, which must have been uncomfortable, balled into fists.

"Everyone who was anywhere near the crime scene in that house yesterday is having his or her fingerprints taken. Miss Allcutt had hers taken last night."

I nodded to confirm this statement.

Lola eyed me slantwise, but said, "Very well."

"Uncuff her, but watch out. She's dangerous."

"Bah," said Lola.

But Matthews had no trouble at all taking her prints. She didn't screech once, and she didn't lash out either. Matthews handed her a wiping rag after he'd done his duty, and Lola wiped her hands, a sour expression on her face.

"They're feelthy. I need to wash my hands."

"You can wash your hands later," said Rotondo. "Right now, you need to talk."

The actress huffed out an exasperated breath but didn't attack anyone.

So far, she was behaving herself. She sagged into the chair as if she'd been starved and beaten for a month or three and couldn't seem to stop glaring at her blackened fingertips. Her makeup, which had been running wild yesterday, had smeared even further overnight, and her eyes had big black circles around them. These weren't like my own black circles, which had been created by means of my having had too little sleep. Hers were makeup-based circles. She also had smears of black down her cheeks. She was about as far from the young, beautiful Daughter of the South she'd played in *The Fire at Sunset* as a person could get.

Rotondo cleared his throat. I already had my pad and pencil poised. Ernie leaned back in his chair. The two uniforms stood at attention flanking the actress's chair.

"Very well," said Rotondo, starting the interview. "You knew Mrs. Winkworth before yesterday, right?"

Lola managed to work up a pretty good glare, which she

229

flung at the detective. "You know I know her."

Her Spanish accent was thick this morning.

"Had you seen her between the time that picture was filmed on her estate and last night?"

"No."

"I understand you and Mr. Nash had words in Mr. and Mrs. Nash's suite of rooms on the second floor of the Allcutt home, is that right?"

"We spoke."

"And you got upset because Mr. Nash told you he wasn't renewing your contract. Right?"

Her head lifted another notch. "I will make him change his mind."

"I'm not interested in what you aim to do," said Rotondo with a sharp bite to his voice and a dismissive wave of his hand. "You were upset by the news he gave you. Isn't that right?"

She pursed her lips and sat there like a sullen cat. I thought for a minute she'd refuse to speak, but she finally said, "Yes."

"What happened after Mr. Nash delivered the bad news to you? What did you do then?"

"What I do? What I do?" A small flash of anger made the two uniforms at her sides stiffen. She must have noticed, realized they'd cuff her wrists again and probably cuff her ankles to the chair if she kicked up a fuss, and decided not to make a scene, because she slumped again. "I run off."

"You ran out of the Nashes' suite of rooms?"

"Yes. I run out."

"And then what did you do?"

She shrugged. "I go downstairs."

"Okay. Back up a minute. You encountered Mrs. Winkworth before you went downstairs, didn't you?"

Another shrug. "I guess so."

"You guess so? You either did or you didn't," said Rotondo in a tone I wouldn't have defied had it been aimed at me.

I guess he was good at his job. If I were Lola de la Monica, I'd have been shaking in my shoes—except she wasn't wearing any shoes that morning. I stared at her feet, shocked. One didn't generally see women with bare feet. I wondered what she'd done with her shoes and stockings, although I knew better than to ask such a trivial question under the circumstances.

"Yes," Lola said sulkily. "I meet her. She was in my way, so I go around her."

"You went around her?"

"Yes."

"And where did this encounter take place."

"At the top of the stairs. In the hall."

"You said she was in your way?"

"Yes."

"Did you move her out of your way by shoving her over the railing?"

Lola leaped to her feet so suddenly, I jumped in my own chair. I think everyone did. Matthews and his crony each grabbed an arm, but she didn't start fighting. She only screamed. "No. No, no, no, *no*! I don't push no one!"

"But you admit you were upset," Rotondo persisted.

"Of course," she said, sitting again with a thump that must have hurt her bottom, which wasn't well padded. I didn't suffer from that problem myself, not that it's important. "I lose my job."

"Huh. Sounds to me as if you flung your job away with both hands." Rotondo peered at Lola de la Monica so long that if I had been she, I'd have started squirming. Not Lola de la Monica. She just sat in her chair and stared back at him. I guess one could have called a stalemate if one were inclined to do such a thing.

Finally Rotondo said, "Well, you're not going to go anywhere until we get this matter cleared up." He turned on me, and I stiffened rather as Lola had. "Is there any place in your parents' house where Miss de la Monica and the rest of the suspects can be kept until we solve this case?"

Where they could be *kept*? Merciful heavens. "Um . . . I suppose so. It's a gigantic house with far too many rooms. I expect there's an extra one or two where we can store suspects if you need them stored."

"It would be helpful," said Rotondo.

Lola spat out, "*Stored*! Bah."

Mother and Father were not pleased when Detective Rotondo, a couple of uniforms, Ernie, and I darkened the doorway to their upstairs retreat. They got downright surly when they learned their lovely winter home in Pasadena was going to be used to house suspects in a murder case for a day or two.

"This is outrageous!" said Mother.

"It's uncalled for!" said Father.

"It's the only way we can keep everyone together and figure out what happened," said Detective Rotondo in a matter-of-fact voice.

In an odd way, I admired him. According to Daisy, he was a regular guy from New York City, yet here he was telling a couple of people who could buy the entire City of Pasadena if they wanted to that their beautiful, enormous house was going to be used as a makeshift jail until the police solved a murder case. It was an impressive performance, and it got better.

"You can't do that!" said Father.

"How dare you!" said Mother.

"I have a warrant," said Rotondo, holding out a piece of paper with official-looking typing and seals and so forth on it. "It says I can use your home as my headquarters until the Winkworth case is solved. It's better to keep all the suspects together in one place, and three of them were already staying here."

Three of them? I counted in my head: Brandon Roberts, Riki Saito, and . . . *Harvey?* Good Lord, this detestable detective didn't still consider *Harvey* a viable suspect, did he?

Shoot. Maybe he did. Maybe he had to. Goodness, there were certain aspects of this policing business that eluded me entirely. Of course, the detective didn't know Harvey as well as I did, but for anyone to consider Harvey an honest-to-goodness suspect in a murder case was . . . well, insane. I figured it would be better not to say so.

"Contemptible effrontery," said Father.

"It is unacceptable," said Mother, repeating herself.

Rotondo didn't even shrug. "I'll need a maid or someone to help my officers find rooms for the suspects."

"Well, really!" said Mother.

"I will speak to your superior, Detective," said Father

"Fine," said Rotondo. "Here's his number." And darned if he didn't hand Father a business card.

Hmm. Maybe I liked the detective a little bit after all.

Rotondo, his uniformed minions, Ernie, and I all turned and walked away from my incensed parents. I know it's awful of me, but my heart did a little pitty-pat in my chest after seeing how completely and easily the police contingent in the form of Detective Sam Rotondo had silenced my parents. Would that I could do the same.

I heard the telephone ringing somewhere in the house, and then Riki's voice, answering it with the usual folderol. "Allcutt residence." No mere "Hello" or "Good morning" for my parents. A second or two later, I heard Riki say, "I'll get her for you, Mrs. Majesty."

Daisy! I glanced at Rotondo, but except that his frown deepened a trifle, he showed no outward sign he wasn't pleased that his beloved was calling a female member of this household. I hoped it was me.

"Miss Allcutt?"

Riki appeared ill at ease as he spotted me among all those imposing men. Personally, I'm not at all imposing, darn it.

"Yes, Riki?" I used a friendly tone with him to let him know I didn't believe he'd done anything wrong, much less committed the vile murder of a little old lady.

He didn't relax perceptibly. He merely said, "Mrs. Majesty would like to speak with you."

"Thank you, Riki." I glanced at my companions. "Where are you going? I'll take this call and be right with you."

Rotondo looked as if he might object, but Ernie said, "We've got to find a maid and deposit the suspects."

"Right. Go into the kitchen. Mrs. Thorne can help you find someone to assist you there."

As for me, I took myself off to the telephone room under the staircase.

"Mrs. Majesty? Daisy?" I said when I'd raised the receiver to my ear.

"Mercy?"

"Yes."

"Oh, dear, is Sam there?"

"Yes."

"That means he hasn't solved the case yet, doesn't it?"

"I'm afraid so. But he's brought all the suspects here, so they'll all be together under one roof."

"Oh, boy, I'll bet your parents loved that."

I laughed. "About as much as you'd expect them to."

"Sam gets pretty high-handed sometimes."

"He did a brilliant job of handling my parents."

"Um . . ." A tiny spate of silence ensued. See? Told you there were a bunch of them that day. "Um, Mercy, would you mind filling me in on what's happened so far? Sam will never tell me, and he'll growl at me if I ask him."

"Men. They're all like that, aren't they?"

"My father isn't. He's the nicest man on the face of the earth."

A shaft of envy pierced my heart. "You're so lucky! My parents are both stuffed shirts, and they totally disapprove of me. But I have to get back to Ernie and the police crew so I don't miss anything. Let me tell you what's happened so far."

And as briefly as I could, I filled Daisy Majesty in on the high (or low, depending on your perspective) points of the investigation to date.

"Good Lord. Lola actually attacked a policeman?"

"She did. Ripped him up with those talons of hers."

"What a . . . well, I can't think of a nice word to describe her."

"That's probably because there isn't one."

Daisy laughed and said, "Well, thanks for telling me what's going on. I appreciate it."

"Happy to." Something then occurred to me that might have been silly, but didn't feel silly at the time. "Um, Daisy, do you think we might get together one of these days? Just to have lunch or something?"

"Sure," she said instantly. "In fact, I'd love to invite you to Thanksgiving dinner at our house because my aunt is the best cook in Pasadena, but you probably have to take Thanksgiving with your parents."

"What a lovely invitation! Oh, I'd be happy to do that."

"But what about your parents?"

Hmm. That was right. My parents would definitely have seven fits if I dined elsewhere on Thanksgiving. After all, I'd driven all the way from my cozy home on Bunker Hill to Pasadena in order to do so. "Well, I'll try to think of some way out of dinner with my folks. It sounds like you have a happy family, and I'd love to see how one works."

Silence ensued. I know, I know. But those many silences really stick in my mind from that awful day.

Finally Daisy said, "That would be wonderful. We always take Thanksgiving dinner at noon, so that we have lots of time to digest and sing songs and stuff like that afterwards. And that man. Your boss? Mr. Templeton? He can come, too."

That sealed the deal as far as I was concerned. "Thank you. And I mean it about wanting to see how a happy family works. Mine isn't, and it doesn't. Work, I mean."

"How . . . how sad," she said, sounding honestly distressed.

"It's not so bad. I escaped, after all, and if I'd had any gumption, I would have told my mother no when she ordered me to attend Thanksgiving dinner in Pasadena."

After another word or two, we hung up, and I felt better about life for some reason. Well, I knew the reason. I was going to jilt my parents and their stuffy confines and dine with a real, honest-to-God, happy family on Thanksgiving! I could hardly wait.

CHAPTER TWENTY-FOUR

But in the meantime, I had work to do, so I hurried to the kitchen.

Celia, her eyes so puffy, I was surprised she could still see out of them, was curtsying when I entered the room. Ernie was there, too, along with a bunch of policemen and Mrs. Thorne.

I don't know where the police had been keeping Miss de la Monica confined, but she stood in the kitchen, too, still barefoot and handcuffed, her hair a scraggly mess and with makeup sliding down her cheeks. Not precisely glamorous.

"There are three rooms upstairs in the servants' quarters," Mrs. Thorne was telling the uniforms on either side of the actress. "You can stash them there." She stopped speaking and directed her next question at Detective Rotondo. "What about Roberts? Is he allowed to remain in his own apartment over the stable?"

"No," said Rotondo. "He's already proved himself a flight risk."

A flight risk? Well, if he said so.

"Very well," said Mrs. Thorne upon a sigh. "Celia, make up the last three rooms in the servants' quarters for Miss de la Monica, Roberts, and . . ." She looked a question at Sam Rotondo.

"Mr. Mann," said the detective.

"Mr. Mann," repeated Mrs. Thorne.

"Yes, ma'am," said Celia, curtsying again. I noticed that she didn't look at Rotondo, Ernie, the other policemen, Miss de la Monica, or me. Maybe she really couldn't see, although I suspected she hated us all for daring to suspect her beloved of doing a dastardly deed.

After Celia, the actress, and her two police escorts left the kitchen, Rotondo turned to me. I blinked at him, not having expected this attention.

"Can you decipher another person's shorthand notes?"

The question startled me. "I . . . I don't know. Whose notes? What shorthand method does the person use? I use Pitman. I learned at the YWCA back in Boston." When the detective's eyebrows started straightening out, as if he aimed to lower them and frown at me, I quit blathering.

He thrust a shorthand pad at me. "Take a look at these and see if you can decipher them. Ludlow's not in today—according to Doc Benjamin, Lola managed to scratch one of his corneas, and he has to wear an eye patch— and I was hoping you could transcribe these notes."

"She scratched his *cornea*?" I repeated, horrified. "That's terrible!" I glanced after Lola as she exited the room with her escort. She only stared at the floor as if she didn't give a care what her deadly talons had done to Poor Ludlow.

"Yeah, but that's not important right now."

Bet it was to Ludlow.

"Can you read them or not?"

I opened the notebook and looked. Hmm. Ludlow used the same Pitman method of shorthand I did, and from what I could tell at first glance, he was pretty good at it. "Um . . . yes, I believe I can transcribe these notes all right."

Rotondo actually smiled at me. "Thank you. We're going to go upstairs with each suspect and have him or her describe his or her actions that night. If you could type up these notes and bring them to us as soon as you can while we do that, I'd really appreciate it."

But I wanted to be in on the reenactments, too! I cast a pleading glance at Ernie, who shrugged and said, "Those notes are
more important, Mercy. Trust me."

Hmm. Did I trust him? I wasn't sure. Nevertheless, after I
heaved a large-sized sigh, I said, "Oh, very well. I'll do my best
to get them typed up quickly." I cast a hard look at Ernie. "And
if you go anywhere else for any reason, let me know where
you're going, all right?"

He saluted me. "Yes, ma'am."

Honestly. Some days were just awful, and this one was turning into one of the awfullest.

I decided to heck with the fancy main staircase with all the
policemen lumbering around doing their silly reenactments
with their silly subjects, and slowly climbed the servants'
staircase. It was a long slog to the second floor and I was tired,
but I got there eventually. Out of curiosity, I peered around the
corner of the hallway and sure enough, there were Rotondo, a
couple of uniforms, and Ernie with a frightened-looking Riki
Saito. Riki gestured toward my suite, Rotondo said something,
and Riki obediently led the way to my bedroom. Buttercup
would love the attention.

Phooey. That looked much more interesting than typing
notes. However, as someone, I forget who it was, once said,
more or less, mine was not to wonder why; mine was but to do
and . . . well, never mind the rest of it. I didn't plan on dying
that day.

Therefore, I left Ernie and the police and the various suspects
to their work and returned to my father's office. The book I'd
placed on the chair earlier remained, so I didn't have to seek
out another one.

Ludlow's notes were easy to read, although he used some
shortcut terms I couldn't decipher. They were most likely related

to his job and he'd created them because he used them so often. I decided to type down what they looked like and let Detective Rotondo figure out their meaning. Perhaps Ludlow used some sort of code another policeman would understand.

The notes weren't too boring, and I did get to read some of what I'd missed during last night's interrogations, so I kept myself fairly well amused as I went about my work. When I was about halfway finished transcribing Ludlow's notes, Celia came into the room and stopped short when she saw me. Guess she hadn't anticipated finding me in this room, and she didn't appear enraptured to have discovered me.

"Good day again, Celia."

Her eyes were still puffy, but she was no longer crying, thank God. Rather, she gave me as good a glare as she could through the slits her eyes had become and said shortly, "What's good about it?"

Oh, dear. She was mad at me. Well, fine. I didn't care.

"Not a thing," said I, and went back to typing. Celia might not like me, but her gentleman friend possessed as good a motive as anyone else for killing that loathsome old woman. Imagine an old biddy like that searching out the dirt in people's lives. What a ghastly person. I was surprised her daughter and grandson were such nice folks.

Celia was in a mood. I could tell because she went about her work noisily, something servants don't generally do if they want to keep their jobs. I got the impression that by then, she didn't consider me the type of enemy who might get her fired. I hardly noticed anyway, because I was busy, and the typewriter was making a racket all by itself.

So I was merrily typing away, and Celia was trying to annoy me, and it wasn't working, when suddenly Celia said, "Oh!" rather loudly, and I stopped typing and looked up from my work.

A silence ensued as we stared at each other. I'm sorry, but it's the truth.

Then Celia, who'd been dusting the mantelpiece and had just moved the clock, held a paper out to me in a hand that shook. "You-you'd better look at this, Miss Allcutt."

Squinting at her, I rose from my father's desk chair, walked to Celia, and took the paper from her hand. When I read the writing on the paper, my mouth fell open. You can bet I raced out of that room as fast as I could, and I hightailed it around the corner and to the head of the circular staircase as if my skirt were on fire. Out of breath and huffing, I burst onto the scene and found . . . the staircase, still dusty with fingerprint powder, and not a single solitary human being in sight.

Those blasted men had skipped out on me! And Ernie hadn't told me where they were going! Darn him!

Staring at the paper in my hand, I pondered what to do next, and decided to make a search for the men who'd deserted me, blast them all to perdition and back again.

I started inside the house on the first floor. No one but servants going about their business. So I made a cursory survey of the grounds. Nobody at all. I didn't even see a gardener. Therefore, I went back indoors and climbed the servants' staircase to the second floor. Not a person was stirring. I couldn't swear to the mouse situation, but I was pretty sure there were none of them hanging around either.

So. Now what? I knew what I'd have wanted to do if Ernie was with me, but he wasn't. Was it wise of me to do what I wanted to do on my own? Silly question. Of course, it wasn't wise. I should wait for Ernie, or at least a policeman. On the other hand, I didn't want to wait, blast it. Not only that, I didn't know where the wretched men were! Lying curs.

Crumb.

Well, nothing ventured, nothing gained. I went back to the

servants' staircase and climbed the stairs to the third floor, where all the assorted suspects were being kept. I was kind of surprised to see only one policeman posted at the other end of the hallway. Because Ernie was elsewhere, curse the man, I decided to approach the officer and ask him which was the room I wished to visit. If he hadn't been there, I'd have had to knock on all the doors to find whom I sought. It was possible he'd tell me I wasn't allowed to talk to the suspect, but I was the daughter of the house, and if he gave me any grief, I'd act like it.

His name tag thing said he was Officer Perkins, so I smiled and said, "Good afternoon, Officer Perkins. I have a message to give to Miss de la Monica."

Perkins frowned down at me. Have I mentioned I'm about five feet, four inches tall? Well, I am, and there are a whole lot of people in the world who can look down upon me. I don't appreciate it, either.

"What do you have to say to Miss de la Monica?"

I straightened, although I doubt it made me appreciably taller. "I am Miss Allcutt, and I have a question for her. There's something I need to clear up." Inspiration struck. "I'm transcribing Officer Ludlow's notes because he's unavailable to do so himself." There. That was the truth, even though it had nothing to do with my present actions.

"Well . . . I guess it's all right then."

My heart had taken to stomping around in my chest cavity like a herd of wild boars, which I understand can be savage beasts with sharp, perhaps cloven hooves. But I said, "Thank you," and stepped aside so that he could lead the way to Lola's door.

He knocked once, sharply, at the second door on the far side of the staircase, then didn't wait for a response, but stuck the key in the lock and shoved the door open. I was just in time to see Lola leap from the small bed in the room and shoot a furious scowl at Officer Perkins and me.

"What you want?" she demanded in full Spanish mode.

She'd cleaned herself up and no longer looked like the wicked witch out of *The Wizard of Oz*. I turned to Officer Perkins. "Thank you very much. You needn't stay with us."

"I don't think—" he started before he saw my imperious glare, the one I'd borrowed from my mother.

"You may leave the door open," I said, both to give him a sop and to make certain I had a means of escape should Lola fly off the handle. I didn't trust her to behave in a proper manner. She never had yet.

"All right." Officer Perkins sounded grumpy, but he left.

After waiting long enough for him to exit the room, I said, "Miss de la Monica, I need to ask you something." I stopped talking and thought how best to present the evidence on the paper Celia had found.

"Bah," said Lola. She plopped back down on the bed, crossed one leg over the other, and dangled a naked foot at me. At least it was a clean one.

"Was Mrs. Winkworth, uh, trying to blackmail you?"

Lola's eyes narrowed to slits almost as small as Celia's. "What does that mean? That blackmail?"

"Was she trying to get you to give her money in order to keep the secret of your past life?"

Her legs uncrossed, and she braced herself on the bed with her two arms as if she aimed to spring upon me and tear me to shreds. Quite a catlike creature, Lola de la Monica. "Past life? What are you talking about, past life?" Her Spanish hadn't slipped, so she was evidently still in control of her emotions.

Just in case she wasn't, I stepped back a pace or two in order to be closer to the door and lifted the paper Celia had found. "This paper says that your real name is Mary Rosanne Mackey,

you come from Trenton, New Jersey, and that you were the illegitimate daughter of a woman named Irene Mackey, prostitute,
of Trenton."

"It *what!*" Lola stood, although she didn't come forward.

Therefore, I stepped back yet another pace and continued
reading. "It goes on to say that you yourself turned to prostitu-
tion when you were a girl, had an illegitimate child, and then—"

But I didn't get to finish reading aloud the words typed upon
the paper bearing Mrs. Winkworth's letterhead and crest (if
crest it was). Lola uttered a piercing scream and made a dash at
me, her arms out, talons bared, prepared, I'm sure, to rip me
into bloody strips after she'd shredded the paper I held.

I turned around so fast I nearly broke my neck, flew past
Officer Perkins, who'd planted himself next to Lola's door, and
dashed toward the servants' staircase, Lola in hot pursuit.

I heard Officer Perkins say, "Hey! Stop, you!" Then I heard
Lola screech again, a scuffle, and a loud thump. I didn't turn to
see who'd been thumped but got to the stairs and ran down
them as fast as my legs could carry me. By the time I got to the
second floor, I knew it was Lola who pursued me, because her
curses were loud and strong and extremely twangy, which probably meant the paper was correct and she was from New Jersey.
I spared a moment to wonder what she'd done to poor Perkins,
but only a moment. I shot through the door onto the second
floor and raced to the circular staircase, where I knew a large
police contingent was probably gathered once more.

They were still gone.

But Lola wasn't. She still pursued me like a cheetah after a
gnu. She was taller than I, she had longer legs, she had a lot to
lose, and she was bent on murder. Again.

"That bitch called me a fallen woman!" Lola hollered as she
raced after me.

"*Police!*" I bellowed. "*Help!*"

"Fallen woman! I showed *her* a fallen woman!"

Lord. She was gaining on me.

"In fact, I *made* her a fallen woman!"

Where the heck were all the policemen? Where the heck was Ernie? And Rotondo. Damn them all! Why was there *never* a policeman around when you needed one?

I didn't have time to worry about it. By the time I reached the spot where Mrs. Winkworth had gone overboard, shoved, I now had no doubt, by Lola de la Monica, Lola was on me. She pounced like some kind of rabid animal, shrieking, "And now I'm going to make *you* a fallen woman!"

My last coherent deed was to toss the paper over the railing. Lola might kill me, but at least the police would know why she'd done it and know, too, that it had been she who'd killed Lurlene Winkworth.

We fought like a couple of maddened lionesses, but it wasn't much of a contest. As I mentioned before, Lola was bigger than I, height-wise. I might have had the weight advantage, but I sure didn't have those deadly fingernails. And her *voice?* Lord above, I hope never to hear language like that screamed in *such* a ghastly accent again in my lifetime. All traces of Spanish had fled, and she sounded just like some of the people who populated the Eastern seaboard, and who'd attended classes at the YWCA where I'd learned shorthand and typing.

But people had heard me scream. Or maybe they'd heard Lola. I don't know who'd heard what, but I did hear voices coming from below, and I heard somebody—I think it was Detective Rotondo—holler, "What the hell?!"

And then my heart nearly leapt out of my chest when Lola pulled a maneuver I hadn't anticipated. She bent over, got hold of my legs, and, with a vicious heave, slung me over the staircase railing!

It was pure dumb luck that I managed to grab a couple of

the wrought-iron curlicues that comprised the elaborate scrollwork of the railing. Once I realized I wasn't still falling, I hung on like grim death.

Naturally, Lola, who wanted me dead more than anything else just then, tried to pry my fingers off the curlicues. She also kicked my hands, although she was barefoot. Still, her kicks landed and they hurt. But I heard feet pounding up the stairs, and clung like a barnacle to the hull of a boat as she slashed and gouged at my hands with those talons of hers and kicked me with her bare feet.

And then I heard something I'll never forget if I live to be a hundred and twenty.

Just as Ernie tackled Lola de la Monica, sending her sprawling in the upstairs hallway, my mother's voice rang out, louder and clearer than I'd ever heard it before. "Mercedes Louise Allcutt! I can see up your *skirt!*"

CHAPTER TWENTY-FIVE

Thank the good Lord and Officer Perkins, I didn't have to dangle long. Ernie sat on a squirming Lola—whose language and accent hadn't improved since he'd felled her—while Officer Perkins reached over the railing and said, "Can you grip my hands? One at a time? I'll haul you up."

So I did. And he did, assisted by none other than Detective Sam Rotondo, who'd run up the stairs after Ernie. And I didn't die that day, squashed like Lurlene Winkworth on my parents' parquet hall flooring.

It took me quite a while to wash my face and doctor my many scratches and bruises, but eventually, looking rather like Officer Ludlow had looked after Lola had attacked him, I was ready to rejoin the human race. Ernie, much to my surprise, had remained with me as I did my doctoring.

"When will you learn not to tackle tigers on your own, Mercy?" he asked as I painted iodine on a particular painful gash in my cheek.

I glared at him in the mirror. "Don't you start with me, Ernie Templeton. I *tried* to find you when Celia gave me that paper. I looked *everywhere* for you and your stupid police buddies. You *said* you'd tell me if you went anywhere. You lied to me, darn you."

"It wasn't a lie. Rotondo decided to check Roberts's apartment, and he wasn't about to wait around while I reported to you."

I sniffed meaningfully. "And your little *fib* almost got me killed."

"It wasn't a fib, and it wasn't my fault you decided to face a murderess on your own."

"Bah."

We didn't speak again until I was finished with the iodine, the gauze padding, and the tape, and we left the bathroom to join the others.

The police had bundled Lola de la Monica off to the Pasadena Police Department, I presume in handcuffs and foot-cuffs. My ears still rang from having been shrieked into by her, my whole body ached, and I hoped she die a slow and painful death, sanctioned by the State of California.

Detective Rotondo had gathered everyone remaining in the house together in the dining room. Mrs. Thorne had mixed some iodine with warm water, and I soaked my scratched-up hands as he summed up the case for everyone present, and that included . . . well, everyone. Including Delbert Mann, Riki Saito, Harvey, Chloe, Roberts, Celia, and Mother and Father, both of whom looked on with supreme disfavor.

Pinning Delbert Mann with his best detectival glare, Rotondo said, "So, Mrs. Winkworth was up to her old tricks and had dug up dirt on Lola. Why didn't you tell us, Mann? You typed this thing, right?" He flapped the paper someone had picked up from the hall floor at Mr. Mann.

"Y-yes. She made me type it."

"So why didn't you tell us?"

Delbert Mann, pale as a ghost and frightened, said, "I-I didn't know what to do. I didn't know if it was true. The information that paper contained, whether it was true or not, would have ruined Miss de la Monica's career."

"Her career was already ruined," I said, disgusted with his cowardice. "Harvey fired her." I saw Ernie open his mouth and gave him a good hot glare. I didn't care right then that Lola wasn't technically fired.

"But I didn't know that. I just . . ." Mann's words trailed off. As they well should. He'd been at fault, and I'd almost died for it.

"That's called obstruction, Mr. Mann," said Rotondo, his face and voice both grimmer than ever. "You can be prosecuted for it."

Mann looked suitably miserable. "Are you going to arrest me?"

I stuck my oar in again, because I was so angry with the cowardly custard. "Darn you. If you'd only told us what you knew, I wouldn't have been nearly murdered today by that fiendish woman! You *should* be arrested! Look at me! She scratched me all up, and I'll have bruises for weeks!"

His head hung lower.

My mother said, "Mercedes—" but didn't get any further, because I turned on her like a snarling lion.

"And don't you *Mercedes Louise* me, Mother! I've been through a lot today, and I don't feel like putting up with *you!*"

"Mercedes," said my father. He, too, shut up when I transferred my snarly-face to him.

"I think," said Ernie, "that Mercy deserves to be upset. That was a stinky thing to do, Mann, keeping all the dirt on Lola to yourself. There was no reason not to tell us Mrs. Winkworth had found out about the woman's past."

"What did she aim to do with the information?" asked Rotondo. "Do you know?"

Mann shook his head. "I doubt she'd have blackmailed her. She has more money than God. I think she just liked knowing everyone's deep, dark, dirty secrets."

Ernie snorted. "Lola had a whole bunch of those."

"Her name's not Lola," I growled. "It's Mary Roseanne

249

Mackey, and she's a prostitute from Trenton, New Jersey. And so was her mother. A prostitute, I mean. What's more, she abandoned an illegitimate child in Trenton in order to make it big in Hollywoodland."

By the time I was through with that speech, everyone in the room was staring at me in varying degrees of horror. I don't know if they were appalled by Lola's history or by my bold recitation thereof. Frankly, I didn't care. I was furious.

"Yeah, that's what the paper says," said Detective Rotondo. "We haven't yet verified if any of it is true. And we don't yet know for sure that Lola—Mary—Roseanne—whatever her name is, killed Mrs. Winkworth."

"What do you mean, you don't know?" I all but yelled at him.

"Calm down, Mercy," said Ernie.

"Calm *down*? Darn you, Ernie Templeton—"

"No one saw her do the deed, Mercy. You've told us that you heard her confession, and we believe you, but no one else saw or heard what she said. The judge would call any recitation of what you heard hearsay."

"Hearsay?!" I shouted. "*Hearsay*? You mean a judge wouldn't *believe* me?" I was incensed.

"It doesn't matter if the judge believes you or not. You're the only one who heard her confession. The police can arrest her for attempted murder of you, but unless she confesses to a law officer, we still don't have the whole story about the Winkworth dame."

I sat there, fuming, until the sense of his words penetrated my anger, and I realized he was right. I deflated. "Crumb."

"Yeah," said Ernie. "Something like that."

"Well, really," said Mother.

"Yes, Mother, really," I said, fed up to the back teeth with her, my father, their idiotic mansion in Pasadena, and pretty much everything else. "I know you don't care, but I was almost murdered today."

"Well, *really!*" said Mother again. Limited vocabulary, my mother.

"The only thing *you* cared about was that someone could see up my skirt when I was holding on to that staircase railing, trying not to fall while that insane woman was doing her best to murder me! I swear, if I ever have children, I'm going to try to be as different from you as I possibly can be." I turned to Chloe, who jumped slightly. "And I trust you're going to do the same."

"Well—" Mother began, but Chloe interrupted.

"Darned right I will," said my sister, bless her heart.

"Now listen, you two," said Father.

"Enough!" roared Detective Rotondo. Silence ensued. "Can you come down to the station, Miss Allcutt? We'll need to take your statement and see if we can wring a confession from the Mackey woman."

Without even discussing the matter with Ernie, I said, "Yes." And I stood up, wrapping my hands in the towel Mrs. Thorne had provided for me. My hands hurt like mad, but I didn't want to stay another single second in my parents' home. "Will you please take Buttercup outside for me, Chloe?"

"Sure, Mercy."

"Thank you."

Ernie stood, too. "Want to take your machine?"

"Yes, please. You drive. My hands are damaged."

"Well, *really!*" said my mother for the last time that day, as far as I know.

With a degree of solicitude I'd never have expected of him, Detective Rotondo had us follow his police car west on San Pasqual to Lake Avenue. There he turned right and drove his big Hudson to Beverly Place and Dr. Benjamin's office. Ernie and he parked the machines one behind the other, and then

Rotondo led Ernie and me inside. Although there were several people sitting in the doctor's office waiting to be seen by him, Rotondo spoke with the lady at the reception window, and she led us to see Dr. Benjamin. He bandaged my hands and gave me some salve to rub on them. I thanked him, and so did Detective Rotondo, and so did Ernie. Then we headed to the Pasadena Police Department.

As soon as we walked through the door, Officer Perkins came up to us. "She folded," he said, grinning.

I didn't know what that meant, but both Rotondo and Ernie joined Perkins in his grin.

Still feeling touchy, not to mention in pain, I said, "What do you mean, she folded? What does that mean?"

"She confessed," said Ernie, clearing up the matter for me.

So I grinned, too.

Ernie drove the two of us back to my parents' house in my darling Moon Roadster, and I remembered the promise I'd made to Buttercup before all heck had broken loose.

As Ernie opened the passenger door for me and I got out of the machine, I asked, "Want to go for a walk with Buttercup and me? I promised her a good long walk after all this was over, and I don't think I can hold her leash until my hands heal." I gazed sorrowfully at my hands, which looked sort of like white mitts at the moment. I didn't want to think about what the rest of me looked like. I already knew my face was pretty well shredded.

"Will your folks mind?" asked Ernie mildly.

"I don't care whether they mind or not," I said, my voice fierce.

With a chuckle, Ernie said, "All righty, then, let's walk the dog."

Naturally, my mother tried to stop us. "You're not going out looking like *that!*" she told me.

"Yes, I am," I told her back.

And I did. And so did Ernie. And Buttercup was ecstatic. I don't know how long we walked, but it was almost long enough for me to stop being mad and scared and upset.

"I'm really sorry that bitch assaulted you, Mercy," Ernie said at one point.

"Me, too. Although I'm glad the murder is solved. *And* I'm glad I approached her, even though she did almost kill me. At least I provoked her enough to do something, and thereby showed her as the killer she is."

"Good God."

"Don't you *good God* me, Ernie Templeton. It's the truth. I was instrumental in solving yet another vile crime, and you can't deny it."

"I'm not denying anything. I only wish you'd solve vile crimes in ways that don't put you in peril, is all."

"Hmm. Well, maybe, but it got the job done."

"And it almost got you killed."

I couldn't deny it. But by that time, my state of exhaustion had returned. I guess it had been driven out of me by sheer terror and leftover adrenaline for a while. So we went back to my parents' house, a place I'd never in a million years call home.

Chloe met us at the front door. She gave me a huge hug, and I burst out crying. How come kindness makes people cry? I know I'm not the only one. Fortunately, my bandaged hands were almost as good as a handkerchief, and my crying spell didn't last long. When I was finished and I'd blown my nose on the handkerchief Chloe handed me, I noticed Ernie standing just outside the door, his hands stuffed in his trouser pockets. He looked ill at ease, which was most unlike my terminally nonchalant employer.

Catching a stray tear with the back of my hand, I said,

"What's the matter, Ernie?"

"Nothing. I just thought maybe I'd better head home now."

"Head *home*?" I cried. "You can't leave me here alone with only Chloe and Buttercup for comfort!" I thought of something pertinent. "Besides, my parents haven't paid you yet, have they?"

He shrugged. "No. But I can send 'em a bill."

If I'd had fingers instead of bandaged sausages, I'd have grabbed him by the lapels and yanked him inside. Instead, I said, "You're not going anywhere, Ernest Templeton. You're coming into this house right this second, you're going to take dinner with us, whether you want to or not—and I wouldn't blame you if you didn't want to—you're going to get paid by my parents, and you're going to sleep here overnight." Then I remembered something that made my heart swell with joy. "And tomorrow at noon, we're going to take Thanksgiving dinner at Daisy Majesty's house!"

"You're what?" said Chloe.

"We're what?" said Ernie.

"Mrs. Majesty invited the both of us to take Thanksgiving dinner at her house tomorrow. She says her aunt is the best cook in the world. Besides," I confessed, "Daisy may be a widow, and she may have lived through some awful times, but she has a happy family, and I want to see one up close for once."

Chloe and Ernie stared at me for a second or two.

Then Chloe said, "May Harvey and I come, too?"

CHAPTER TWENTY-SIX

Mother and Father were furious when, on Thanksgiving morning, I packed up my clothes and Buttercup, and took my things downstairs and put them in my Roadster.

"You can't leave on Thanksgiving day!" Mother said, her voice rather louder than usual. She generally didn't need to raise her voice, her commanding presence and imperious tone being enough to cow most mere mortals into submission.

"Oh, yes, I can," I told her. For some reason, I didn't fear her any longer. I guess almost being murdered sort of puts the other things in one's life into perspective. My mother was a true pain in the neck, a miserable stuffed shirt, a more or less indomitable force of nature, and she deplored the heck out of me, but she no longer scared me. Much. "I've been here since last Sunday, and so far you haven't said a single kind word to me. I'm sick of you, your attitude, Father, and this stupid house, and I'm going somewhere else for dinner."

I hadn't told her or Father where Ernie and I intended to dine that day, mainly because I didn't want Daisy to suffer any repercussions if my mother became tetchy about my actions. Daisy wasn't at fault here. Neither was I. If my parents wanted happy, dutiful children who delighted in spending holidays with them, they could be happy, decent parents, darn it. And they weren't.

"Mercedes Louise Allcutt," said my father in his sternest

255

voice, "if you leave this house today, you will never be invited back."

I smiled the first genuine smile I'd ever smiled at either of my parents. "Promise? Then I'm definitely leaving. Thank you!"

Chloe stood behind my parents, Harvey with his arm around her shoulder. I felt sorry to desert her under these unfortunate circumstances, but not even for Chloe would I bear my parents for another day.

Ernie snickered behind me. He'd already stuffed his disreputable suitcase into his disreputable Studebaker, had cranked it up, and was ready to lead the way to Daisy's house. *With* my father's check in his pocket.

My hands were yet heavily bandaged, but I could work the steering wheel stick shift pretty well. I still looked like heck, but I was sure Daisy would understand. With luck, Detective Rotondo would have already told her what had transpired regarding the solution to Mrs. Winkworth's murder.

Stepping out of Harvey's embrace, Chloe came up to me. "I'll miss you, sweetie, but I understand." She gave me a gentle hug—she'd seen most of my bruises and scratches last night, so she didn't dare squeeze—and a kiss on the cheek. "Harvey and I will stop by your Bunker Hill place on the way home tomorrow. Is that all right?"

"That would be wonderful," I told her, hugging her back and getting teary-eyed for a second. I loved my sister. I guess my entire family wasn't horrible. Just most of it.

So, with Chloe and Harvey waving and Mother and Father glaring at our backs, Ernie and I tootled off to the Majesty house. I later learned that, since her husband's death, Daisy was the only Majesty there. The rest of the family was comprised of Gumms. Not that it matters, but I thought I'd mention it.

Ernie drove west on San Pasqual, past Lake Avenue, and on until we got to a street called Marengo Avenue, where he turned right. So I turned right. I don't know how many blocks he drove, but eventually he pulled up across the street from a pretty little bungalow. There were a lot of bungalows in Pasadena, I'd noticed. This wasn't a fancy neighborhood like that of my parents, but it was lovely. The street was lined with some kind of trees that dripped and drooped and almost created a canopy over the entire street.

I noticed Detective Rotondo's big black Hudson parked directly in front of the house, and I also noticed ramps leading up to the front porch. Daisy later told me her father had built those ramps and the ramps in the back of the house, in order to accommodate her late husband's wheelchair. I thought that was most enterprising of him. My own parents would have made a servant build any ramps required at their house. Houses. Pfft.

Daisy's family was as delightful as I'd expected it to be. Her brother and sister and their various children ran rampant all over the house, something Chloe and I had never been allowed to do; and her dog, Spike, and Buttercup played until they were both exhausted. The meal was excellent. I do believe that Mrs. Gumm (Viola, not Peggy, who was Daisy's mother) was an even better cook than my own Mrs. Buck. I don't think I'd ever eaten such a delicious meal.

After dinner but before pie, which everyone was too full to eat right then, the men retired to the living room, where Ernie and Sam Rotondo set up a card table, and all the men played gin rummy. The women, me included, washed the dishes, dried them, and put them away. Well, except for her aunt, who'd cooked the feast. No one expected her to clean up after it.

Although, because of my bandaged hands, I wasn't allowed to wash, I did dry and put away. I felt so . . . I don't know. Normal. Like a real person. Like an honest-to-goodness member of the worker proletariat for perhaps the first time in my life.

Then, after the last dish was put away and all the dish rags, cloths, and aprons were hung up, we ladies joined the men in the living room. Daisy took a seat at the piano, got out some music, and began to play. The men abandoned their card table, and we had a jolly old sing-along.

First Daisy played "Baby Face," then "Five Foot Two, Eyes of Blue," "Ain't We Got Fun," and I don't even remember all of them. I discovered that Ernie had a fine tenor voice and—shock of shocks!—Detective Rotondo had an even finer bass voice. When they sang "Bye Bye Blackbird," they harmonized so well, they might have earned a recording contract had anyone in the music industry been present.

After "Bye Bye Blackbird," Daisy resumed the upbeat jazzy rhythms popular in the day. Eventually, Daisy's brother Walter and his wife, Jeanette, started dancing the Charleston, but there wasn't really enough room, and Walter smacked one of the children with his foot, and the child (can't remember which one) started crying. So that was the end of the dancing. I was disappointed, although I couldn't have danced even if there'd been plenty of room, because I was stiff as a board and my hands were still bandaged.

We were all laughing, singing, and having a simply wonderful time when someone knocked at the door. Spike and Buttercup went wild, both barking and carrying on, until Daisy hollered, "Spike! Sit!" And Spike sat. I stared upon him with amazement as I scooped my own wriggling bundle of fluff into my arms, where she continued to squirm.

Daisy saw my expression, grinned, and said, "Obedience training. It's the cat's pajamas."

If obedience training had taught her dog to sit and stay even in the midst of a riotous family party, I guess it was.

Daisy gave a startled exclamation as soon as she opened the front door. "Harold! Monty! Come in, come in! What are you two doing here? Oh! Mrs. Hanratty! I didn't see you there. My goodness, whatever . . . oh, how *adorable!*"

And darned if Harold Kincaid, Monty Mountjoy, and Mrs. Hanratty didn't enter the already-crowded Gumm/Majesty residence, Mrs. Hanratty with about the most darling little doggy I'd ever seen in my life in her arms—well, except for Buttercup, of course.

"This," said Mrs. Hanratty in her funny, honky voice, "is for Mercy. I suppose it's really for her sister and brother-in-law, but I wanted her to have it as a thank-you for solving my mother's murder."

"Oh!" I cried, surprised as all get-out. "How kind of you."

"Nonsense," said Harold, smiling happily. "Daisy telephoned me last night to tell me what that evil bi—uh, I mean that witch Lola had almost done to you, and I called Monty, and he told Mrs. Hanratty, and she telephoned a friend who breeds English toy spaniels, and here we are!" He made a gesture like a carnival barker, presenting the puppy to us.

So, since he'd put on a show, and we were all happy, we applauded. I guess the puppy didn't appreciate the noise, because it yipped and we stopped clapping.

"Thank you very much," I said, moved almost to tears— again—by the kindness of some people. Because I couldn't very well take the puppy from Mrs. Hanratty while I held Buttercup, I offloaded Buttercup into Ernie's arms. He looked surprised, but he didn't drop her.

"What a dolly," I murmured as I held the little bundle of fluff.

"She's a true beauty," said Mrs. Hanratty with authority. "This bitch is from a long line of champions, and she's one of the best I've seen of her breed. English toy spaniels have been recognized by the American Kennel Club since eighteen eighty-six, and they're perfect companion animals. I can't think of a better breed to give to a young family."

A black-and-tan pup, her coloring was a lot like Daisy's Spike, but her fur was soft and long and curly. Because I couldn't help myself, I asked, "What about a toy poodle? Buttercup is perfect for me."

"Poodles are very smart dogs, but they can nip if they're provoked," said Mrs. Hanratty, repeating what she'd already told me before. Personally, I didn't think that trait was such a bad one, but I didn't say so. I'd wanted to nip a few people myself once or twice. "English toy spaniels were bred to be the perfect companions. They require little care, barring brushing. They're loving and sweet and easy to train, unlike Daisy's Spike."

"Spike learned very well when he went to your class," Daisy reminded her.

"True, true," said Mrs. Hanratty, "but that's only because you worked with him every, single day. Dachshunds tend to be a little stubborn."

"Ha!" said Daisy's father, Joe.

"But come in and sit down," said Daisy, I guess remembering her duties as a hostess. "We're about ready to have pie and whipped cream."

So Monty Mountjoy, his mother, Mrs. Hanratty, and Harold Kincaid trooped farther into the house, and Aunt Vi (Daisy's, not mine) served us about the most delicious pumpkin pie I'd ever eaten. I had to put the pup down as I ate pie, but I kept my eye on her, since both Spike and Buttercup were interested in meeting her. Neither Spike nor Buttercup meant her any harm, naturally, dogs being ever so much kinder to each other than are we humans to one another.

Daisy wouldn't let me help wash the dessert dishes, citing my hands. Truth to tell, time was passing and, since I'd be drawn and quartered before I went back to my parents' Pasadena house again, I decided I'd best be on the road back to my Bunker Hill abode. Ernie agreed that it was time to be tootling off, since driving in the dark was so dangerous.

"I'll take the pup in my machine," he said, eyeing Buttercup doubtfully.

"Thank you, Ernie."

"Let me get you a towel for her to sit on," said Daisy.

"Oh, you needn't bother," said Monty, who hadn't spoken a whole lot up until that time. "Mother came fully equipped."

"True, true," said Harold. "She's got a doggy bed, bedding, and a collar and leash out in Monty's car."

And darned if the two men didn't exit the pretty little bungalow and came back with all the accoutrements a puppy, or a puppy's owner, could want.

That time, I did cry, but not for long, thank God. Ernie didn't even roll his eyes at me.

We said our good-byes, and I probably thanked Daisy and the Gumms too many times, because Sam Rotondo—he'd never be Detective Rotondo to me again—told me, "Cut it out now. You two have to get on the road."

So Ernie and I drove off, I with a light heart and Ernie with a tiny little English toy spaniel pup. I'd actually seen a happy family at play. Amazing.

When I pulled into my driveway on Bunker Hill an hour or so later, Lulu was there on the porch to greet me. Her brother Rupert was with her. I guess, since their family was in Oklahoma, they'd taken Thanksgiving at my house, which was perfectly fine with me.

I was so happy to be home, I felt like kneeling down and kissing my driveway. Now, if only my parents would honor their vow never to invite me to their home again, I'd consider myself a very fortunate girl. Somehow, though, I doubted they'd stop trying to make me over into their own image that easily.

ABOUT THE AUTHOR

Award-winning author **Alice Duncan** lives with a herd of wild dachshunds (enriched from time to time with fosterees from New Mexico Dachshund Rescue) in Roswell, New Mexico. She's not a UFO enthusiast; she's in Roswell because her mother's family settled there fifty years before the aliens crashed. Alice would love to hear from you at alice@aliceduncan .net. And be sure to visit her Web site at http://www.alice duncan.net and her Facebook page at https://www.facebook .com/alice.duncan.925.